ABSOLUTE POWER

TALES OF QUEER VILLAINY!

EDITED BY
ERICA FRIEDMAN

COVER BY
AGNES CZAJA

Absolute Power: Tales of Queer Villainy!
Edited by Erica Friedman

Book design by Charles "Zan" Christensen

Absolute Power: Tales of Queer Villainy!
ISBN: 978-1-9438903-8-5
ISBN (digital): 978-1-9438903-9-2
First Northwest Press edition, December 2016.
Printed in Canada

Many thanks to my wife,
the most villainous woman
I have ever known.
—Erica

THE LINEUP

INTRODUCTION 2
Erica Friedman

FINAL GRADES 4
Erica Friedman

DATE NIGHT 16
Tristan J. Tarwater

EDEN'S REVENGE 30
Missouri Vaun

GENTLEMAN JACK 46
Barbara Ann Wright

FALLEN 64
Audrey Chase

THE DEVIL INSIDE 84
J.D. Glass

GLITTER BOMB 100
Emily Kay Singer

FOR WANT OF A HEART 118
A. Merc Rustad

ABSOLUTION 136
Claire Jackson

**SO MANY THINGS SEEM
FILLED WITH THE INTENT** 158
Jude McLaughlin

THE PRADO BY CHANCE. 180
Leia Weathington

JAGUAR LIGHT 196
Susan Smith

CHROME CRASH 210
Mari Kurisato

I think there's something really powerful and refreshing about a woman who is unapologetic.

—Rachel McAdams

INTRODUCTION
Erica Friedman

What does villainy mean to you? This is the question I ask myself every time I read a book or story that purports to portray a supervillain. Is being a villain just being power-hungry or does a villain need to be sociopathic? Does it make a person a villain to want revenge for horrible wrongs, or is that just boring? Is villainy something human and profound or is it something so intrinsic to the human condition that we don't really understand it any more than we understand "love"?

So often supervillains are labeled evil, but turn out to have rather banal dreams of "ruling the world" or "enslaving humanity." I have often thought about the idea of ruling the world and my reaction has always been… "but think of the paperwork." Even worse are villains who rant about proving their superiority, only to be taken down by a buff babe in a spandex cape.

So what is evil? What makes a person a "villain?" Is it intent to harm… or is it something deeper than that?

Each one of the authors in this amazing collection has taken a completely different approach to answering this question. They have gone above and beyond expressing the idea of evil and supervillainy. They get to the bottom of why villains are the way they are, and what they hope to gain from it. These are dangerous women… and they'll be glad to let you know exactly why you should fear them.

Evil. Was it born this way? Maybe these villains knew from the very beginning, maybe not, but by the time you get to meet them, they've come through the crucible and learned to accept themselves for who they are.

FINAL GRADES
Erica Friedman

Erica Friedman is a professional psychopomp, author, speaker and blogger. She writes the world's oldest and most comprehensive blog on lesbian-themed Japanese cartoons, comics and related media at Okazu.yuricon.com. Erica has written about Yuri for Japanese literary journal *Eureka*, *Animerica* magazine, the Comic Book Legal Defense Fund, Dark Horse, and contributed to *Forbes*, *Slate*, *Huffington Post*, *Hooded Utilitarian*, *The Mary Sue* and *Afterellen*.

Welcome incoming class, to what promises to be a life-changing education for you. Many of you have thought about this day since you were young, vowing revenge on all who refused to acknowledge you as their masters. Some of you applied on a whim when petty crime no longer seemed to have appeal. But, I assure you that what you learn here will change the world.

I look down upon you now, your eyes filled with the kind of self-confidence that only youth and dreams of grandeur can provide and I have to laugh. One day, many years ago, I was like you, ready to take on and destroy the world. I stared up from those very chairs, plotting the death of the Chair who held the position at the time, dreams of world domination filling my head. I see you in the blue and gold cape, rolling your eyes like you've heard this a million times. You haven't and no one is fooled by your bravado. When you stand here on the podium over my dead body, then you can posture.

Yes, you burn with passion, yes, you desire vengeance and control, of course you have devastating plans and amazing powers, but there is so much more to supervillainy than that. You need many things in order to be a successful villain.

In your time here, you will understand the difference between becoming a genius inventor or a powerful overlord, how to command, control, outthink and overpower. And you will learn to understand the importance of choosing your archenemy well.

You'll learn from the very best—me—on how to dominate the media. You don't think it's accidental that you are all here, do you? You were drawn by the dominance I have of the news that reports on me with such glowing terms—words designed to thrill people like you, and strike terror into those unlike us.

Not all of you will graduate, of course. Our hallowed halls flow with the blood of many just like you, megalomaniac children bent on conquest, without so much as a catchy name to their name. If this worries you, leave now, you are not suited for this school. We have 118 students enrolled for this year. The best graduating class I ever had was a single person. That is the benchmark you must seek to match.

In conclusion, Welcome to Hypnotika's School of Supervillainy. When you leave opening ceremonies, you will be assigned your rooms. Those of you who make it safely to those rooms will begin class tomorrow promptly at noon. We expect you to stay up late working on your first death ray "inventions".

◆

The sound of a single person clapping made me look up from the paper on which I had printed out my speech.

"Come back to bed, sweetie, you've been working on that speech for hours." A yawn, then a sigh. "Why don't you just use a previous version?" Then a handwave. "Forget it, I know why. 'Each student deserves the best, that's why they are in my school.' I know, I know."

I smiled at her. "That's what I love best about you. You're so diligent all the way down to the bone, you can't even allow yourself an honest moment of petulance." I put the paper down, took my glasses off, walked over to the bed and leaned over her. "I can be convinced, you know. Rather easily, I'm afraid."

"That's what I love best about you," she said, "You're so easy to corrupt." Her lips met mine and the speech was forgotten.

◆

It's always a pleasure welcoming in the new class at the school. I mentally mark off the ones who won't make it a week, and bet with myself which ones will be plotting behind my back before the month is over.

But the true test of my skill comes when teaching. I don't get involved in the nitty-gritty of class often anymore, but another one of our instructors had been arrested last spring and I thought it would be fun to try my hand once again.

"And who can tell me what I just said?" I look around the class at a sea of bewildered faces. "Anyone?"

A hand goes tentatively up. I don't need to look at the seating chart. He's pale, with splotchy skin, and isn't going to amount to much. "Dastardo?" I call.

"Something about…"

"Stop." I dismiss the rest of the statement. "If you can't remember, don't guess."

A noise from the back of the room makes everyone turn and look. There is a gasp. As I expected. I smile at her, holding out my hand. She walks towards the front of the room without looking at any of the students, but their eyes are fixed on her. It's understandable. She is dazzling. The colors of her prismatic costume shimmer and change, as does her hair. Her alien skin is the color of red clay, her eyes dark and terrible.

"Oh my god…" The first whisper.

"It's Bedazzle…" the second, then the room erupts as I take her in my arms for a slow, luxurious kiss. Showing off is an important skill they must learn, and I have a lot to show off. Her red skin and the deep brown of my own complimented each other beautifully. I knew the effect our embrace would have on the class. I relished it.

"Hello class." She says in dulcet tones, as she pulls away from me, smiling apologetically at the effect she has on the students.

"…"

There is stunned silence. I keep my eye on the class waiting out the wave of shock.

"But.."

"You're…!"

"How…?"

I make mental ticks against the gasps. Nope, nope, not her, not him, nope, nope, bummer, I thought she might have some promise, nope, nope.

"I get it."

Ah-ha, as I suspected, it's one of the two in the corner, a young Korean woman. She's been quiet this whole time, but now, her voice rings out.

"She's never been a good guy." I love this kid. She gets it in one and doesn't waste time with the explanation.

I nod. "Explain it to your classmates. Stand up."

She does, awkwardly, a little unsure, until she starts speaking. She speaks over the heads of her classmates (both figuratively and literally) at me. "You told us yesterday, didn't you?" She checks her notes. "…*the dominance I have of the news that reports on me…*" I went back last night and rewatched the news. You're always the bad guy, but the press admires you. They praise you with faint damns."

I really like this kid. With an approving smile, I nodded. "Sit back down."

Turning to the class, I gestured at her. "May I present the world's most famous superhero, my wife, Bedazzle."

Only a gape or two, all from students who already had mental ticks against them. Best thing I can do is cut them from the roster right away. Poor things don't have a chance. There's still time for them to go into finance, they always need petty evil. For the rest... we shall see if they can fully comprehend what they've learned today. My bet is that only one has.

❦

Week three of class is the hardest. I've tried to encourage students to think beyond the boundaries, to see through subterfuge, to attack smartly, create new forms of mastery. As week three comes to a close, there's always a few who need to be reminded and a few that need to be stopped from hurting themselves.

"How many of you remember yesterday's homework?" I begin.

"Are you ever going to teach us how you do that?" Steel Fist is a bit dopey looking, but has sharp mind. He always remembers *when* I use my powers, even if he can't remember what I made him do or why. He'll make a good henchman.

"No, never." I smile brightly. "Not even on my deathbed. Which brings me to the homework assignment. I am deeply disappointed at the number of assassination attempts I have had to fend off in the last week. Only three? I know I gave you until the end of the month to complete the assignment, but expected more alacrity. Remember, I'm the only thing between you and taking over this school... and this city."

Manipulation. They didn't understand my powers at all, not yet. They heard the words, they thought they understood them, but they didn't. I looked around the class. Only one pair of eyes met mine with a keen look. She sat in the corner today as always, her body language completely different than just a few weeks ago. Now she sat back; casual, surprisingly comfortable in herself. She looked at me from under half-lidded eyes, with just the slightest smile. Of all the students, only she, maybe, understood. A little, perhaps. Not fully, not yet.

I moved quietly to the side as the projectile lodged itself in the wall and sighed heavily. "Today, we're going to talk about plans to take over the world. Put that weapon down," I spoke over my shoulder as I wrote on the chalkboard. Poor Miasma had no choice, but scowled as she did. If I was going to be destroyed, it wasn't going to be by a first-year lab project.

I spared a glance for the young woman in the corner, now going by the name Blood Rose. I had encouraged them to change names until they found one that suited them. "Names are powerful. You can strike fear into hearts by using the familiar, or the unfamiliar." Her given name, Jangmi, she explained, meant rose in English. "Blood" she felt was self-explanatory. In subsequent weeks, three missing students had had their desks marked with flowers. I quite liked her style. Blood Rose had raised her hand. "How did you and Bedazzle meet?"

Fair question. Probing, too personal behind the banal, I might give away some weakness. I approved. But they had much to learn.

I met her when my parents (who are already long dead, thanks for asking, Darknight) brought me into the city for the very first time. I had always loved the circus, and had begged for weeks and weeks to be able to come in and see the big show in the city arena. After doing my chores—well, getting them done, in any case, I rarely did them myself—and convincing them I had been a good girl, which was easier for me than actually being a good girl, they agreed to take me.

The city was amazing. I had never seen that many people in real life. I had to work at getting people to give things to me—they were more suspicious and less attentive than people were in my hometown. But there we were at last, to watch the Circus. The clowns came in on the back of the animals—I briefly considered convincing the animals to eat them. One of the clowns had red skin, the color of clay. I was fascinated because I thought that was his real skin color. He had a "family" of red-skinned clowns, a wife clown and a child clown. I watched them with attention, wondering out loud where they had come from. My parents told me that the red color was merely paint and I was deeply disappointed.

You may have read about this in the archives actually—do any of you remember reading of the acrobats in the City Circus staging a mutiny and holding a hostage up on the high wire? Yes, well, apparently I had gotten quite bored. Mea culpa. But that isn't the point.

The point is that the hostage, one of the animal trainers, began to fall. I wasn't watching the hostage situation; it wasn't panning out to be as entertaining as I had hoped. Instead I asked to go to the restroom and was walking around, looking for a way backstage. I was hoping to prove my parents wrong about the red-skinned clowns. I heard someone scream, and felt a rush of wind as the young "child" clown ran past me and leapt into the air, pulling off her clown suit as she flew. Her hair was more magnificent than I could describe. I had thought it a wig, but now it flamed and shimmered like a jewel. She caught the animal trainer and ran for the back door before the crowd could stop her.

I was waiting in the back by the trailers.

"Is that… you?" I asked, reaching out to touch her face.

She nodded. "We're… from another planet."

"My name is Hypnotika," I told her, using the name I now use. It was a secret name then, one that I never shared with anyone. She told me her name was Opal and made to run off. Before she disappeared into the trailer, I said, "Can I write you?" and quickly, because I could hear sounds of people coming close, had her write her address on my hand. And then she was gone, and I was pushed away by the crowd.

❦

I took a deep breath. "And that was how we met."

A few moments of silence, breaths that had been held let out slowly, a softening of opinion, a slight melancholy and a little thrill. After a pause, Man-o-War asked, "That really happened?"

I stood up from where I had been seated and stretched. "Well the hostage part did, anyway. Okay, back to class."

The lesson today was about never trusting anyone with the real story. Reality was less exciting, if slightly more fascinating, than fantasy. But people preferred fantasy.

❦

Midterms, or what the surviving students liked to call "the field trip", was always well-received.

The premise was simple. Students teamed up—voluntarily if they wanted, involuntarily if they didn't—and were sent out to commit a crime of their own creation. The rules were simple—there were no rules. Why would there be? I explained at least once a semester to someone who was lagging a little behind the rest. The only thing I promised was that I would not actively call the police. I had to promise this or they would never hand in their plans as part of the assignment. I loved reading the efforts the students put into their little robberies, attempts to influence through blackmail or threat of violence or pestilence or bomb threats. So cute. Every once in a while, I thrilled to the idea of a full-blown coup d'etat, but even those didn't give me have the joy that reading Blood Rose's plan did.

"Oh what a darling!" I took my glasses off and sighed deeply.

Opal joined me at the desk, reaching over my shoulder to take the report from my hand. She read in silence for a moment, then her eyebrows shot up to her iridescent hairline. "Wow." Was all she said.

"Right? This isn't a undergraduate crime spree, this reeks of actual genius." I laid the pages out and glanced across them. "Traffic control, crowd control, arms control. Inducing panic to influence stock prices and food supplies. Nothing's perfect, of course, but this might work." I nodded, as I reviewed some of the steps. "This one has serious potential." I looked up at my love.

"So… what do you think?" Opal looked at me, a very serious expression on her face.

"Too complicated in the short time she has, and there's no way she's got all the resources," I smiled brightly. "But I admire the gusto with which it's all written." I grinned down at the plan and nodded. "I can't wait to see what the results are. All things being equal—which they never are—taking her out of rotation may be the final exam."

"I was just thinking that," Opal rolled her shoulders. "Well, the police reports are starting to come in. I'm going to go grade your midterms for you." Her smile (which was quite literally pearly) was incandescent as always. "Wish me luck."

I kissed her deeply. "Never. But do be careful."

I sat all afternoon and evening watching the media networks under my control alternately panic and reassure the populace, with tales of a mysterious crime spree and the comforting figure of the city's protector, Bedazzle, stopping each crime before anything more than slight damage might be done. As perpetrators were caught and detained, I crossed them off the class roster. By the end of midterms the class would be significantly smaller, but I had no doubt that Blood Rose would be among them.

🌹

One must maintain a high level of alert and attention. Over the years, I have honed my abilities to a level of sensitivity that most people would consider magical. Not only could I manipulate others, I was instantly able to identify when a will other than my own enters my perimeter. It was refinements such as these that allowed me to retain my position unchallenged for so long. As every villain knows—it is not enough to simply have a power, one must train it like a muscle for it to be meaningful. One of the many reasons I opened this school in the first place.

All of which is to say that I knew she was coming well before the knock on my door.

"Come in." I was at my office desk. I filed the paper I had been reading away, brushed off my skirt and looked up as she entered. The midterms had been tremendously successful. Classes were much smaller now and I was able to give personal attention to each student. The survivors were the best this generation had to offer. I expected her to come. Of this year's class, she was among the stars. She and the few others left alive had tremendous potential. Potential that I had been pushing to its limits. Potential that would succeed magnificently or fail tragically in the coming final exam.

"Good evening Blood Rose, how may I help you?" She nodded unsurely and entered. I noted her awkwardness, so much like she had been that first day. I almost leapt up to hug her, she really was just so adorable.

"I wanted to talk with you about…" she closed her eyes, then opened them again slowly, looking at me with a nervous expression. "…about the final exam." I nodded, motioning for her to take a seat. Instead she stood across from me, fidgeting ever so slightly. I smiled brightly, with just a hint of predator.

"I've been working on the plan I submitted with Maximon, Poison and The Gaul. We were wondering," a nervous giggle escaped her lips, which she tightened quickly. "I would like to request an addition to the group. We'd like Madame Sans Merci on the team. If we can get her to join us, I believe we have everything we need for the plan to succeed." A quick gasp of breath and she finished with "We'll trade Darknight. He isn't happy about it, but we don't need super strength for this plan."

As she spoke, I watched her carefully. Folding my hands on the desk, I considered the nature of her request... and my own nature.

Clearly, she saw this in me. I wasn't unaware of my appetite, just fascinated that she thought it tended towards the innocent. I allowed hunger to show on my face before I responded. Looking her openly up and down, I replied, slowly, softly, "And what do you propose to offer in return for this change?"

As I suspected, her reaction was to look at me shyly. "What would you like?"

"Blood Rose, come here." I waved her over. It was a policy of mine to always use their chosen names. I never forgot the thrill I felt the first time I was called Hypnotika. This wasn't a secret identity—it was, for the first time in my life, me proclaiming my *true* identity. It was freeing. I promised myself I would always give the students the chance to feel truly themselves. She stood in front of the desk, I waved her around the back and stood up, looking into her eyes.

Blood Rose drew closer, still sticking to the "cutely awkward" script, her hands played with the edge of her blouse. I took one of the hands in mine, lifted it to my lips and said, "Graduated Top of the Class in high school, Magna Cum Laude in college, honors in post-graduate work, awards in every job you've ever had," I kissed the back of her hand again. "But your chameleon power is wrong this time. I have no use for innocence."

I dropped her hand and watched as she transformed. Her stance, her face, even the tilt of her shoulders, her expression grew harder, her hands slimmed out, her legs lengthened. The woman standing before me was comfortable in her body, comfortable using it. No longer a waif looking for guidance, ready to be seduced, but a seductress herself. The hand she lifted extended out towards me. Moving slowly, she snaked her hand along my neck, pulling herself closer, Slowly, so slowly, she brought her lips up to capture mine.

I love every seduction attempt of the semester. Each one had a unique feel about it and this one was no surprise. I had known that it would be Blood Rose from the first day of class. But I couldn't wait to see what she had planned.

Her lips were cool, soft, sweet. Her scent was, unsurprisingly, rose. We tore at one another, pulling at clothes, not stroking each other, but raking with claws and teeth. Magnificent. I pulled her onto the floor, stripping her of her ill-conceived costume. This one deserves something slinky, something gold and crimson or black and classic. She fought me, just a little, but I could tell that she hoped I would take control, her eyes staring into mine, the whole time. When she climaxed, she gripped my arms hard enough to bruise, and I bit at her, knowing she would never forget the lesson she was about to learn. Her eyes were closed, as she panted, my fingers still inside her. I heard the door open. It was time.

"Jangmi," I spoke gently. "Open your eyes." Slowly, they fluttered open, almost soft for a split second. Then they focused and saw what I knew she would see. I pulled my hands away from her, and lifted them to where Opal took them in her own and slowly, deliciously, licked them clean.

I pulled away, as Bedazzle began to generate a ball of power in her palm.

"Blood Rose. You are incredibly intelligent, with an extremely useful skill. But you missed something critical that first day. You... all my beloved students... missed the obvious. You thought you were here so I could train you. Think about it. Why would I do that? How could I hope to retain a position of power when younger villains would always be challenging me for my position?"

I narrowed my eyes. "This isn't a school, Blood Rose." I smiled. Not nicely. "This is a gladiatorial ring where I dispose of potential rivals." A flicker of recognition in her eyes, as she stared at me, then Bedazzle, then me once more. Then fear. "Now you understand. You're looking at the only student who has ever survived this course."

"The good news is that you'll pass the final," I said, as I placed one hand on Opal's shoulder. The beam was gorgeous, a glorious cascade of light and color. As it slammed into Blood Rose's chest, shattering her sternum and forcing her a foot into the floor, I finished. "But you won't graduate."

❦

"You looked like you were having fun," Opal pouted as we called for cleanup.

"I was. She was absolutely delicious. You're not jealous, are you?"

"I'm only jealous that you get to have all the fun, and I have to be the good guy."

I stretched, and wrapped myself in a robe from the closet. "You know, that might be a good idea." I came back and pressed myself against her with a kiss. "How do you feel about turning evil? TV ratings have been down this year."

Opal put a clay red finger to her lips thoughtfully. "I don't know, do you think I'd make a good supervillain?"

"The best. In fact, you could be even eviler than me. And I'm bored with this mayor, how would I be as a hero, a savior of the city?"

"The media will love you."

We kissed again, laughed, then sat down to plan the graduation ceremony, and the subjugation of humanity, together.

DATE NIGHT
Tristan J. Tarwater

Tristan J. Tarwater is a writer of fantasy, comics and RPG bits. Her titles include *The Valley of Ten Crescents* series, *Shamsee: A Fistful of Lunars*, and *Reality Makes the Best Fantasy*. She has also worked for both Pelgrane Press and Onyx Path. Born and raised in NYC, she now considers Portland, OR, her home. When she's not making stuff up, she is usually reading a comic book, cooking delicious meals for her Spouse and Small Boss or petting one of her two cats. Her next RPG character will most definitely be an elf.

Yvette stood in the restaurant bathroom, looking over her makeup. She was fifteen minutes early for her date, as planned. Perfectly manicured nails gripped the counter top as she leaned forward, eyes wide. Her eyeliner on her left eye was extended slightly further than the one on the right. Her lipstick was perfect. The color was called Not Shy and the red, matte shade went well with her complexion. She had considered having her eye makeup tattooed on. It would make it less likely to smudge after all the explosions. But there was something Yvette liked about the ritual of putting on her makeup. She had the same feeling when she slipped on her diamond-threaded cowl and tunic, emblazoned with her symbol: an E within a black gear. Estratega's makeup smudged. Cause and effect. Tonight, Yvette couldn't be too perfect. She had a date.

Being an expert strategist was a time consuming power. Her schedule kept her busy and Yvette didn't often make time for amorous perusals of her fellow citizens. She had many projects and heists to plan and many of her fellow villains often contracted her to look over their own diabolical schemes, a rather lucrative part of her operation. In addition, she had her assistant to mentor. Spontaneity worked for those with more flamboyant, physics-defying powers. No plan was foolproof, but only fools didn't plan.

She brushed her bangs out of her face. She had looked at the menu online before she arrived but would be looking at it when her date arrived. Yvette would order the red rice with chicken. It had the potential to lead into a conversation about cooking, which was always disarming. Yvette had checked out Bri's CatPics account and there were more than a few home cooked meal pics. It'd be a safe topic. She pulled down on her leather skirt, smoothing it over the curves of her hips and ass. The goal of the date was a few hours of company and an equal time of sex, to be repeated at regular intervals over the next few months. That should suffice.

Her phone buzzed. Yvette picked it up, swiping to see the message.

<Hows the date going??????? ;)>

Diamond Point. Her sidekick was back at the lab, making more materials for replacement costumes. It wasn't glamorous work but it had to be done. Yvette could hardly believe she had time to go on a date but things had lined up. Her dating app had them at an 89% match and Yvette found

Bri more than pleasing to the eye. A shipment of corundum was postponed and so the block of time had opened up.

<Hasn't started yet. Get back to work. Spaghetti already in microwave.> Yvette sighed, hitting send. Diamond Point was a… useful sidekick. He kept her from having to do menial material heists, which cut into her real passion: taking advantage of security loopholes to amass a fortune, exposing hypocrites in all levels of government in the most damning and soul destroying way possible and fighting Lady Brawn, who she loved to punch in her stupid face. Yvette took a deep breath, trying to push thoughts of Lady Brawn out of mind. She wanted this evening to be pleasant. Perfect, even.

Yvette tucked her phone into her purse and walked out of the bathroom, into the restaurant. She stopped short, seeing Bri already at the table. The waitress must have seated her. She was early.

She didn't look exactly like her SM profile pic, which was to be expected. Angles, lighting and poses all distorted faces and arms. But Yvette had checked her presence online and found her to be within reasonable parameters of what Bri had presented. Signature big earrings dangled from her ears. She made them as a hobby. She was dressed slightly more casually than Yvette. But she was early. A pleasant surprise.

Bri waved at her, smiling broadly. In person, her smile was dazzling. Yvette walked over, her flat shoes clicking on the linoleum floor.

"It's so nice to meet you in person," Bri said, rising from her seat. She reached out her hand for a shake. Yvette took it and leaned in, Bri picking up the cue and exchanging kisses on the cheek. Bri was taller than her.

"I know, same," Yvette said, sitting on her chair.

"And thank you for picking the restaurant," Bri said. "I'm usually not so indecisive!"

"Well, you're new to town," Yvette said with a shrug, picking up the menu. She knew she was going to order the rice but still. It was what one did at restaurants. "Easier than you reading a thousand YumTown reviews." It helped that Yvette knew the layout of the restaurant, including the kitchen and basement. "I hope you like Puerto Rican food."

"I've never really had it, to be honest," Bri said. "I looked at the menu on the bus, but this guy was sitting across from me playing some game on his phone really loudly? It was so annoying."

"Ugh, I hate that," Yvette said, rolling her eyes. "I don't need to know you just got a high score on your shitty matching game."

"Do you play phone games?" Bri asked. "Maybe you're playing Space Belligerence 3, we could co-op sometime?" She smiled.

"I don't usually play games on my phone," Yvette said, looking down and folding her napkin. "I like board games, though."

"Oh, board games! Are there any good board game stores in town? I used to play Sovereign Squares back in New York."

"You play Sovereign Squares?" Yvette asked, narrowing her eyes. Sovereign Squares was her favorite game. She had her game set up under a force field back at her lab to keep Diamond Point from knocking into it. He was getting better, though he hadn't gotten close to beating her yet. He didn't understand the importance of securing resources early on in the game.

"Is that so hard to believe?" Bri said.

"No, it's just… I really like Sovereign Squares!" Yvette said. "I've been playing since I was in college." Yvette had brought her set with her to Spain, to the Andalusian Sinister Scientist Camp. She remembered the only person who would play with her was Vicente Amaro, The Red Fist. Her first boyfriend. The person she had dated after that, a civilian named Harriet, hadn't liked board games. "I have the Wetlands Expansion."

"I was about to get it, but then with the move and all, you know," Bri said, shrugging. "But I might pre-order the Cloudforest Expansion, now that I'm settled."

"If you go to Red Castle Games, they'll order it for you," Yvette offered. "It's a good store, locally owned."

"If this date goes terribly, I can always take it out on you on the battlefield," Bri said with a wink. Yvette noticed her eye shadow, gold and purple.

"I'll remember that," Yvette said, looking back down at her menu.

The waitress approached, notepad in hand. "Are you ready to order?"

"I'll have the arroz con pollo and the Puñeta," Yvette said, the words rolling off her tongue.

"I'll have the number 5," Bri said, pointing. "And a Crown Ale." The waitress scribbled something in her pad before she took their menus and walked away.

"Didn't want to try and say it?" Yvette said with a smirk.

"And have you judge me?" Bri said. "I took French in high school, not Spanish."

"So, you're fancy?" Yvette spoke French. Among other languages. None of those were pertinent to the date so she kept that info to herself.

"Oh my god, really?" Bri laughed. "My mother wanted me to learn it. I think she thought I'd move to France some day."

"Why is—" Yvette stopped. A flash from within the building across the street. An explosion. Massive.

Yvette grabbed her bag and dove to the ground. The force hit the restaurant. Glass screamed as it shattered, falling all around her. Next came the panicked screams of those around her. Alarms sang all around her, high pitched peals adding to the chaos around her. Yvette coughed and sat up, glass sliding off of her.

"Are you alright?" she asked Bri. Her own words were muffled in her ears. Bri was still sitting in the booth. Glass glittered in her dark hair.

"I'm fine," she said, her head moving side to side, as if slightly dazed. She shook her head. "What happened?"

Yvette stood up, glass and debris crunching under her boots, slinging her bag over her shoulder. She could already see people on the street. Mostly she noted the glow of their phones. They were filming something. "Let's find out." She walked out the shattered window, ignoring the blood and sobbing of the restaurant goers. They weren't important.

Yvette pulled her glasses out of her bag and slipped them on, looking where the phones were pointed. A lone figure stood at the top of the building. She feigned brushing her hair out of her face and zoomed in on the person standing there.

Diamond Point.

I thought I told him to stay home, Yvette thought to herself. She clenched her teeth, stress already starting to pool in her jaw. He was wearing his white and black demolition suit. She could see the smirk on his face. He was proud of himself.

"Diamond Point!" someone in the crowd said. How had the crowd gathered so quickly? Yvette tried not to roll her eyes.

"Oh my god, Diamond Point?!" another voice came.

"Estratega should be close by," she heard Bri say.

"I bet," Yvette said. "We should try to get out of here, we don't know what he's going to do."

Her phone buzzed in her bag.

"Come on," she said, grabbing Bri by the arm with one hand, while slipping her phone out of her pocket. It was a message. From Diamond Point.

<Impressed?????? :)>

Yvette's face twisted in disgust. Bri looked over. "Everything alright?"

"Yeah, just… text from a friend, trying to see if I'm alright." Yvette said.

"I should do the same, hold on," Bri said, pulling out her phone. Yvette took the opportunity to bang out a quick response to Diamond Point.

<No. I thought I told you to stay home and make materials. Is this related to that assignment in some way, y/n?>

Yvette hit send and turned around. "Told my friends I was okay. Finally glad for mass texts today, right?"

"Oh, damn, I didn't even think to do that," Bri said, frowning. "Hold on." Bri turned to her phone. Yvette's phone buzzed. She turned before she looked it.

<All part of my plan, boss. Incomincf.>

Yvette scowled at her phone. Then she grabbed Bri and pushed her into an alley. She held her arm up to shield them.

Another explosion. Loud. Screams. Bri said something but Yvette couldn't make it out. The roar died down. Fire crackled and she could smell the rank odor of burning construction and plastic. In the distance sirens wailed.

"I need to stop him," Yvette growled in her throat.

"Stop who?" Bri said.

"No one," Yvette said. "An idiot." Her phone buzzed again.

<Incoming*, sorry>

"Hey," Yvette said, turning towards Bri. The other woman was shaking. Blood trickled, bright red from her scalp, shining in what remained of the street light. "You're bleeding. Are you alright?"

"I am?" Bri brought her fingers to her scalp, pulling her hand away from the blood. "I am."

"I think you're in shock," Yvette said. She stepped away from the building, an ambulance blaring down the road. She pulled out her EMP taser from her purse and discreetly pointed it at the vehicle. It screeched to a halt, the driver side door opening and an EMT popping out.

Without hesitating, Yvette scooped Bri up, carrying her towards the ambulance, both EMTs staring at her. "My date is injured," Yvette said, the confidence in her voice breaking through their stupor. "She may have a concussion." One of the EMTs scrambled to the back of the ambulance, pulling out a stretcher. A firetruck and several other ambulances crested over the hill, blaring past them. Yvette didn't flinch.

"Here's her purse," Yvette said, pulling Bri's phone out. She tapped her number into the phone and handed it to the EMT. "My number is on the phone. Just hit 'call' in thirty minutes with her condition. I'll pay you if you do." The EMT took the phone and stared. The other was already shining a light into Bri's eyes.

There was nothing else to say. Yvette knew how to contact her. The closest hospital was St. Vitus. She would check there later. After she dealt with Diamond Point.

It was simple enough to get past the police officers trying to cordon off the area. Look like you were supposed to be there. Once she was past the yellow tape she peeled off her skirt. The fabric of her stockings was flexible but impermeable. She tossed it in the dumpster. Off came the rest of the street clothes, including the jewelry. The diamond weave fabric of her bodysuit darkened and hardened as she slipped on her two bracers, the lights on them glinting into more obvious operational capacity. She threw her purse, including her phone, into the dumpster.

She tapped on the screen on her left bracer. He was three buildings over by now. Estratega flicked a fire ball into the dumpster, aiming her grappling hook towards the edge of the building. If she got to the roof, she could easily make the leaps and get to Diamond Point. Behind her, she heard the gentle 'whoosh' of the ball igniting, incinerating the contents of the dumpster and her belongings.

With hardly a sound, the hook shot up. The console beeped as it made contact, a light turning green to let her know it was safe to ascend. Estratega took hold of the rope and gave it a squeeze, the rope receding into the console, pulling her up the side of the building.

Another explosion. Behind her. Estratega cursed quietly as dust and bricks enveloped her. Something hit her in the back. She reached the top of the building and hoisted herself over the side, looking at Diamond Point's handiwork. The building was collapsed. The inside rose from the ground like a broken tooth, wiring and plumbing spurting sparks and water noisily on the cool evening. She was on the rooftop of a different building. She was safe. She walked to the edge to give a glance at the ambulance she had left Bri at, noting her presence before she bolted across the roof.

Left, right, left, right, left right, SPRING. Estratega leaped across the narrow alleyway, landing in a roll before she spring up and ran again, her feet pounding against the tar and gravel. Left, right, left, right, left right. She kept her breathing even, sucking in as she sprung again, leaping across to the next one. Diamond Point came into view.

He was standing by the air conditioning unit, holding one of the thermal detonators in his hands. His white bodysuit glittered, the black diamond icon plastered on his chest. His hood was down. Stark white hair, like spun silver, spilled boyishly around his ears. When he finally looked up and saw her, he smirked.

"You didn't answer my texts," he said.

Estratega wanted to kick him in the face. But he was her sidekick, and that wouldn't do. Not now. "I was busy getting exploded on," she said, her jaw tight as she did. "I told you, I was going on a date tonight."

"On this side of town?" Diamond Point said. "I'm surprised by that."

"I left the name and number of the restaurant on the fridge," Estratega spat.

"Oh!" Diamond Point said. He smacked himself on the forehead with the palm of his hand. "I thought you were going to El Rincon on the west side. Oops." Diamond Point looked down at the detonator, fiddling with the touchscreen. "Oh well. Sorry I ruined your date."

Another explosion.

"What the fuck are you doing?!" Estratega screamed. This was the last straw. "I told you to stay at the lab! You have materials to make. What is the strategic value of these buildings you are destroying?"

"There's a secret tunnel under these buildings that leads to Dark Blade's hideout, one of them. I figured if I blew them up, the city would find the network and—"

"Push her deeper underground, you idiot." Estratega grabbed Diamond Point by the shoulders and slammed him against the wall. "Where did you even get the information about Dark Blade's hideout?" she asked. Dark Blade sometimes worked with Lady Brawn. She mostly dealt with gangsters and sometimes overlapped with Estratega's corporate espionage but she wasn't someone Estratega wanted to piss off.

"What, she's probably buried under the rubble!" Diamond Point squeaked. This close up she could see the silver irises of his eyes. He smelled like vanilla musk and candy bars.

"Am I interrupting something?"

Estratega spun around. Her mouth dropped open. A woman wearing scintillating armor stood on the roof. She smiled at Estratega. Something about her smile was familiar.

"Facet?" Estratega said. "What are you doing here?" Facet was another gem-generating powered person. Last Estratega had heard, she had gone dark but before that had operated on the East Coast.

"Checking out the local competition," she said with another smile. It was more brilliant than her armor. She wore large earrings. "Didn't mean to interrupt you and your boyfriend."

Estratega let go of Diamond Point, the young sidekick slumping to the floor. "He's not my boyfriend."

"I thought you were into women?" Facet said as she strode forward.

"What is this about?" Estratega said, standing up straight. She felt short compared to Facet. Not that it mattered. Well, maybe a little. "Please leave so I can discipline my sidekick appropriately."

"You're the only one's getting disciplined," a voice said from the shadows. Estratega gritted her teeth as she spun around.

"Dark Blade?!" Diamond Point squeaked.

"AND ME." Lady Brawn slammed into the ground, kicking gravel up into the air.

"You have got to be fucking kidding me," Estratega said. She tapped on her bracer, pulling out the small cylinder that was the hilt of her laser foil. "Shouldn't you be helping the people down there?"

"Local officers have that under control," Dark Blade rasped, stepping forward out of the shadows, yet seeming to bring them with her. She was clad from head to toe in black body armor, a sword insignia on her chest. If her eyes had a color, Estratega couldn't see it. "We're dealing with the real problem."

"AND THAT'S YOU," Lady Brawn shouted.

"Oh my fuck, we know," Estratega said. She dashed at Lady Brawn with her sword, slashing and thrusting with the blade. Don't let your anger make you sloppy, she told herself. Lady Brawn had incredible strength but also wore a special girdle provided by some stupid super hero agency. It helped her regulate her strength so she didn't spend it all at once. Estratega knew there was a weakness in the girdle. She always tried to hit it, but it was hard getting around Lady Brawn. And Diamond Point was terrible with his projectiles, still.

Estratega grunted as a force knocked her sideways. High pitched thrumming told her Diamond Point was doing his best. His hand to hand wasn't bad. And he was hard to knock out. Literally. There were a lot of his powers he had yet left unexplored. Now would be a nice time for him to figure some of the more deadly abilities out. Estratega grit her teeth as she staggered up, bracing herself as Lady Brawn slammed her fist into Estratega's jaw.

I had not planned for this, Estratega thought to herself, her ears still ringing. Was it from the blow? Diamond Point? A multi-hued glow began to spread over the rooftop. She could hear Dark Blade and Diamond Point exchanging punches and kicks.

"Hey, Brawny," came Facet's voice. It was more melodic this time, like chimes. Lady Brawn actually spun around. "Look at the pretty colors. Opal Chaos."

Colors filled the air like they had form. Everything was the wrong color. Lady Brawn threw her hands up in front of her face and stepped back, trying to get away from the light.

The opening.

Estratega picked up her foil, gritting her teeth as she thrust forward between the third and forth bolt. More easily than it should have, the point broke through the metal, inches deep, sinking into metal and flesh and bone. Lady Brawn screamed, jerking against the blade. Estratega twisted the foil once for good measure before she drew it back, red, slick blood sizzling on the blade. Dancing around Lady Brawn, Estratega made a fist and delivered a punch across Lady Brawn's jaw. The hero's head snapped to the side with a labored grunt.

Lady Brawn fell to her knees. "Lady!" Dark Blade yelled. It was more like a scream. Diamond Point took the opportunity to kick the distracted hero in the face, sending her sprawling across the floor.

"Let's go," Estratega said. "This way." She taped on her bracers, upping her endorphin and adrenaline. She needed to ignore the pain to get away. Speeding across the roof, she only hoped Facet was following after her. And Diamond Point.

It never felt good to run away. But it felt good to be alive. And for small victories. A smile crept up onto her face as she leaped between two buildings, remembering her small triumph over Lady Brawn. Facet had helped her with that.

"Hold on!" Someone grabbed her by the shoulder. Estratega stopped and spun around, facing Facet. "I think we've lost them."

"I've got to get home before my adrenaline runs out," Estratega said. "I've got a bit to cover."

"My place isn't that far from here," Facet said. She smiled. "Maybe we can lay low. You and I can play Sovereign Squares."

Estratega blinked at the dazzling woman before her. "Bri?"

Facet smiled. It was the same smile Yvette had seen in the restaurant as they talked. It was Bri. "Yeah. Thought you could use some help."

"I thought you were hurt in one of the explosions," Yvette said. Confusion twisted her expression. Had Bri's disorientation been an act?

"Just a scratch," Bri said. "I heal up quick."

"You're dating Facet?" Diamond Point said. "Oh my god, this is so cool."

"Walker, shut up," Estratega said.

"As long as you're not dating Diamond Point," Bri said, side-eyeing Diamond Point.

"I'm not," Estratega, not masking her feelings as to how much the very thought disgusted her. "Though," she added. "I do date men. Occasionally. I'm attracted to both. Though I don't get much time to date." She nodded to herself, pleased to clear the air about it all. Seemed like the best strategy.

"I'm not into dudes," Facet said, crossing her arms over her chest. Even in her costume, she wore big earrings. "And I'm a one woman woman. I might make more of myself in times of war, but in love, there's just me."

"Oh my god, she's talking about the Multi-Facet Attack, where she makes copies of herself. I can't believe you're dating Facet?!" Diamond Point said. "This is so cool!"

"Shut up," Yvette said. "And we're not dating, we went on one... interesting date." Yvette smirked, looking up into Bri's eyes. "We'll take you up on your offer of shelter."

"I've only got a civilian set up right now," Bri said, starting to walk to the staircase of the building. "Stuffs still in boxes. Just warning you."

"Yvette hates that," Walker said.

"This is the third time I am saying it, shut up," Yvette said. "I'm still angry with you for blowing up all those buildings. We're lucky Facet showed up. And you know I don't like to leave things to luck."

"I know, I know," Walker said quietly. Facet ripped the door off its hinges and the three of them began their descent down the stairs, the sirens of the catastrophe barely audible in the staircase.

Yvette smiled as she walked behind them, Diamond Point chatting loudly as he walked, asking Facet questions. Every once in a while, Bri would look back and give her a slight, smile. Not as brilliant as the other ones. But sweet.

Yvette smirked. Her date hadn't gone to plan.

But it was perfect.

EDEN'S REVENGE
Missouri Vaun

Missouri Vaun hails from rural, southern Mississippi. She spent twelve years finding her voice working as a journalist in places as disparate as Chicago and Jackson, Miss., all along filing away characters and concepts until they seemed to rise up, fully formed. Her stories are heartfelt, earthy; speak of loyalty and our responsibility to others. She and her wife celebrated their sixth anniversary this summer. They live in northern California. You can visit her site at missourivaun.com

She hated him. No, hate wasn't strong enough. She reviled him. Yeah, she reviled him. She watched as Mr. Perfect, David Fleming reached inside his overcoat to retrieve a wallet, exposing the impeccably fitted custom suit underneath. Then he turned to leave the café with his six-dollar coffee without tipping the barista. He never noticed her. She figured her breasts weren't big enough to get his attention, or maybe it was the way she dressed.

As he passed her chair she stood abruptly and bumped into him, causing David to spill coffee down the front of his shirt.

"Fuck!" He shook the scalding beverage from his dripping hand.

"I'm so sorry." Eden made a fumbling attempt to wipe at the frothy spill with a few napkins and slipped her fingers lithely inside his jacket.

"Don't worry about it. Christ! Just watch where you're going the next time." He stepped around her and cursed under his breath as he exited leaving a small puddle of milk and coffee on the floor for someone else to clean up.

Eden picked up her laptop and moved to a corner table at the back of the coffee shop. She replaced her ear buds under her dark hoodie and looked through David's wallet. His arrogance made him such an easy mark it almost took the fun out of it. Almost. She'd buy enough random shit online to get his account frozen. He'd likely have to spend the rest of the afternoon straightening everything out with the bank, after he'd reported his cards and ID stolen. Eden was happy to have ruined David Fleming's day.

She didn't look much like her sister, Jordan, so David hadn't recognized her. He'd never have noticed her if she hadn't bumped into him. Eden Sorrow could have added the gift of invisibility to her list of qualifications, but she had other skills she'd more cleverly honed. Invisibility simply aided her ability to move freely in and out of venues she would normally never frequent, like expensive coffee houses in midtown Manhattan.

Like most unhappy thirtysomethings, Eden had not always been this way. She'd begun as so many before her, with hopeful optimism that the world was good and just and people who hurt others were held accountable. This was of course a naïve assumption. She knew that now. Her sister's death had shown her the truth.

David hadn't noticed Jordan for her looks either. He'd noticed her for her talent. And then he'd stolen it from her. He would live to regret his thievery. His six-dollar lattes were about to become a distant memory.

Eden had carefully catalogued Mr. Perfect's daily routine, and it gave her great joy that he had no idea what was coming. The gift she was about to bestow upon the masses. The truth was David Fleming wasn't alone in his callous use and dismissal of those he viewed as lesser. He was a product of a colossal systemic fucked-up-ness that seemed to permeate most of the modern world. Capitalism was eating away America's soul. David Fleming had been the catalyst for something that had become a much larger crusade for Eden, the demise of the so-called free market system and the wealthy assholes who profited from it.

Capitalism was, in her opinion, ephemeral. A network of virtual goods that only benefitted an entitled few who propped up the whole system. Eden Sorrow had a skeleton key to that virtual world and she was about to use it.

She downed the last sips of her overpriced black coffee, adjusted her hoodie, stowed her laptop in her shoulder bag, and headed for the subway. It would take three, maybe four hours to get back to her place near Lake Desolation. If she caught the train now she could beat the commuter traffic from Kingston heading north. She had to prepare before tomorrow's big show, and she wanted to make sure she didn't overlook even the smallest detail.

Thinking of tomorrow's event as a show made her smile. What she had in mind was a curtain drop on the final act of a play that had wearied its audience into numb passivity. Tomorrow, the curtain would fall and the stage lights would go dark, for good.

※

Grey Bishop pulled off the highway onto a wet, rutted gravel road. The battered mailbox at the end of the drive had the number 69 stenciled on the side with no name. At least the scenery on the way up from the city had been nice. The most recent April shower had cleared during her three hour drive to reveal spring's arrival in the newly sprouted greenery along the state parkway.

If Grey had been in the mood for a scenic drive this would have been the perfect day. As it was though, she was annoyed to be saddled with what was likely to be a wild goose chase. The Feds usually investigated anything they deemed a significant cyber attack. The fact that they'd turned this hunting expedition over to the locals meant they didn't perceive this lead to present a credible threat.

She'd drawn the short straw so here she was in the middle of fucking nowhere to question a woman named Eden Sorrow. What kind of name was that, anyway? She pulled her unmarked dark sedan up in front of a century old farmhouse in need of paint. The minute she stepped out of the car she regretted wearing her good shoes. *Fuck.* The mud made a sucking sound when she pulled her shoe free. She took tentative steps toward the porch, trying to avoid the worst of the mud.

Before she knocked, Grey leaned sideways to peer into one of the smudged front windows. She didn't see any movement. She gave the yard a slow sweeping glance. A Mercedes was parked inside what had probably at one time been a barn. Not a nice Mercedes, one of those puke yellow early 80s diesel jobs that every greenie was now converting to biodiesel so you smelled French fries if you tailgated.

Grey knocked and waited. After a moment she tried again. This time she heard footsteps and the door opened. The file said this woman's hacker handle was NrdGrl so she'd expected a pimply faced, nerdy science type. The centerfold for sexy librarians greeted Grey instead. She certainly didn't need to hide behind a laptop or an anonymous hacker handle. She was about five-eight, with a slender girlish build, light brown hair with blond highlights, and dark framed glasses. The frames offset the bluest eyes Grey had ever seen. She was wearing an oversized oxford shirt and an extremely short plaid miniskirt with Converse sneakers.

After too many moments of silence, Grey realized she'd been caught staring. She cleared her throat. "Excuse me, I'm looking for Eden Sorrow."

"That's me."

"I'm Detective Grey Bishop." Grey flashed her badge. "Do you mind if I ask you a few questions?"

"What about?"

"Some recent activity in your area of expertise."

"Okay, I guess." Eden shrugged and stepped to the side of the door. "Would you like to come in?"

"Yeah, thank you." But then she hesitated and looked down at her muddy wingtips.

"You can take them off just inside the door."

Grey nodded. She'd definitely lost a few intimidation points by following Eden further into the house in socks.

"I won't take up much of your time. I just have a few questions." Once inside Grey tried to visually document every detail of the room. There wasn't much to see. Her first impression was the décor didn't fit the owner. This place looked like someone's grandparents had decorated it, complete with a faded floral print sofa and doilies on the coffee table.

"Would you like some coffee? I was just about to have a cup." Eden left her in the living room and headed toward the kitchen at the back of the house.

"Sure. Thanks." Alone in the room for a moment, Grey leaned into the two adjoining rooms for a quick look. The socks made it easy to move about without making too much noise.

One room looked like a study. An open laptop rested on the desk. The wallpaper featured a pink skull with crossbones. *Cute.* The other room contained a neatly made bed and one small dresser. It looked oddly unlived in.

Grey returned to the main living room before Eden did. As Eden handed her a mug of black coffee she motioned for Grey to sit.

Eden sank into an armchair and watched the detective as she shifted on the sagging sofa, crossing and then uncrossing her legs. Eden could tell that she made Grey nervous. She liked that. Grey was tall with dark brooding eyes, fashionably disheveled short brown hair, leanly built with slight curves in all the right places. The stiff white dress shirt was open just enough to reveal a tempting view of her delicate collar bone. Grey Bishop was incredibly sexy.

"Sorry, I drink mine black so I never have cream on hand." Eden nodded toward the coffee in Grey's hand.

"Just the way I like it."

"Is Grey your real name?"

"It's a family name."

"Interesting name for a woman."

"I suppose." Grey sipped the coffee and averted her eyes. Eden was fairly sure they'd been focused on her legs. "Miss Sorrow, I came to ask you about the power outage that happened a few months ago."

"Power outage?" Eden played dumb. She wasn't about to reveal anything to this cop, regardless of how hot she was. As Grey leaned back into the sofa the handgrip of her sidearm was barely visible in a brown holster beneath her dark jacket.

"We're investigating the possibility that the outage was caused by a computer virus. You work with computers, right? Your hacker handle is NrdGrl?"

"Yeah, that's me. You know, being a hacker isn't a crime."

"I didn't say it was."

"In fact, a unifying trait among hackers is a strong sense of curiosity. We just like to see if we can figure things out. Curiosity wasn't a crime the last time I checked either."

"Do you know anything about the outage, Ms. Sorrow?"

Did Grey know something or was she just fishing? Eden decided the detective had no idea what really went down.

The blackout had been caused by a software bug Eden planted into the alarm system at a control room of the FirstEnergy Corporation in Ohio to find out how vulnerable the system was, apparently, very. Alarms were supposed to prompt technicians to reroute power from overloaded grids. The lack of alarms left operators unaware of the need to re-distribute power, which triggered a race condition in the control software. Unexecuted functions backlogged and what could have been a manageable local blackout cascaded into massive widespread distress on the power grid. Boom. The lights went out for ten million people in Ontario and forty-five million in the States. Eden's little test run had gone brilliantly.

"I don't know anything about the outage, except that I lost power out here for more than a week." Eden sipped her coffee and waited for Grey's next stupid question. Then something occurred to her and she smiled, maybe Grey liked to play dumb also.

"That's an interesting ring." Grey said and took a sip of her coffee.

For a moment Eden forgot that Grey was someone to be wary of. The comment was casual, almost personal. She fingered the bulky silver band on her middle finger. A lightning bolt was cut into the face. "I like electricity. Lightning fascinates me." Why had she shared such a personal detail with Grey? Maybe she was leaving Grey clues to her psyche. Did she want Grey to save her? No, not really. She didn't need to be saved.

"I like lightning storms too." Grey's voice sounded wistful and for a moment her gaze seemed far away. She cleared her throat and leaned forward, downing the last of her coffee. "This place, it doesn't look like you, if you don't mind me saying so."

"It belonged to my grandparents. I don't come up here very much." Eden shifted in her chair. She had things to do, and Grey was a distraction. "I'm sorry I can't be of more help, but there's a project I really need to get back to." Eden nodded in the direction of the laptop on the desk in the adjoining room.

"Of course." Grey stood and walked toward the door. She slipped on her muddy shoes, but before stepping off the porch she turned to Eden. "Here's my card. If by chance you come across any information about that blackout, please give me a call."

"Sure." Eden stood in the door, rubbing the embossed letters of the card between her fingers as she watched Grey drive away. She didn't think for one minute that Grey bought her story about this place belonging to her grandparents, but by the time Ms. Detective figured anything out it would be too late.

Eden locked the door, picked up her laptop and stepped into the closet of the bedroom. The real reason she'd bought this place was fifty feet underground. The closet had a false floor that opened onto a narrow stairway. At the bottom built into the concrete floor was a circular steel door that looked as if it belonged on a submarine. Eden swung the handle around four times and the hatch popped loose, behind it was a room full of equipment.

She'd lucked out when she found this place. It had belonged to a survivalist prepper and his wife who thought having a black president was the last sign of the apocalypse. The husband had been an engineer and had built a fallout shelter with everything someone would need to survive a nuclear bomb, a zombie invasion, extreme climate change, or any combination of the three. But then he'd died. Turned out cancer claimed him before the apocalypse could. His wife didn't want to keep the place after that. She sold it to Eden for cash and moved south to be with her kids.

Her sister's life insurance policy had given Eden more than enough to buy the place. She couldn't have constructed a better hideout if she'd tried to build one herself.

The wife had sold her everything, including the firearms that her husband had amassed. Eden wasn't really interested in guns. She preferred Tasers, but the battery of firepower did have a certain intimidation factor. In a small room off the main control center were two pre-ban AR-15s with 50 magazines, other handguns ranging from .22 to .44 magnum, several hunting rifles of various calibers, four surplus bolt-action .30 caliber rifles and stores of ammunition. The man was serious about guns.

The farmhouse had water from nearby wells stored in uphill tanks and a 5,000-gallon underground water storage container fed by recovered rainwater from the metal roof. Electrical panels configured to allow essential circuits to be powered by a propane generator, or by photovoltaic panels.

In the control room there was a suite of base and mobile radio gear, with matching low profile dipole and vertical antennas that blended in with the surrounding trees.

Above ground the house looked like shit, below ground it was like a fortified doomsday shelter.

The only thing Eden had to take care of herself was converting her car. She'd attended a few prepper meetings herself and learned that the best candidate for surviving an electro magnetic pulse blast would be a governor based diesel because it had a compression ignition, rather than a spark ignition. She just had to get a mechanic friend to replace the cables for the starter and batteries with heavier gauge protected wires with shielding grounded to the car frame.

Eden picked up a small, framed photo of Jordan. She traced her index finger along the shape of her face. She'd been so beautiful, so full of life. David Fleming had taken all of that away.

Jordan and Eden couldn't have been more different. Where Eden was introverted, Jordan was the life of any party. She was a talented clothing designer and had just gotten a spread in Designer Weekly leading up to fashion week. Jordan was living her dream, until David bought her clothing line, her brand.

Only, to Jordan, her creations weren't a "brand," they were her life. Those designs were part of her. The fashion industry was brutal and unforgiving and once you fell from grace it was nearly impossible to regain that position. Jordan had sunk into a deep depression that ended in suicide.

Eden couldn't save her. The familiar knot of grief rose in her throat.

Jordan was a talented woman who had always played by the rules, done what she was supposed to do and had succeeded, only to be brought down by a shallow, fake-tanned shyster like David Fleming.

Eden brushed a tear away with her hand.

Tomorrow would be the end of David Fleming. Eden could only hope that he was in the elevator shaft in his high-rise building when the device detonated. She liked the thought of him being trapped for hours, days even. Then he'd have some time to think about everything he'd done.

She logged into her computer and input keystrokes. Once she hit execute it would only take the missile twenty minutes to reach the proper altitude over Kansas to do the most damage. The powers that be would be scrambling, looking for someone to blame. They'd likely assume it was Russia or North Korea rather than someone in their own backyard. The government was too distracted by their war on terror to see the terror they'd fostered at home.

Back at the station, Grey was puzzling over her encounter with Eden. Everything about that visit to the farm had been wrong. She decided to dig a little deeper. The file on Eden Sorrow now seemed woefully incomplete. There had to be more of a story.

She sipped coffee as she scanned the screen for threads to follow. Then something caught her eye. Another name, Jordan Sorrow. Grey clicked through several screens until she found the coroner's report on Jordan's suicide. Foul play wasn't suspected but why would a seemingly beautiful and successful woman kill herself?

Grey spent two hours reading everything she could find about Jordan Sorrow, whose life read like a screenplay for a movie. Hers was a rags-to-riches tale of a talented designer making it big in the competitive fashion industry. Then her line of clothing was bought by David Fleming, who turned it into a mass-market sensation before moving onto his next acquisition. Fleming's business model sounded more like the entertainment industry, using actors and other famous types to promote his clothing lines.

A few fashion insider blogs hinted at some confrontation between Fleming and Jordan Sorrow. Would someone really kill herself over fashion? Maybe Grey just didn't get it. She didn't give ten minutes of thought to her daily wardrobe. White shirt, dark suit, black shoes, done.

Okay, enough of Jordan Sorrow. Back to what she was really looking for before she'd spiraled down the rabbit hole.

Grey pulled up property records for the farmhouse. Just as she'd expected, it hadn't belonged to Eden's grandparents. The property had been cited in a complaint a few years back. The previous owner had pulled a gun on someone from the utilities company and then he was later fined for carrying a sidearm into a pastry shop in Saratoga Springs.

Grey was unable to find much on Eden Sorrow directly. Her file was thin for a reason. Either Eden had never done anything or she'd never gotten caught. She'd attended NYU and graduated with dual degrees in political science and computer science. And then nothing. It was as if she'd evaporated into thin air after graduation. The only reason she'd shown up on the FBI's radar at all was because she'd been named by a fellow hacker in an investigation into a breach of security with Suisse Bank, funds were missing from the accounts of several investors, one of whom was David Fleming. A connection between Eden and the missing funds had never been found. Still, there must have been some connection with Jordan's death otherwise why would Eden have paid any attention to David Fleming?

Grey now had more questions she wasn't going to get answers to unless she went back to the source. But was there enough evidence to warrant another drive out to Lake Desolation or was her libido leading her around again? A mental picture of Eden's legs tucked beneath her, wearing that very revealing mini skirt was seared in Grey's brain. She logged out and leaned back in her chair to stretch, her back was stiff from the drive and sitting for two hours hunched over the keyboard.

"Hey, Bishop, we're heading over to Mike's Pub. You coming?" Frank, a burly fellow with a perpetual five o'clock shadow was pulling on his wrinkled jacket nearby.

"Yeah, sure." A drink sounded appealing, preferably something strong enough to get her mind off Eden. She wasn't sure why, but the woman had gotten to her and she feared she wasn't going to be able to stop thinking about her anytime soon.

✄

Eden checked the coordinates again. Once the launch sequence was initiated it would take only twenty minutes for the missile to reach the airspace over central Kansas.

The Starfish Prime detonation over the Pacific Ocean in the sixties had disrupted radio and electronic equipment eight hundred miles away in Hawaii and this was going to be a much larger HEMP device. The high-altitude electromagnetic pulse weapon's detonation would be picked up by power lines which would act as antennas to conduct the energy shockwave into the electronic systems of cars, planes, computers and communications equipment. Everything would be affected.

North America would get the reboot it so badly needed, a huge wake up call for the comatose masses. And David Fleming would lose everything. That was the cherry on top. He'd have no access to funds or services. He'd be like a helpless fucking baby. Did the man even have any friends he could turn to? She doubted it.

She paused for a moment wondering what Jordan would say about all of this. She'd probably say Eden was going too far. But Eden was tired of finding small ways to hurt David. The whole system needed to come down so no one else could be hurt by it.

She leaned back in her chair and laughed, maybe she was spending too much time alone. Grey's card caught her eye and she picked it up and ran her fingers over the number. Maybe she should call the sexy detective and turn herself in. Yeah, that sounded like a truly inspired idea. Once the power grid went down there'd be no more online dating or chat rooms or cell phones. She'd be left with nothing but freeze-dried dinners and shelves full of her favorite books. Maybe she should consider finding someone to share her fall-out shelter with. She wondered if the sexy detective liked to read. Eden picked up the phone and dialed Grey's number.

The phone rang once, twice.

"Hello?"

Eden could barely hear Grey's voice above the cacophony of background noise. "Detective? This is Eden Sorrow."

"Hang on." After a moment, the noise lessened. "Sorry, I had to step outside so that I could hear you. Who is this?"

"Eden Sorrow."

"Hi."

"Hi." She'd obviously caught Grey by surprise. Cute. "Listen, I realized that I do have some information that might be helpful. Could we meet?"

"Sure. I could drive back out tomorrow but it would be early evening before I could get there."

Perfect. Just in time for the light show. "That would work. I'll be here."

Eden clicked off. She couldn't help smiling as she dropped the landline phone back into its cradle. She walked through the main control room of her underground playground, through the pantry filled with freeze-dried and canned goods and into the small bedroom space. She pulled a book from a nearby shelf and fell backward onto the bed. She would read a bit of Cormac McCarthy's *Blood Meridian* before she fell asleep and dreamed about the end of the world.

✼

Eden sealed the hatch and climbed the narrow stairs to the main floor of the house. She'd input the launch sequence and the virus that would keep anyone from stopping it, should any system alarms get triggered. Grey was late. If she delayed much longer Eden would have to drive out and pick her up because as soon as the HEMP detonated Grey's car would be dead and she'd be on foot.

She backed the old Mercedes out of the barn and drove toward the main road. She reached the end of her long narrow drive at the same moment that Grey's dark sedan turned off the paved road. The lane was too narrow for either of them to pass so Eden switched the car off. She reached for a small, black, insulated box on the passenger seat before she got out.

"Sorry, it took me longer than I expected to get here. Are you leaving?" Grey stood behind the open door of her vehicle. The sun had dipped to the horizon. Darkness was moments away. Grey reached back and switched off her headlights.

"I was driving out to find you."

"Really? Why?"

"Well, any moment a high altitude nuclear electromagnetic device is going to detonate and when it does, your car won't work."

Grey stepped to the front of the car. They were standing about ten feet apart. Eden could see the confused look on Grey's face, even in the waning evening light.

"What?"

"Yeah, hopefully we'll be able to see the debris fireball stretching along Earth's magnetic field. Within three minutes of the detonation we should be able to see an air-glow aurora even from here." Eden watched Grey reach for the holstered weapon under her jacket. She pulled the gun, but kept it low at her side.

"Eden, what have you done? An EMP device will knock out everything." Grey took a step forward. "You don't want to do this. This will have long-term, catastrophic consequences for everyone."

"I know. It'll cause cascading effects on all interdependent infrastructures, possibly lasting for months. Pretty rad, huh?" Eden didn't want to gloat, but she couldn't help smiling.

"Eden, people will die from lack of services. Innocent people. David Fleming won't be the only one who suffers."

Ah, so Grey Bishop wasn't dumb after all. Good. Smart women were so much more attractive.

"But he will suffer and that's what really matters." Eden rubbed her hand over the box she held. She was impatient, but she knew she had to wait for it.

"So you'd take down the whole world just to hurt one person?"

"Americans always see themselves as the whole world." Eden shifted her stance and cocked her head. "I'm fairly certain China will be unaffected by the blast."

Grey turned as a flash of light erupted to the southwest. Bands of light danced as the glow silently expanded over the horizon. It looked like all the photos Eden had seen of the northern lights. She enjoyed the view for a moment, then, while Grey was still distracted Eden removed the Taser from the small box and fired it at Grey.

Grey absorbed the electric jolt like a solid kick to her chest. It tossed her backward and she hit the ground hard. Her whole body vibrated. Her skin felt numb and hot at the same time, every muscle rigid. She couldn't make her arms move. Eden stood over her looking down. She kicked the handgun away from her paralyzed hand with the rubber toe of her sneakers.

"The explosion releases a blast of gamma rays into the mid-stratosphere, which ionizes and the electrons interact with the Earth's magnetic field to produce a much stronger EMP than is normally produced in the denser air at lower altitudes. Thus the amazing light show." Eden switched the Taser off.

Grey no longer felt the charge pulsing through her body, but her limbs were weak and her rattled brain struggled to understand what Eden was saying.

Eden knelt beside Grey, pulled the handcuffs from her belt, and Grey felt the vague sensation of the cuffs closing around her wrists.

"You know that power outage you asked me about? Did you know that with the power grid down the Milky Way was visible to the naked eye? Without all the air pollution and light pollution I saw the Milky Way from my front yard. It was beautiful." Eden dragged Grey toward her car. With some effort she hoisted Grey's weakened body into the back seat and closed the door.

Grey sensed motion as the car turned around. The cool leather of the back seat was soothing against her heated skin and the smell of French fries filled the airspace leaking in from the sunken space between the back seat and the trunk of the car.

Handcuffed, twitching and weak in a near fetal position, Grey came to the disturbing conclusion that Eden Sorrow was insane. The hot ones always were.

GENTLEMAN JACK
Barbara Ann Wright

Barbara Ann Wright writes fantasy and science fiction novels and short stories when not adding to her enormous book collection or ranting on her blog. Her works have been *Tor.com*'s Reviewer's Choice, finalists for Foreword Book of the Year and Golden Crown and have won two Rainbow Awards for Best Lesbian Fantasy.

No one lets their gaze linger quite like a woman. Respectable ladies can't display the leer of the working girl, but that's what makes their surreptitious glances so delicious. They peek out from behind fans or from the sides of hats and bonnets. The most naïve, innocent girls will stare outright before a pink flush and averted gaze, and then the game is all about looking while pretending to do something else.

I don't blame them for gawking. Indeed, it gives me quite the thrill. I cut a fine figure in my black suit and hat, my silk shirts and vests, a colorful cravat to tie the whole thing together. My skill at dressing is no doubt one of the reasons so many choose to stay in my room even after they find out I'm a woman.

My charm has more than a little to do with it, too. The northern ladies like my drawl; the southern ones appreciate a gentlemanly manner. And those ladies in the one horse towns of the frontier take to anyone who eschews rough and tumble ways for courtly manners and a kiss of the hand. Of course, a little handy cash never hurts either.

But mostly, they love me because of the power.

As I pass down a particularly dusty street in the thriving town of Sedona, Arizona, I tip my hat to the ladies and count every little glance. I also tap a bit of power, watching as those I pass raise their noses just a trifle. Heads turn, and brows wrinkle as if trying to remember where they might have smelled my tantalizing scent before. Having never actually smelled it myself, I couldn't say. Those I've asked—usually as we are entwined in the sheets—have never given me a sufficient answer. One little coquette I picked up in Texas said it smelled like raw sex, and then she put her hand over her mouth and giggled until I had to have her again.

At the moment, I just like the attention. When I stroll into the bank, it's a different story. As soon as the door closes behind me, I turn the power up nearly full blast.

Heads swivel my way like clockwork. A male and female clerk as well as a male customer step toward me, hunger lighting their faces. The pair behind the counter fumble through the locked door until they can breathe deeply in my presence.

The men advance quicker than the woman, but I point to the floor. "Sit a while, fellas, and I reckon you'll get everything you want."

They obey immediately, desperate for a touch, a caress, anything, but I'm in control here, and they'll do whatever I command as long as the promise of me remains. Sometimes, their lust is so strong, they even start in on each other, but that's none of my business.

The lady is petite, with a plump figure I could spend a few pleasant days exploring. She steps nearly to my chest and breathes deeply, eyes closed. I put a finger under her chin and tilt her head up. "Darlin', why don't you and I see about that vault?"

She giggles as she leads the way. I chase her, patting her rump, giving her a tickle. When she unlocks the vault, she steps in backward, biting her lip and crooking her finger for me to follow. Hot damn, she makes me wish I could stay a spell, but I need to work fast or the whole town will get involved. Too many people ensnared in the power is nothing but trouble. The orgy of Kansas City nearly did me in.

The clerk sits on a stack of crates and undoes several of her dress buttons as I fill my satchel with dollars and gold. She's a fine distraction, and I wonder briefly what she'll tell herself when I'm gone. The power does wear off, and at times there have been regrets. Even for all the pleasure I can give, some ladies are just never happy. I rub the clerk's cheek, and she makes a little mewling noise.

"Now just stay here a while, darlin'," I say. "I'll be right back."

"Hurry!"

The two men look up as I pass, but I gesture for them to sit still. With extreme pouts, they obey, and when I step out into the dusty street and sunshine, I turn the sign on the door to "Closed." It's always bought me a little time.

When I return to my horse, already packed for my escape, it seems a shame that it's so easy. Maybe I should settle somewhere, get a big estate in Georgia or South Carolina and have a harem like in a cheap novel. But I could never be content in retirement. The gold rush in California beckons. They say a man can make his fortune there, but I intend more than that. Amassing wealth is easy. I intend to be a queen. Unfortunately, a queen needs capital.

No outcries sound behind me as I ride out of town. I imagine the bank will be left like all the others, blinking and stammering and trying to comprehend what happened. Good Lord, it still makes me smile.

After a day, I arrive in Jerome, my next target town, with several banks ripe for picking. As I check into a mid-priced hotel in the evening, another guest gives me an over the shoulder, covert study. She's handsome in her widow's black, and she's added touches of color that say mourning is nearly done. I lean on the counter and study her outright. I think she's suffered enough.

When the desk clerk goes to the back, I check to make sure we're alone before I let my power slip loose. The widow turns with a surprised look, as if she's having feelings she'd never thought to have again. She could resist me. It's happened once or twice, but I find most people don't bother to try. When I invite her up to my room, she blushes and stammers, but ultimately agrees, hungry as the rest of them.

Behind closed doors, she is all greedy kisses and fumbling fingers as she divests me of my coat and vest. At my shirt, she lingers, discovering my breasts. She gasps and stares with wide blue eyes.

I nod over her shoulder. "There's the door if you want it, darlin', but if you stay, I promise you the time of your life." I even turn the power down a smidge. Being able to pass for a man is too handy to make me ever give it up, but it does make this stage a mite awkward. I always give them the chance to escape, though. It's the gentlemanly thing to do. My pride will brook no less.

Just like all the others, she refuses the offer, dives back into the scent of my power, and claims my lips again.

Hot damn.

For a few days, I gladly help the Widow Tucker sneak from her room to mine. All part of a gentleman's duty, as I see it. Well, there's also the fact that if I keep her happy, she keeps mum about my abilities. It's three full days before I'm ready to come up for air, ready for my next score. In between bouts of ecstasy, I've studied all three banks in my temporary home, memorizing their light hours and who's on duty when. The widow has suspected from the beginning that our time together is short, but I don't think she knows how much. During one smidge of pillow talk, she told me she's never felt so free. I told her I was always happy to oblige. Today, however, I'm going to disappear.

If she misses me, she'll get over it. I suppose it's a shame that some of them are heartbroken, but that's the way of the world.

As I approach my target bank, I spy a very attractive woman lingering outside. I slow to take a good look. She's as tall as I am, quite unusual. I doubt she has to wear lifts in her shoes to achieve it. She wears a dove-colored riding dress, very sensible yet well made. It flatters her trim figure. Her hat is stylish, New England if I had to bet, and I've seen the insides of enough pieces of clothing to know the difference. She is beautiful in a fierce way, and her lips are set in a little frown that says she's not prepared to take any nonsense. God help me, I love the schoolteacher types.

When I tear my eyes away from her body, I notice she's affixing a sheet of paper to the wall in front of the bank, a paper with a very familiar face, the one I see in the mirror every morning.

I don't stop but walk on by, turning away from the woman and more importantly the picture and wondering how in the hell I let this happen. All the people in all the banks I've visited should have recalled only hazy details about my person. A large shot of my power puts people in quite a funk, but the picture is a very good representation. She must have spoken to a great many people, amassed a large amount of clues, and it means I should leave sooner rather than later, but I circle around the back of the building and pull my hat low over my face, determined to find out just what this fierce woman knows.

I poach a discarded paper off the front bench of a general store and approach the bank again from an alley to the side. I sidle close to the front of the bank and peek around. The sheriff has joined the fierce woman, so I lean against the side of the bank and lift the paper to cover my face while tilting my ear toward the pair.

"And you're sure this Gentleman Jack is coming here, Miss Shepherd?" the sheriff asks, pure skepticism in his voice.

"After Sedona, this is the most likely target," Miss Shepherd replies in clipped New York tones.

"No offense to your bosses, Miss Shepherd; the Pinkerton Agency knows what it's doing, I'm sure, but Sedona was nearly a week ago. If he's been here, he's come and gone."

"Have any of your banks been robbed by someone who can charm the clerks into giving him the money?"

"Well, no."

"Then he hasn't been here."

The sheriff sighs, and I've heard the tone before. It screams, "God save me from dealing with women." I wonder if Miss Shepherd will lose her patience and give him a good kick.

"You don't even have a last name for him," the sheriff says.

"Nor a first." Her tone says patience is a virtue, one that's quickly running out. "He has used Jack in the past, but I'm sure it's not his real name. However, faces are easier to remember if they come with names, especially catchy ones, so I give you Gentleman Jack."

He must mumble something because she adds, "I beg your pardon?"

"Look, maybe I should talk to your boss, Miss Shepherd."

The sigh she utters seems to trail a hundred other sighs behind it. Even though the Pinkertons see the wisdom in hiring female agents, not everyone agrees. I almost feel sorry for her, but I can't help but take joy at anything that stands in her way.

"Unfortunately," she says, "Mr. Gerand isn't available at the moment."

"But he is here, right? Overseeing all this?"

She hesitates before uttering, "Of course. I'll let him know you inquired."

It sounds like every other lie I've heard from people who consider themselves truthful. As far as I know, Pinkertons like to travel in groups, at least when they're advertising what they are. Miss Shepherd might be striking out on her own. I can't contain a smile. Hell, this might be easier than I thought.

When she stalks away from the sheriff, I give her a ten count before I follow. A little alone time and I can find out if she really is on her own. Maybe I can even send her on her way with a powerful jolt, telling her I'll be waiting wherever I send her to. If I time it just right, maybe it will carry her days away, and I can ride on, skip a few towns and get nice and ahead of her before she cottons on.

She enters one of the better priced hotels, and I follow, lingering in the lobby as she climbs the stairs and enters her room. I stay put, perusing my paper until the clerk disappears on some errand, and then I'm up the stairs like a shot.

Miss Shepherd's door is slightly ajar, and I knock softly, sending it swinging inward. There's no one about, but I would have seen her emerge. Maybe some errand took her to the back stairs?

When I turn that way, I hear the click of a pistol being cocked. I turn slowly, and Miss Shepherd is standing in the door to her room, a small revolver aimed at my chest. She cocks her head and stares at me, but she can't feel as confident as her straight back suggests, for a thin sheen of sweat glistens on her upper lip.

I let my power ooze out slowly, not wanting her to make any sudden moves with that pistol in her grasp. To my quiet horror, she only cocks her head further and frowns. Her nostrils flare, but her eyes retain the same determination.

"Good God," she says, "I thought you must be using some sort of spray, but that's just... you, isn't it?"

I take a step back and turn up the power a bit more. "How are you..."

She twitches and raises the gun higher. "An oil of my own concoction. After hearing about your exploits in Missouri, I thought it prudent."

Not sweat under her nose, then. She's been on my trail a long time. Ah well, it has been awhile since I had to rely on charm alone, but I reckon I can manage. I lean against the wall, letting her know I'm not about to lunge. She doesn't seem in a hurry to take me to jail. Indeed, that intensity in her eyes speaks to curiosity more than anything. That I can work with. Still, I let my power build up slowly, just in case.

"How did you find out about me?" I ask.

"I've interviewed some of your victims."

"Lovers, Miss. I have never in my life forced a woman."

She frowns harder. "So you say. Do you truly believe that robbing a woman of her virtue and then leaving her does not make her a victim?"

"Which of them claims I stole their virtue?"

Her silence says none.

I give her a sideways smile. "The virgins who have made my acquaintance can console themselves with the fact that after having me for a lover, they can still claim to be untouched by a man."

Her frown deepens, and her eyes give me a quick pan up and down, but it's not a hungry glance, not yet. Whatever concoction she has devised is strong indeed, but I am determined to defeat it.

Her eyes widen once they've finished their survey. "Good God, don't tell me you're—"

I put my finger to my lips and wink. She flushes six ways to Sunday as she no doubt pictures me entwined with some of the ladies she's interviewed. I hope it's giving her quite a show. The pistol is trembling a smidge now, but I don't know if it's from my power or her thoughts.

She rallies quickly, taking a deep breath. "I suppose I'll have to stop calling you *Gentleman* Jack."

I shrug. "I quite like it."

"And how do you…" She gestures at me vaguely. "Do what you do?"

"Shouldn't you be taking me to your superiors?"

Another pause. "Can't a woman be curious?"

"You're here alone, aren't you?"

Her fingers grow white-knuckled around the pistol's grip.

I shake my head slowly. "I don't aim to hurt you, Miss. But if I'm your pet project, investigated outside the gaze of your superiors, how are you ever going to explain me to them?" She still doesn't answer, and I lean forward just a little. My power is almost as high as I can take it.

"They'll have to believe me," she says softly. "This time."

"Had trouble believing you before, did they? Maybe you tried to warn them about me, only they didn't listen. It's only your keen open mind that's figured it out."

She can't seem to break her gaze from mine, and that pistol is really shaking now. Her mouth slips open a little, and her breath is coming faster. She lowers the gun suddenly and launches toward me. I catch her in my arms, and then her lips are on mine as if she's dying for lack of a kiss.

But as considerable as her charms are, I'm not looking for companionship just now. I grab her shoulders and thrust her back. "Go inside and wait for me, darlin'."

"No, now!"

By God, her will is as strong as iron, even under the influence of my power. When it wears off, she is going to be as angry as the devil himself. I've had more than a few like her. Even under the power, they have to be in control. Usually, I don't mind, but I want her too embarrassed to pursue me, not angry enough to hunt me to the ends of the earth. If I stick around, and we make love, she might strangle me with her bare hands.

"I will be there as soon as I can, darlin'." I steer her into her room and take the pistol. She uses her newly free hands to caress my body until the blood is pounding in my ears, but I push her roughly into the room, making her trip onto the bed and bounce over it onto the floor. I slam the door between us and high tail it out, running until I reach my horse and gallop out of town.

Luckily, since I was planning to rob the first bank, I'm already packed. Even though I had designs on the other two, I always think it best to be cautious, and this morning is proof that such forward thinking serves me well. I lick my lips and reflect on Miss Shepherd as I ride. Seems I haven't been forward thinking enough. Missouri would have garnered a lot of attention, but events there got out of hand before I realized it. The orgy told me a lot about my powers, how they might be put to greatest use. It was after that night of debauchery that I first considered becoming queen of California. I knew what I could accomplish if I truly put my mind to it, and it seems other people have realized it as well.

Well, one anyway, a woman smart enough to invent measures to guard against me, even if she thought my power was derived from some kind of spray instead of myself. And now she knows even more. It's a shame her bosses don't believe her, but I suppose it's good news for me. Still, the thought of someone dismissing her chaps my hide a little. I don't know if they fail to believe her because she's a woman, or because someone like me seems ridiculous to anyone who's never been under my spell, but if Miss Shepherd showed them evidence, only prejudice could make them turn a blind eye. Maybe someday, when my power and my influence are undeniable, her bosses will pay me a visit, and I can show them the truth, up close and personal like. After a few days of panting for me and being denied, maybe they'll crawl back to Miss Shepherd sighing a hearty mea culpa.

I try to remember if I told anyone in Missouri about my revelations, if anyone knows about my ultimate destination. To be on the safe side, I turn south toward Tucson, only stopping to resupply before I head on. It's been a long time since I camped out in the wilderness for an extended period, and I must say, I've lost my taste for it. I've become accustomed to fine sheets and making love to beautiful women at least once a week, and I begin to resent Miss Shepherd as I'm limited for weeks on end to dust and cold nights. My wardrobe begins to look very much the worse for wear. I wonder what Miss Shepherd would think if I sent her a tailoring bill, care of the Pinkerton Agency.

When I judge I've gone far enough to put her off my trail, I stop at a small town, not even bothering to learn the name as my horse trudges through the outskirts. I don't think of Miss Shepherd as I hitch my horse, take a very welcome bath in the town's best hotel, and head out to the nearest saloon. I don't think about her while I drink whiskey or play cards. She doesn't even cross my mind as I meet the eyes of the ladies plying their wares around the saloon floor. No, it's not until I seriously consider taking one to my room that the specter of Miss Shepherd dashing into my arms won't leave me. I retire to my room alone. I'm so tired, I think sleep will come immediately, but it waits a long time, and Miss Shepherd follows me into my dreams. Of course, those dreams are of the hot damn variety, but all in all, I'd rather she left me alone.

Imagine my surprise, then, when I ride out in the morning, ready to turn west again, and find Miss Shepherd standing beside a horse and cart. She lingers in the middle of the miserable excuse for a road, turned away from me, a large portmanteau open at her feet. I dismount and edge close to her, leaving my horse standing alone. Her suitcase is a curious one, with racks of glass bottles nestled inside. It's scratched and battered appearance makes it seem older than her, all but the gleaming brass plate on one side bearing the initials BLS.

Miss Shepherd takes one bottle and dribbles a few drops of liquid onto a circular piece of fabric held in a small embroidery hoop attached to a long pole. This she lifts into the air and waves slowly back and forth. She frowns up at it in quiet intensity as she walks across the road, waving the hoop before her.

I peer at her cloth, wondering if it's some kind of ritual or if she's gone quite mad. Then like a bolt of lightning, I reckon how she's followed me, how she probably found me in the first place. Even keener of mind than I previously thought, she has engineered some way to track me via my power, using her bottles and concoctions to sniff me out.

Inside its hoop, the cloth slowly turns blue. She begins to lower it, but when the color darkens from light blue to indigo, she pauses. I take a step back, but she whirls around, stabbing a finger in my direction, and I jump as if she's shot me.

Her smile is pure satisfaction with a tint some might call evil, and I know I should run, but I am rooted to the spot. I see no pistol. Maybe I took her only one. Maybe her others are hidden, but since she doesn't seem to want to draw right that instant, my feet don't want to take me anywhere else.

"Miss Shepherd," I say, touching the brim of my hat.

"Gentleman Jack." She straightens, and the look of satisfaction softens to something more respectable. If she's surprised I know her name when we haven't been introduced, she doesn't show it. "Did you think you'd seen the last of me?"

"That seems a line more suited to a woman seeking vengeance than a lawman looking to make an arrest."

She lifts an eyebrow. "Law woman."

I step toward her, and she matches me step for step until only about a foot of air separates us. "So," I say softly, "are you going to try and shoot me again, or are we going to come right to the kissing?"

She obliges me with a bit of a blush, but not nearly the brightness I was expecting. "I should shoot you just for that."

"I do believe you kissed me, darlin', not the other way around."

"You made—" She takes a deep breath. "You used your... ability on me."

"People can resist me if they want. It's happened before."

Her eyes blaze, and it seems as if she might yell at me, but I nod at the contraption still in her hand. "You are a scientist crossed with a bloodhound, Miss Shepherd. I tip my hat to you."

She straightens a little but does not lose her glare. Her fist, however, uncurls. "I simply use the lessons my parents taught me."

"Your bosses seem like even bigger fools now, to dismiss what you had to say."

There is a hint of a smile on her lips, but she does not let it bloom. "You're under arrest."

"Even though you know they still won't believe you?"

"They may not recognize what you are, but they know what you've stolen. And I'm sure the witnesses can identify you, even if they can't say what you did to them."

I take a long look at her lips, remembering their softness as well as noting that she's used her oil again. I wonder if she's figured out how to make it stronger. One of her hands is now lost in her skirts, perhaps fishing for another pistol.

"Are you going to pull a gun?" I ask. "Or just woman-handle me into your cart?" I glance at the empty road behind her. "Or do you have an invisible posse?"

She quirks an eyebrow. "Better."

"Oh? Do tell." My power is already creeping up. She has to know it's just a matter of time.

Her nostrils flare, and she leans back as if she might step away but holds her ground. Her mouth parts like it did just before we kissed. I wonder if our kiss affected her as much as me, and now she's looking for a reason to let go.

I'm just starting to ask her when her hand whips up from where it was hiding. A splash of liquid hits me across the face, and the lights go out immediately.

When I wake, I go still. I've woken up in enough strange bedrooms to know it takes a minute to process my surroundings. The first thing I notice, my hands are shackled in front of me. Also not a first, though I usually go for velvet rope instead of cold steel. I'm lying on something that's moving, probably Miss Shepherd's cart if the hard surface is any indication. Now that's a new one on me. I crack my eyes open, but there's something over my head, something thin enough to let a bit of light in.

I hear the steady clop of horses' hooves, one in front of the cart and one behind. I can't hear anyone moving, which leads me to believe Miss Shepherd is still alone. If she had riders with her, someone would be making a noise or two, and I can't hear any person over the wheels on the road. I stretch a bit. My feet are unbound, but I don't want to run for it while shackled. I'm either going to have to find a way to convince Miss Shepherd to let me loose or wrestle the keys to the shackles away from her. I suspect neither is going to be easy.

At the first bump in the road, I cry out harshly, yelping as if I've been struck. Miss Shepherd mumbles to the horse until it comes to a stop, and I moan softly, shaking my head back and forth.

"I thought you'd sleep longer than that, Gentleman Jack," she says, and her voice moves from the front of the cart to the side. "I gave you a rather large dose. Perhaps your power helps you recover?"

I moan again softly and mutter, filling my voice with the sound of tears.

"Are you all right?"

When I don't answer, I hear her step closer. She mumbles something about not foreseeing any adverse effects. When she lays a hand on my arm, I cry out as if she's burned me, and her touch retracts immediately. After another mumble, she eases a bag off my head, and I lurch away from her, turning my power up full blast.

More liquid sloshes over the area where my head had been, and I open my eyes enough to see her raised arm, bottle in hand. When my power hits her, she staggers, holding on to her head. I've never used so much of it before, but I find I don't like being tied up with someone I don't trust.

Miss Shepherd doesn't stick around but runs for the side of the road, sliding into the ditch. I lay flat in the wagon as a shot rings out from her hiding place, tearing a hole in the road.

"That could have been your head," she says, "but I'd rather take you alive."

"And I would rather stay alive," I say, casting about for some avenue of escape. My horse is tied behind the wagon, but escaping on it or with the cart would leave me vulnerable.

"There's a bottle in the portmanteau with a white label," she calls. "Dose yourself out in the open where I can see you, or I'll shoot."

"I'll stay in the cart, thanks, where you can't hit me, and since you can't come close without being vulnerable to my power, it seems we are at an impasse."

"I'm happy to starve out here if you are."

My eyes alight upon her portmanteau, but I don't consider her orders for one second. I shuffle over and open it, hoping to find some acid or something to burn through my shackles, but the labels on the bottles are written in some sort of code. The handwriting is large and strong and speaks more of a man's hand than a woman's. I remember what she said about her parents leading her to science. Maybe this case once belonged to someone else, someone she cares for. Maybe these bottles are the only concoctions she has.

On my belly, I slide the open case to the back of the cart and lean it precariously over the edge. "I've thought of a third option, Miss Shepherd. How about you throw me the pistol and the key to the shackles, or I tip all your bottles into the road?" I peek around the edge of the cart to see her craning to see over the side of the ditch.

Her eyes fly open as she sees her equipment poised to drop and smash to the ground.

"I don't want to do this, darlin'. Do as I ask, and your treasures remain safe."

She frowns hard, but I think I see her lip wobble. Whether it's the portmanteau itself she's concerned with or the contents within, she clearly treasures it.

After a heartbeat, she says, "Go ahead," and the sound is more than a little breathless. "The chemicals will mix, and you will be blown to kingdom come."

I pause and stare, but her gaze is fixed on the case, not on me, and she doesn't look exactly confident. No doubt she's bad at cards, too. "All right." I tip the case farther and hear her gasp.

"Wait!"

I swallow my grin. "If you free me, I won't use my power on you. I'll just be on my way."

She lets out a breath. "You give your word as a gentleman?"

I give her a kindly smile. "Just so."

She takes a key from her pocket and throws it over to land in the cart. I don't move for it immediately, thinking I see the potential for her to rush me once she thinks the portmanteau safe. "And the pistol," I remind her.

She glances at it and at the cart, but she turns and flings the pistol far from both of us, into the scrub. I have to chuckle and think I should never doubt her intelligence. After all, I didn't promise not to shoot her. I sit up in the cart, leaving the portmanteau in danger from my feet as I unlock the shackles about my wrists.

She stays away as I ready my horse, the portmanteau still in my hands. She edges closer though, her eyes on the bag.

"Set it on the ground," she says, "and be off with you."

I hold it out in front of me. "Come and get it."

With anger blazing in her eyes, she stalks toward me with her chin tucked in, and her nose wrinkled as if trying to avoid a bad smell. It'd be offensive if it wasn't so entertaining. "A true gentleman would never threaten a lady's things."

I wink. "How true are we talking about? You already know my secret."

"A true lady, then."

"Maybe I'm something in between." She reaches for the case, but I don't let go. She bares her teeth as if beginning to hate me. That's fine. When it comes to passion, there are two sides to the coin. "And since I'm not a gentleman…"

Her eyes widen, but it's too late. My power washes over her, as strong as I've ever made it, and she's in my arms again, the portmanteau crushed between us. I'm polite enough to maneuver it out of the way.

She's kissing up and down my neck, but I hold her wrists in order to keep my own head as she tries to caress me. "I want you to remember this, darlin'," I say, "something to tide you over on all the lonely nights to come."

"Please, please," she mutters between kisses. Good Lord, if she hated me before, she will be positively wild with it when she remembers that she *begged* me.

"I don't think you'll ever stop hunting me after this," I say, nuzzling her ear. "Now…"

"If you want to keep your career, you probably should, but I doubt you will. My advice, look for me only in your spare time. Hell, I'll send you a letter now and again if you like, once I'm the queen of California."

She jerks against my grasp, trying to get her hands on me, and I let her kiss me again, slipping my tongue into her mouth as she moans her need.

"I'll even let you be the head of my harem," I say.

She closes her lips around one of mine and nips me fiercely. One of her hands slips free and grips my chin, and she glares into my eyes. "No, you're all mine."

Now that is a surprise, but as she dives in for another kiss, I don't think too hard about it. I let go of her other hand and root through the portmanteau to find the bottle with the white label. Then I back her to the cart, making her sit on the edge. She pulls me close, fitting me snuggly between her legs, her lifted skirts.

I fight down my own desire. "Goodbye, Miss Shepherd."

"No, no!"

Well, one more kiss for the road. "I hope we see each other again in California. We could have a lot of fun. With you around, I reckon I wouldn't need any other women, and that's a fact."

Before she can kiss me again, I splash her with the liquid, and she goes limp. I hold my breath and back away, studying her limp form, skirts raised above her knees, face slack in sleep. It's very undignified, and I have a feeling that if I left her like this, she'd kill me just as surely as if I'd let her make love to me. And I don't want her going past hatred into loathing. I didn't think I'd ever care for a chase, but it's turning out to be more exciting than I thought. I take one final look at her legs before straightening her out in the cart and covering her up. I'm finding anticipation more thrilling than I thought, too. I clap the shackles over her wrists and pocket the key.

As I drive the wagon back to the little nameless town, I picture all the ways I can lead her off the straight and narrow and right into my arms, and hot damn, it makes me shiver something fierce. By the time I turn her over to the sheriff as a potential bank robber, I'm positively shaking. I make sure to threaten the sheriff with fire and brimstone if he doesn't treat her like a lady. I throw the Pinkerton name around as liberally as fine seasoning, and by the time I'm done, he seems ready to piss himself, falling over his own feet to assure me he'll obey. He even brings in another lady to sit with Miss Shepherd until she wakes.

I nod as I leave them, making sure the portmanteau is tucked safely with Miss Shepherd's other possessions so she'll have it when she wakes, but I don't leave a letter or account of what happened, no evidence that could potentially impugn a lady's honor. It's the gentlemanly thing to do, after all.

FALLEN
Audrey Chase

Audrey Chase is a caseworker by day, writing addict by night. Despite the many original works sitting on her computer, this is her first submission to a publication.

This shit again.

She rises from her throne and takes the steps down.

They stride toward one another, eager for confrontation. She swings and misses. He's fast, but not so fast as he's claimed to be. The marble floor is cold against her bare feet. He comes into her domain masked, as if she doesn't know who he is or recognize the cologne he thinks he's scrubbed away. He thinks the cape and the mask hides it and how his natural voice sounds when it isn't gruff and hurting.

The worst thing about their squabbles isn't only how utterly predictable they are. It's the mess that remains after she thrashes him. The contractors will arrive, see her place, make repairs and then she'll kill them. They never put up a fight, which is a greater crime than all the murder these humans get so up in arms about.

He shouts her name. She doesn't remember what he's pissed off about this time. This thing or that thing? This person or persons or city or cities? He doesn't understand how small it is to her, these people she regards as little more than ants.

She dwells on it and he lands a shot, his balled fist cracking into her face. His eyes are hooded but she sees the smile on his lips, behind that grizzled face and rash he calls a beard. "Goddess, my ass." He flicks his fingers, trying to get the feeling back into them.

She's getting real damn tired of all these anti-heroes trying to take a bite out of crime. She heard that expression once. Some giant stuffed bear, or was it a dog, on a television set, playing detective. Sadie knows she could bite a piece of him off and that gravelly effect he puts into his voice to sound hard would be reduced to high piercing shrieks and whimpering. She's heard it before. All men scream the same.

"It's over," he says.

They all say that. Usually when they think they've won. This is what humans call hubris, and she's seen it lead them to enough death that she can fill catacombs with their bones. Maybe it's unfair of her to let them keep trying. Maybe it's wrong to let them play mouse to her cat. She's beginning to think this one has outlived his use.

She lifts her hand. He raises his cloak swiftly. He's waiting for the lightning. He's come prepared. She's used it against him before. He flopped around the floor like a dying fish. Those were the days of foreplay. Seconds trickle by. She waits. He lowers the cloak. He looks at her wary and curious, like some kitten she's about to drown.

She whips her hand to the side. The red line blooms along his neck. He staggers back, hands at his neck, gurgling. She moves closer, her feet slick with his blood. She takes hold of his cloak and rips it from him, a flick and she's wound it around his neck, pulling back on it as if it were a noose.

In no time he's on his hands and knees. She tsks, pressing a knee to his back pulling tighter on the cloak. "Why have you come here?" She presses her lips to his ear, his blood spilling on her fingers. "Is it because I'm a woman?" Would he battle a god on his own, with his party tricks? "Do you think I'm soft because I felt that way once when you were inside me?" She pulls tighter. She doesn't know if she's interested in his response. "You once said that you hated how indecisive I was. Why not make up my mind? Why not choose? You asked if I was afraid to be who I really am." She yanks his hood back and takes a fistful of his hair. If he could breathe he'd have yelped. "Do you think I fear *anything*? I've made my choice. I've chosen that I will do as I please, as I always have. There was a time you made me feel... wrong." She considers. "But I want you to know that *you're* wrong. No, don't argue," she pushes his face down so his forehead nearly touches the marble floor. She considers that he might suffocate or bleed to death before she finishes, but he's always had a nasty habit of interrupting her so she delights in this moment. "I'm fairly sure you *do* know that I could crush your head into the floor like a walnut. I can reduce you to a smear on my marble floor. And then Luther of Cross City will be no more. But first, I want you to know that I've found your weakness. I like her very much. Eleanor." She brushes her lips along his neck. "She's going to come so hard for me, she'll forget her own name. She'll shout for a goddess. She'll shout for me. And your name will be forgotten."

He flails about, trying to get away. She admires his determination against such a hopeless situation. "Should I kill you now, knowing you were helpless to save her? Or should I heal you and let you try to stop it? That will hurt more than anything, won't it? I've taken some of your friends already. What's another? How many cuts until you break? I'm curious."

She kicks him to the side and he flounders forward, twitching on the floor. She watches him, trying to come to a decision. Maybe she is indecisive.

✿

The bell chimes when Sadie walks in. This one isn't electronic; it's brass, making an exclamation that is too bright for the hour. There was a time they met her with trumpets.

The gas station is 24-hours. Eleanor works the third shift. Sadie imagines that's how she and Luther met. The lights are an appalling fluorescent, highlighting the many imperfections of the drab beige linoleum floor. Eleanor watches with mild curiosity before nodding. Early twenties. Pale and darkeyed, arms and neck marred in vibrant tattoos, pierced nose. Sadie thinks she can understand how these short-lived creatures long to stand out.

Eleanor's feet are perched on the counter, a newspaper in hand. *Masked Vigilante Still Missing.* Sadie walks the narrow aisles looking at the mishmash of products. The food section has shriveled hot dogs and nachos with toxic sludge cheese. So much disgusting food and yet people are so fat.

She pauses, noticing the domed overhead mirror reflecting her long, wavy blonde hair and bright blue eyes. People make assumptions about her based on her physical appearance.

"Is the card reader down?" Eleanor calls out. She stands somewhat resentfully. "At the pumps?" she fishes behind the counter and pulls out a small black binder. " I don't want to have to call those tech-support assholes again."

"I don't need gas." Sadie walks past the soda coolers and watches her. Luther crawled here months ago, knocking over three shelves in the process. Sadie stopped giving chase and watched. Eleanor brandished a nail-spiked bat until he convinced her he was the good guy. "Quiet night?"

"No frat boys or rednecks yet, which is good. And no super powered freaks. Better."

"You run this fine establishment?"

She doesn't miss the sarcasm. "I've worked here six months. That makes me the sheriff. Shitty sheriff, though. It's been trashed a good twenty times."

"The cameras don't stop all the criminal activity?" She points to the mirror, to the other camera she knows isn't running. The gas station is mostly used for drug deals. No self-respecting citizen visits. The frat boys she mentions come to beat the homeless for sport. Eleanor is right to be suspicious. "Do they give you trouble, these super freaks?"

"Sometimes."

"Why don't you leave?" she fills a styrofoam cup with lukewarm coffee and brings it to the counter, pulling a twenty out of her purse. "Everyone else comes and goes." Eleanor cashes her out. "This must be some kind of record."

"I'm the veteran so I get to play manager. Not bad for a high school dropout."

"Is it common for high school dropouts to have a death wish?"

"You don't need a death wish in this town." She looks out the window. "It falls out of the sky. Or crashes through the walls. Anyway, fuck them. Why should I run? That's what they want."

"At least we have the vigilante."

"No one's seen him."

"Do you know him?" Does she know?

"Haven't seen my brother in a while. Maybe it's him," she comments dryly.

"Is he single?"

"My brother's too busy playing with the family inheritance to bother running around the city in the dark. Tell me you have better taste."

"I have better taste."

That pulls a smile out of her. "Anyway, these freaks don't usually hand out business cards or show their faces. Hides the allure."

Sadie can't argue. The mask *is* the most compelling thing about them. Behind their cloaks they're ordinary. "So you think they're alluring." She touches the newspaper, turns it. There's a picture of Luther, donning his mantle, cloaked in the shadows. These heroes and anti-heroes love the shadows. Sadie's always longed for the light. It's been too long since she's seen it. "Look at that jawline. Do you go for that kind of thing?"

"I don't trust anyone who has to hide their face."

"Maybe he wants to protect his loved ones."

"From what?"

"The boogeyman." She takes the change Eleanor offers. "He'd have enemies."

"Like what? Good fashion? Why do they all run around dressed like it's fucking Comic-Con? Look, no offense, but are you lost?"

"Lost?"

"You're not from around here. Do you usually stroll around at five something in the morning? Coffee's shit," she apologizes. Sadie has a drink and agrees with the assessment. "Heading in to work?"

"I'm taking a break from work."

"What do you do?"

"I'm a supervillain." Ellie rolls her eyes. "I'm Sadie." She looks at the cheap plastic nametag on Ellie's shirt, handwritten in sharpie, at an angle. 'Eleanor'. "You don't look like an Eleanor."

"Don't really know me well enough to say. But you're right, the name's shit. Ellie. Ella. Anything but Eleanor." She shifts her weight from one leg to the other, crossing her arms on the counter. "You in a hurry? I'm out in twenty. Car's still in the shop from when those super freaks took a nose dive off the building next door. Assholes."

"Do you need a ride?" She doesn't drive, but she's sure she can find something.

"I'm not too far from here."

"Are you afraid of the super freaks?"

"It's not always the super freaks you have to watch out for. Women have to stick together, right? I'll give you a slim-jim. On the house."

She's pathetic at bargaining. "Sold."

✄

Sadie doesn't know how long she's been searching. There's a blank where childhood should be, a blank where family should be. She didn't walk out of the sea. She didn't spring out of Zeus' forehead. She remembers patches from different times, different places. Without context she trips into identities she never knew she could have, never knew she had. Luther wants to reform her.

It's tough without her origin story. How many people did she kill before she realized they weren't tissue? For so long she fought that it was *her*. It happened so often that she stopped caring. You have to stop caring. That's how minds break.

Ellie walks alongside her, bat in hand. Sadie considers taking it from her and making her head crack like a pumpkin. If she pulled the bat free she'd likely take a chunk of her skull with it. She decides against it. She likes Ellie's jaunty step, the pink sheen to her lips. Anyway, why rush a good thing? There are so few good things to this world. These lives are painfully brief. "Have you ever used that?" Sadie asks.

"I've swung a bat."

"What if someone took it from you?" These people think they're invincible. They don't know invincible. She doubts they'd like it.

She shrugs. "People are always going to take. I won't let them without a fight."

Sadie doesn't tell her the weapon is useless against a powered being. They walk some distance further. The sky is heavy with clouds. Cars propped on cinder blocks smolder in the dark. Small groups clump around trash barrels, lit with old newspapers. Others slump against the walls of brick buildings. People urinate against alley walls without shame.

It isn't long before the crowd notices them. "Hey, baby. What's your name?" One shouts to Sadie. Whistles. Catcalls. Sadie usually stops and visits when she gets these behaviors but tonight she has to pretend. The women of this world, by and large, move on and pretend to not have heard or seen. "I see you, Ellie! Walking like you don't know us. You think you're too good for us now that you're clean?" The group starts climbing to their feet. "I remember when you'd give anything to roll."

"Friends of yours?" Sadie asks.

"A long time ago. Walk faster."

Sadie obliges. It doesn't take too long for the group to circle them. One of them grabs Sadie. The men of this world are overly confident and aggressive, as if everything and everyone in it were their exclusive property.

"Let her go, Johnny." Ellie says, exasperated. There's a spark of panic in her eye, gone as quickly. "Can you give me one fucking night free of all this bullshit?"

"So take a hike," he says. "I've seen you walking around with that thing," he nods at the bat. "As if you have the guts to use it."

Ellie's fingers tighten around the handle of the bat before she lets it go. It clatters to the ground and rolls an inch before coming to a stop. "I'm not afraid of you."

"So stick around. Let's party. It's been a while."

Ellie shakes her head and moves off. Sadie waits for her to stop but she doesn't. She runs as if her life depended on it. Maybe it does. Maybe this is her battle. What a courageous lion, leaving her to her fate. Sadie watches her until she's out of sight.

Johnny releases her, patting down his pockets. "Your girl took off. She'll be back. She always comes back." He looks her over, apparently satisfied. "We'll make our own fun." He lifts a hand to wave his buddies over.

Sadie stoops and picks up the bat. She gives it a twirl. "Hey, Johnny?" he turns to look at her.

The sound alternates between hollow wood and wet meat. Thwack, klunk, thwack. One by one they come at her, then in droves. They scream. It's like a song. It's messy work but the blood that splashes her keeps her warm. She misses warmth. She doesn't know why. It's more like an impression she has, the remains of a dream.

If the vigilante were here, he might stop her, or distract her long enough for most of them to get away. He'd bore her with some high-horse speech. But it's not murder. It's population control. What were these people giving to the world? Parasites. She wipes blood from her face. It drips from her clothing. A few run off and she lets them. She throws the bat down.

A killing spree hadn't been a part of her plans but she rarely plans. Chaos is its own reward. Violence can be cruel and senseless. They're dead because they gave her attitude. They're dead because she didn't like the way they looked at her. They're dead because they were at the wrong place at the wrong time. Ultimately, they're dead because she was looking for a reason. Or didn't need one.

Ellie returns. She takes it in. Sadie watches the light in her eyes flicker and go out like the flip of a switch.

This smaller, personal violence is more gratifying.

Ellie believes her when Sadie says it was the vigilante. People will always believe what they want to believe. What's the alternative? To allow herself to think the woman she invited for a stroll is powered and massacred her group of shitty friends?

Ellie brings her to her apartment. The building door has a lock as secure as a safety pin. The walls are stained and lined with peeling wallpaper. The halls are littered with old mail and used Styrofoam containers. They climb the creaking stairs, arriving at the door that's been repainted several colors over the years. They don't pass anyone. Ellie drops her keys. She grabs them and fumbles with the door before getting it open.

The apartment is deceptively large. Wooden floors and weathered beams shoulder the burden of the ceiling. A loft. The walls stretch out, covered in charcoal drawings. The windows are large but patched together with newspaper and cardboard in places. Cold air worms inside. Sadie doesn't know if Ellie rents or squats.

"You can wash up in there," Ellie points vaguely down a dark hall. Her voice trembles. She drags a chair into the kitchen, clambers onto a counter and reaches far back into the cupboard. Sadie watches curiously to see what she'll pull out. A few baggies. A few capped needles. A few tickets. Ellie isn't expecting her. Sadie's gaze hits her like a wall. She gets down guiltily. "What?" She has a look in her eye, some cornered feral animal.

Sadie thought this woman to be Luther's lover. Is she his sister? How did they turn out so differently? "Johnny said you were clean."

"I was. Am. Who cares. Johnny's dead. Jesus, fuck. He's dead. That fucking vigilante." She's going to cry. "I can't believe this. He wasn't always that way. He was good to me sometimes." She clenches the needles harder in her hand. "God, how the hell does something like that happen? Where was he? How could he do it so quickly?" She leans into the counter, a hand over her face. "I've never seen that much fucking blood." Her tone has gone weepy.

Ugh. "Help me out of these clothes."

"What?"

She searches for emotion, she tries to remember those who have begged before her, what their voices did, what their faces did. Maybe she needs to keep it simple. "Help me."

Ellie puts the drugs to the side. "Right. Shit. This way." She leaves the kitchen and leads her to the bathroom, a claustrophobic hole with missing patches of tile, a small band of curved soap left on the teal colored sink. The tub is off white. Flakes of paint linger on the edges. The showerhead is rusted and limp. Sadie catches her reflection in the mirror. Her hair is red with blood. "The water heater sucks," Ellie reaches past her and turns it on, "give it a few to heat up." Sadie nods. "Are you okay?" Sadie considers the response, the ensuing silence appearing to be response enough for Ellie. "I'm freaking out."

"Should we call the police?"

"They don't care about this place."

Maybe that's why the vigilante spends his time in this part of town—because it's long been forsaken by the police. "Are you okay?" Ellie shakes her head. Maybe tonight is the least of her worries. "Why did you come back?"

"I heard a woman screaming. This is all my fault." It's true. Sadie 'fumbles' with her blouse. Ellie watches uncomfortably before taking her shoulders. "I'm sorry this happened to you." Why? Sadie never understood the point in giving survivors condolences. Or perpetrators. "Lift your arms." Sadie complies, amused at how careful the woman is. The blouse falls to the floor with a wet splat. Every inch of her is stained red. Ellie averts her eyes.

Sadie steps out of her heels, out of her skirt. "You don't have to look away." Ellie's eyes remain concentrated on the sliver of soap on the sink. "Thank you for coming back for me." The gratitude sounds unnatural in her mouth and comes out stiltedly. The unevenness lends her unexpected credibility. "No one's ever done that before." Not that she remembers.

"Don't you have family?"

"Where's yours?"

"I only have my brother." She shrugs in that way people do when they're trying to appear indifferent. "Don't see him much."

"Why?"

"It's just the way he is. It's just the way things are. Look at this place. Who wants to come around?"

Steam fills the room. The blood that was caking to her grows soft and runny again. Sadie takes Ellie's arm. "I do." The tattoos lining her arms prevent the blood from showing bright against her skin. Sadie's left disappointed that she can't dress her in the last remnants of her dead friends. Her fingers glide to Ellie's neck. It's covered in ink too. So many necks she's snapped, torn open, severed heads from. It's so easy that her fingers quake from the habit. The crimson marks stand out like a beacon when she touches her face. It makes Sadie feel clear again. This one's pretty. It's never stopped her. But she's also damaged. So what's the point? What compels him to protect her? Has he?

Ellie meets her eyes. "What do you want?"

"What?"

"I see it. You want something. Everyone wears that look the same way. So what do you want?" There's no anger in her voice, only the monotony of routine.

Sadie's mouth goes dry. She considers inching her fingers up, taking a firm hold of her head and smashing it to chunks on the sink. Against the wall. On the edge of the bathtub. Or she could crush it, fingers breaking through her skull to the gooey matter of her brain. There are so many ways to die when you *can* die that she can't imagine how they get out of bed.

She considers telling Ellie she's here on her brother's behalf. It strikes her as terribly amateurish and petty. Gods may be petty but never amateurish. Maybe time away from her kind (if indeed there are others like her) has made her common. Her hand slips away. This isn't the right time. "I want to get clean."

"You and me both. The shower's right there." She has a seat on the toilet and crosses her arms. She looks away while Sadie strips and steps into the shower. Does she stay with her to make sure she's safe and doesn't pass out? Or does she stay to stay safe and away from her stash?

The water's gone lukewarm. Sadie grapples with some memory of golden light, glimmering like a jewel. How does one get so close to the sun? Rivers of blood trail down her body. The water has gone cold and continues to run off her, diluted now, like watermelon juice. She steps out, leaving red footprints on the thin bath towel placed at the base of the tub. She trembles from cold or excitement or the way Ellie tries so desperately to not look at her.

Ellie stands. There's no towel except for the one on the floor. "I'll get you a blanket. I'll get you some clothes."

Sadie pushes her to the sink. Her palms are still red, leaving a handprint on Ellie's shirt. "Is this how you wanted to take me home?"

Her jaw hardens. "I wasn't planning any of this."

"Oh. I see." Her fingers curl around the fabric of her shirt. Maybe she's being unfair. It wouldn't be the first time. How could Eleanor Foss have imagined that the blonde she met at the gas station was not only one of the supers she's so worried about, but a lunatic on top of that. That's Luther's word. It hurts her how he still doesn't understand her. "This isn't what you do to stop yourself from getting high?"

"Jesus. You sound like my brother."

There's always pain in her eyes when she speaks of him. It makes Sadie hungry. "I'm not your brother." She kisses her. Now that the adrenaline from her killing spree has waned, she's anxious and bored again. It's possible that there is something fundamentally wrong with her. She can get this anywhere she wants. Men and women throw themselves at her, taken in by appearance. It makes it easy. But this woman silently rebels against her and doesn't know why. This woman is Luther's sister and she has a promise to fulfill. Normally she doesn't bother sticking to promises, but ones made in wrath, intended for revenge are important to act on. This is business.

Ellie harbors reservation. It's in the stiffness of her lips, the rigidity of her body. She fights what she wants because there are mourning rituals. The contact is a key. Ellie's lips soften and part. Her breath is uneven and guilty. Sadie hadn't known breath could take on that quality. Stress makes people do unreasonable things. They'll both make that excuse later.

Sadie takes the shirt from Ellie. More piercings. Other than that her torso is bare and soft, warming like a furnace. There's no more need for pretense. This touch, these moments are like brands of sorcery. Her hands settle on her hips, leaving handprints. Ellie notices. For a moment reality threads its way into the moment. Who knew dark eyes could appear so conflicted?

✿

Ellie visits her lair. It's not like Luther's, dark and full of gadgets. It's wide and open. The columns have been restored, the mess cleaned. Sadie looks at Ellie, standing where Luther's blood pooled. It's afternoon but the sunlight is hazy. Sadie despairs.

Ellie holds her jacket close. She looks out the wall-to-wall windows to the clouds. "How do you have a place like this? What do you do?"

"I don't do anything," Sadie goes closer, dressed in her usual garb, the lightweight flowy fabrics. "I bide my time. I meet people."

"But you work. You have to, for a place like this. Or is this all off someone's trust fund?" The bitterness makes her voice jagged.

"Isn't it possible that I stole it?"

"You can't steal places."

"People steal places all the time. Not just places. Cities. Lives. Look at where you live. Look at what's been done to your people," she regrets that wording. "To your economy. You've noticed." She brushes a hand along her hair, sweeping it off her neck. "I know you have."

Ellie holds her gaze for a moment before staring at the floor. Sadie detects a crimson hue. It's possible she imagines it or that only she can see it. Does Ellie feel it? A connection through blood? "You look like the kind of woman Luther likes to have on his arm. Some bust come to life."

"Maybe I am. Do you care about your brother?"

"He's family."

"That matters to you?"

"Doesn't it matter to you?"

No. Yes. No. She doesn't know what family is. Doesn't understand it in any other way than a diagram. But what would Ellie be without her connection to Luther? Dead. And if she didn't matter to Luther? Dead. She thinks of pulling that cloak around his neck until his face went purple and his fists pounding on the ground became light slaps, before he went still and the fight went out of him. "I don't remember my family."

"That sucks. I barely remember mine. It was only ever Mom and Dad. Do you remember fifteen years ago? That… attack on the downtown district?" Haphazardly, perhaps. "I still load up those videos. The news footage and shitty hand cam stuff. Those buildings just… disintegrated. Some of those people trapped inside lay there for days before they died. Everyone thought it was another terrorist attack and we'd be finding someone else to point the nukes to. But how do you point them when the terrorists look like anyone else? Everyone was pissed off and then they forgot about it. Now it happens on a smaller scale and no one cares."

"I care." Sadie survived that day but just barely. Her knees wobbled. Blood ran down her mouth. She wore a costume then. She doesn't remember what it looked like. Her memory went fuzzy that day. She can't remember what came before.

"You just want to get me into bed again."

"I haven't had you in a bed. Did you see anything that day? The day of the attack?"

She shakes her head. "I saw a man. I saw a woman. She had long hair... she was in the sky. So high. She had a cape."

"Who was she?" Some hero, probably. They do fancy their capes.

"I'm not sure. Maybe no one."

"What happened to your parents?"

"Don't know. They never recovered the bodies. Eventually the estate went to Luther. The attacks kept happening. Sometimes bigger. Sometimes smaller. Know what I noticed? The nice areas would get picked up and 'thrive' again while the poorer areas were left to rot. Where were the vigilantes when everyone was starving and homeless and the hospitals were turning them away? By the time I was old enough to claim my inheritance, I didn't want it. Or maybe I was too doped up to care. So there you have it, my tragic backstory." Sadie smiles grimly. *Don't forget all your dead friends,* she wants to add. Not that tragic backstories matter if you aren't powered or special. You're just another person dealt a shitty hand. "Aren't you going to give me a tour?"

Sadie takes her hand, just like she's taken everything from this girl. "Yes. Let me give you the tour."

※

Her ears ring. Blades whirr in the distance. She rises from the bed and dresses, satisfied with Ellie, satisfied on a promise delivered. She walks to the throne room. Her eyes turn to the windows. Soon the helicopter hovers into view. Machine guns rev up and blow out the windows. She takes shelter behind one of the columns. Glass and bullets spray the room. They lodge into the columns, taking chunks of marble off. Glass clinks and clatters. The door to the bedroom opens. "Stay in there!" Sadie shouts. She'd hate for Ellie to die before the grand finale. The door slams shut and Sadie breathes easier.

Why do these assholes have to bother her? They swing inside while the helicopter dives away. She doesn't recognize the woman with the shadow mask and the too tight clothing. The man flips over to her—do any of them walk? She recognizes the outfit. Some modified tweak of the modified tweak that came before. "Haven't I killed you before?" Sadie asks. They're like roaches, these heroes, coming from beneath the foundation. They don't ever seem to die.

He belts out battle cry. A moment later there's a flash and smoke fills the room. She sees their body heat like torches in the night. There's a pinprick, glancing off her arm. It sticks out of her skin like an acupuncture needle. She flicks it away, turns. A bo slams into her face. She grabs the tip and throws the bitch swinging it. She flies with a yelp, landing hard. Another sliver goes into her. This one hits her calf, her back, her neck. This is getting irritating.

Number Three springs, kicking himself off a column, planting his feet on her chest before flipping back. The smoke is dissipating now. There are three of him. They swim apart and then together. Something is wrong. This dipshit could never do this before. Her ankle twists, her balance momentarily compromised.

Her eyes go red. She never tires of the terror in the eyes of her foes when this happens. She glides toward him, picking him up by the neck and lifting him off the ground. His legs kick *Where is he?* The mask screams. She's alive?

Number Three's face is changing colors. "I know you have him," he grunts. "Let him go. Let him—" Her hand tires and she lowers him. He's surprised as she is. A roundhouse and she's kicked back. She staggers. The woman with the shadow mask grabs her arms from behind. Sadie throws her off again. She lunges but she feels slow and heavy. She doesn't catch her. "Where is he?" Number Three demands again.

"We know he's here." The woman says. "We tracked him."

Ah. They do love their trackers. They fight her, moving in tandem. They're fast and time is slowing by the second. Their hits land. The back of her knees, her stomach, her face. The Shadow Mask swings hard, the spikes on the forearm of her gloves cutting into her face and drawing blood. It'll heal but it's the principle. Her knees wobble but she rights herself. "I'll kill you," Sadie says. "I'll throw you with him. He should have known better than to come here alone. Don't you know who I am?" But it sounds like she's begging for answers.

Number Three exchanges a look with Shadow Mask. "He came here alone to protect you."

"Protect *me?* From *what?*"

"From this." He lifts the bow gun. So that's what they've been shooting with. She's going to shove it so far up his ass he'll have to spit it out. He shoots her again. This dart goes into her chest. She pulls it out, looks at it. How can something so small hinder her? "Whatever you were, it's gone."

"Go find him," Shadow Mask says. "I'll keep an eye on her." He runs to the bedroom. Ellie shouts. Sadie half-listens. He won't hurt her. "Where is he?" Shadow asks again.

Sadie smiles. Shadow Mask punches her until Sadie's laughing and her head has drooped to the floor. Shadow Mask flexes her finger. Sadie lifts her head, looking back to Number Three and Ellie. It's been ages since anyone made her bleed. Ellie hangs outside the corner of the room, watching the scene unfold.

"Keep looking," the Mask directs Number Three. She drops in front of her. Puts those bracer blades to her throat.

Sadie's eyes twinkle. "Oh, come now. I know you won't do it. You won't even try. You know you can't kill me." Shadow Mask's dark eyes narrow. Pretty beneath that paint. She cracks her elbow across her face. Sadie slumps and then rights herself. This one has bite. Luther hasn't fully indoctrinated her. "But you want to. You know that your code of honor comes at the cost of innocent lives. What does it feel like, having hundreds on your conscience? I killed your man. You should have heard him scream."

The colors are returning to the world, the dulling of her senses lessening by the second. She can taste the blood in her mouth. Smell it. Hear how this one's heart beats, hear Ellie's breath, so fast, her heart like hummingbird's wings. Poor thing. She can take this woman. She could snap her neck. Ellie might run. Would that ruin the fun? Or would hunting her become another game?

"You took his sister," the Mask whispers. "Why?"

"Because I could."

Her knee comes up hard on her face. Sadie lets herself fall, back colliding hard with the floor. Ellie runs over. If Sadie knew anything of being touched she would be. Ellie stoops beside her, turning heated eyes to Shadow Mask. What a stressful day. She'll relapse at this rate. "Are you okay?" Ellie asks.

It's a stupid question. She starts to nod yes before shaking her head no.

"Who are you?" Ellie gets between her and Shadow Mask. "Why are you doing this?"

"You don't understand the situation, Eleanor. Stay out of it."

"How do you know who I am?"

"I've got him!" Number Three shouts. They all turn their heads. Number Three half carries, half drags Luther. He's got an arm around his waist, Luther's over his shoulders. How romantic.

Shadow Mask's eyes brighten. What a happy reunion. Everyone's together again. Sadie reaches out and takes hold of Shadow Mask's leg. She twists. There's a pop. She screams and falls to the floor. She's put a dent in her night-time vigilante acrobatics.

Ellie looks around, confused. Sadie gets to her feet. Everything's clear again. Whatever they shot her with was good but it couldn't hold her down long. Her body is already knitting itself together. It's almost disappointing. She has to hand it to these humans. What they lack in power they make up in resourcefulness. She knows Luther and his cronies have labs. He's never showed her, never talked about it but she knows that. Knows it somehow. Maybe it's because she's at a higher level. Maybe because she's a supreme being. When they're dead she'll be alone again. It's boring and lonely, maybe even disappointing, but there's comfort in that familiarity.

Shadow Mask twists around on the floor and Sadie marches to them. It's easy to disentangle Number Three from Luther. A punch to his side and ribs crack. It makes her realize that some piece of her must have been holding back with Luther. Odd. "You should start auditions to find a number four," Sadie tells Luther. She hurls Number Three. He flies across the room, out the shattered windows and off the building. "Butter fingers."

Luther's eyes widen. Something goes out of him. So much weight lost in so little time. His skin looks grey. How long has she had him? He wheezes and stumbles forward. She catches him, letting him drape over her arm like a limp towel. He doesn't look half as good on her arm as she did on his. "Before your Number Three died," she tells him softly, "he said you came alone to protect me. Surely you understand now how ludicrous such a thing was." Blood drips off her chin onto his face. Are his vocal cords severed? Will someone else have to take up the mantle? It wouldn't be the first time. "Did you hear her? Your Eleanor. I make good on my promises. You left her so lonely that it was easy. Luckily, you appear to have done all the damage yourself. She's so broken. Killing her would be a mercy."

She peels the hood back from his face and looks at him. His temples are prematurely silver. He's in a dangerous, stressful line of work. He didn't always look this way. His face was unlined once. There was a light inside of him that drew her to him like a moth. It burned her because he always looked past her, to something further that she couldn't find, hasn't found, hasn't even identified. Ellie has it too. That pilot light. So necessary. So easy to snuff out.

There's a small whistle and a dart jabs into her. She frowns, turning her head in the direction to Shadow Mask. No. It's Ellie, armed with a crossbow. She fires again. The second one goes into her arm. Ellie picks up the small kit Shadow Mask is pushing towards her, loads it and fires again. "Stop that." Sadie says. It comes out much slower. She dumps Luther to the side and teeters to her.

She glances at Shadow Mask, stretches her fingers out to give her a kick of lightning—and seizes, her blood on fire at the attempt. What have they done to her?

Her head is going foggy again. She can't afford to have it happen now. It was Eleanor. Ellie. Sadie snatches the bow away, snapping one of Ellie's fingers in the process, making her shout. Sadie crushes the bow. It falls to the ground like matchsticks. She cradles Ellie's neck, focusing on her heat, her betrayal. *Kill her.* Ellie's eyes glisten, angry and sorrowful. "Was it you?" Ellie asks. "Did you kill them?"

The question is so vague Sadie doesn't know where to begin or if it merits a response. "Probably."

"You kept my brother here."

"Don't get sanctimonious now." She looks back. He crawls towards them at a slug's pace. "He killed your friends, remember?"

"I hate you."

Already? The words sting, or maybe it's only the needles of the darts, wedging their way under her skin. One of them is becoming unsteady. Sadie walks her to the edge of the building. The air is brisk. The sky remains too cloudy. She needed to go higher to get to that light. "That hurts me. I thought we were close." Ellie spits in her face. The saliva mingles with the blood, sliding down her face. Sadie goes colder.

"You monster."

The air burns in her lungs. The strength is being sapped from her again. Whatever is in those darts... Ellie pulls at Sadie's fingers, peeling each one from her neck. How. A sharp pain and she looks down. Luther has buried one of his rappelling spikes into her leg. She reaches down to remove the spike and lets go. Alarm crawls into her. Ellie slips out of sight from her peripheral vision, then away entirely. Luther drags himself to the edge of the building to stare down.

Sadie holds the bloody spike like a trident before releasing it. Where has Ellie gone? Down below with Number Three? Color on the pavement? She might have reached her once, saved her once. How long has passed? A splitting of a moment? Minutes? Hours? Years? Everything swims, trailing color.

Luther's crying. It pierces her in places. She walks until she falls. Old memories tug at her: the sun warm on her skin, cities as small as miniature models, something akin to happiness.

Buildings streak past. Wind whips her clothes, her hair. The ground races to meet her. Ellie hasn't landed yet. She's fast, they've said, but she can't catch hold of time. Maybe she'll catch hold of *her*. Or she'll crash and burn. Another villain that was, vanquished by the light. But maybe not. If she can get her bearings. If she can get her second wind. If she can only remember.

THE DEVIL INSIDE
JD Glass

JD Glass is the author of American Library Association (Stonewall) and Lambda Literary Award (Literature) Finalist *Punk Like Me* (currently being illustrated by Kris Dresen for graphic novel adaptation), followed by *Punk And Zen*, then Lambda Literary Finalist and Ben Franklin Award Finalist *Red Light*. She also penned GCLS Finalist *American Goth*, and the critically acclaimed *X*. Selection editor (and contributor) for the GCLS Award winning anthology *Outsiders*, and was listed on The Advocate's Top 100 for *CORE*, Vol.1 Iss.1, GCLS Award Finalist for the anthology, *Nocturnes*. Her work can be found in various bookstores, online retailers, and at dresenglass.com

"Morningstar, your ten o'clock is here." Sinestra's voice sounded more nasally and clipped than usual through the intercom. I grinned, knowing she was probably in a snit because the woman in the waiting room was better looking than Sinestra—well, that was an easy thing, given that first, the meeting was with a mortal, meaning she was at least a hundred years younger, *and* secondly, I knew my ten o'clock had neither membranous wings, nor scales.

I hit the button to let me answer. "Send her in."

"Right away—stupid mortal moisturizer…" I heard Sinestra mutter before she fully released her side.

My door opened and in walked Jessica Mayfair, star reporter, all perfectly-coiffed shoulder length ash blond hair, a recognizably high-end designer bone-colored suit, handbag dangling in just that perfect urban way over her shoulder, and complete with a pencil and handheld device in one hand, and an honest-to-goodness small writing book in the other.

Of course, I knew what she looked like, I had full dossiers—well, of course I did. If there was a being living on the Material sphere, still enduring the trial and travail of "good" versus "evil," I knew everything about them.

Every. Single. Thing.

That candy bar you stole in 3rd grade? Yeah, I know. That, and the magazine sitting under the mattress since the 5th grade, the "uncharitable" things you called several teachers under your breath, and every time you told a lie—even the white ones.

My system's better than the secret browser history sitting on your system, or the software your company is running.

It's *that* good.

Though "good" only means effective, here, that is.

Because, after all, this is Hell.

And this is *my* show.

✦

"Not quite the décor I expected," Jessica said as she approached my desk, hand extended for a firm shake.

"Not enough stone and ironwork for you?" I asked, and gave her my trademark grin. I materialized, then reached for a decanter on my desk. I poured.

"It's very lovely to finally meet you," I told her. "I really enjoyed that piece you did on Shiva and Shakti, capturing both the Maker and the Destroyer, Creation and Change. Made them seem almost—humane, without losing sight of the necessary and therefore Holy darkness of it—I like your style, balanced and fair."

Her eyebrows raised as I held the half-full glass out for her instead of shaking her hand. "Scotch... neat, yes?"

Jessica gave me a cool appraising gaze. "It was an interesting bit of research and conversation. And, not while I'm working, no. Perhaps later, when we're—"

"Off the record?" I finished for her.

Her gaze was still cool and level. "This is... much more Zen-like than I would have expected for the Lord of Lies," she said, ignoring my question, and she raised her chin to challenge me with that label.

"I don't usually use such... *formal*... titles around the office," I said instead, and waved my hand to indicate the crème décor that matched her suit, the clean lines of my desk. I sat on the edge. "Call me... Devi."

⚡

That bitch—or bastard. Whatever, Sinestra thought, shaking her head. Not like "male" or "female" had any *real* meaning in the shape of the True Reality of Things. Still, there were polarities beings tended to gravitate to, and what had the Morningstar asked that stupid blonde to call her? Devi?

Sinestra snorted.

Yeah, it was time someone else took over—for certain, Morningstar was getting soft, and definitely getting a hard-on (or whatever body It was going to choose to impress) over the wordy bimbo.

But everything was in place, and in just under an hour or so...

She picked her cell phone out of groove in her ribs.

She tapped a grey-brown talon against the glass as she waited. She really liked this new smart phone. So appropriate that it had the blonde idiot's dimension's symbol for what these stupid mortals called "THE Fall..."

She had to give the mortals on this level credit—some of them *were* clever. Millennia had gone by, and it took the stupid monkeys to figure out a way to communicate that didn't involve levels of training and trance and all the usual rigmarole.

The Dimensional Ætheyric Method:Network—the DAMN. Thanks to the rare engineer that actually made it to Hell, the system worked like the internet and allowed for time saving, and certainly no ætheyric eavesdropping from whatever Incorporate Beings might be invisibly hanging about.

"Is everyone in position, Pablo?" she texted rapidly.

"Yes, Mistress Avery."

Ah… Avery. That was gonna be her name as soon as she took over. Why not? She liked it—and Sinestra, well that would perhaps become a nickname, another one to add to the list the Lord of Lies—or when it happened to her, the Lady—had.

"Perfect. Be ready for my signal."

She tucked the tech away, then scratched a spot. Damn. Another scale was flaking. That was the problem with Hell, she thought ruefully. Sometimes, things… itched.

Well, as she took over, that was going to change. In the meanwhile, she was going to check in Blondie's coat pocket and see if there was a tube of moisturizer she could appropriate.

Damn monkeys. Sinestra scowled, not aware that in doing so, the wizened leather of her face tightened into lines that made her seem like something out of a movie where if not monkeys, well at least apes, had taken over things.

She opened her desk drawer, then the hidden compartment within. Carefully, she withdrew the dagger, *the* dagger, the one that would make the Morningstar mortal, the one that would allow for a new ruler in Hell.

It would be easy enough. The blade, made of stone from the first cooling of the Universe, it alone would render Lucifer mortal. But—and this was the sticking point, so to speak, if it carried the blood and with it the life energies—the Light energies—of an innocent, such as this mortal was, then in the moments between stabbing and transformation, the Light would kill any Dark immortal being, including and in this case *especially* the ruler of Hell itself.

And then whoever was left holding the blade would take on the mantle.

Which was exactly the plan. All Sinestra had to do was use confusion and misdirection to corner Itself and the blonde lunch meat into the ancient torture chamber, unused since they'd discovered that internet withdrawal was such an effective tool.

Sinestra gave a big sigh. Oh how she missed the screaming...

Oh yes, she thought as she checked the reflection of her shoulder and the curve of a wing in the shine of the stone blade's reflection. Things were *really* about to change...

✍

Frankly, I was a bit surprised, though I counted on my training and experience as a journalist to not let it show.

After all, the receptionist, Sinestra, had been exactly what I'd expected, given that this was Hell, and I supposed the carnation she wore behind one leather ear and tucked into the frame of her cats'-eye frame glasses was her idea of "dressing for the mortals."

But this... this Morningstar... not what I expected.

At all.

She was slender, she was elegant, she was wearing—

"Yes, it's a Calvin," she told me as she pressed the glass into my hand. The glass was cool, the tips of her fingers weren't as they grazed mine.

"Excuse me?" I managed to ask.

This... wasn't like me. I swirled my glass and inspected the contents in an attempt to collect myself. I had interviewed Thor, Shakti and Shiva. I had taken a tour of Valhalla and ridden one of their steeds. I'd even had dinner with a Valkyrie later, privately, but that was another story and—

"The suit—it's a Calvin Klein," she said as she smooth her hands over the exquisite curves, of both the suit and her body. Long... lean, and just enough curve in all the right places... "And yours is... Jones, yes?"

I managed to contain my continued surprise even as I nodded. "Yes." I swallowed. "What... what did you ask me to call you?"

"This scarf, Ms. Mayfair," Devi said instead, as she pulled it from the air, a piece of shimmering gauze so fine it seemed like silver mist. "You need to wear it," she said softly as she neared. I didn't even realize she'd moved. She was so close as she gently wrapped it around my neck and shoulders, I could feel the warmth of her breath against my cheek.

"It'll shield you from, well, me."

She stepped back with a small frown to admire her handiwork, and suddenly, I was clear. She was still beautiful, but I was no longer so... so... focused... on her, and the kerchief itself was so slight and light, it felt like nothing more than the lightest puff of air against my skin.

"What was that?" I asked and I pulled my pen out to write.

"Call me Devi—and that was... my side effect," she said with a small smile and a shrug.

"Side effect? Of... what?"

"There's a reason my half mortal children are so... irresistible," she—Devi—told me with a smile, and a faint glimmer of red outlined her eyes.

"So that part's true, then? You have semi-mortal children, known as incubi and succubi, and they're—"

"Polymorphous and perverse—isn't that what you expect?" Devi said, her smile even wider. This time the glimmer was a definite soft glow.

I was journalist. I had interviewed conscientious leaders and conscience-less thugs, unsung heroes and the lowest of the evil low. And I had to take over this conversation, or I would never get the information I was after.

"I'm after truth—so I have no expectations, Devi. And you can call me Jessica. I will say, though, that you don't seem like what I think the world expects from"—I waved at her—"the ultimate figurehead for evil."

Devi's smile disappeared and her expression grew serious. "You do know it's just a job title, right? I mean yes, of course, there's been a lot of leg work and PR over the years to really embellish the whole Lord and Lady of lies thing, but really, it's just a position with a lot of history and really great branding to back it up."

"And good lighting!" Sinestra said as she entered with some papers. "Good lighting is critical—I need you to sign these, my Liege."

"Oh, yes," Devi said with a sigh as she took the pages and manifested a pen. "Oh yes, good light. That's always critical." She quirked a quick grin at me, then signed. "And so is paper work. Here..." she handed the sheaf of papers back. "That should do, then."

I wrote that down even as I made sure that I had a recording going on with the phone in my bag. "So... are you saying it's all a case of 'bad' publicity?" I asked and watched her closely.

Sinestra and I ignored each other as she stalked past me with her pages. The flower behind her ear had dried and I caught the faintest whiff of sulfur as she passed.

Devi sat on the corner of her desk and smiled at me. "Well, in this business, 'bad' publicity really *is* good. Let me give you a tour of operations, show you how it really works, okay?" She opened the door to the office. "Sinestra, hold my calls and send an email to Gabriel telling him we'll rehearse tomorrow."

"Yes, my Lady of the Shadows," the voice from the front office came back as Devi once more crossed back to me. Another door appeared in the wall, and she opened it.

"Rehearsal—with Gabriel," I said flatly. "You mean, as in the angel, Gabriel?" I asked as she ushered me before her.

"Well of course," Devi answered with a grin I could hear. "He's quite a horn player, and as I'm sure you've heard, there's some types of music folks have been saying for years will land you a one-way ticket here. Not that that's exactly true, but we really do have a great jazz and blues combo going, and we like to keep our chops up. Besides, we've got a gig next Friday night over in Helheilm and some new tunes to share—the Valkyries are big fans."

"Really?" I murmured as we stepped into the hallway. "I've met a few you, as I'm sure you know."

"I did read the article," Devi agreed. "And how did your... dinner... with Sword Time I believe her name is, go?"

"Skalmöld," I corrected as we walked. The hallway we'd entered was a dark and flickering red, and while it still appeared like a normal building, I could smell the faintest whiff of something... I stopped in my tracks as I fully registered what I'd heard. I faced Devi. "You... are in a band? This is quite an unexpected side to the legend and lore of the De—"

"It's Dutch and the Blazes," she said and this time, I couldn't tell if the red glow was her eyes or a reflection from the flicker on the walls as we once again moved down the hallway.

"What is?"

"That's the name of the band," she told me, and the white gleam of her smile was unmistakable. "We have some rotating guest spots—there's a lot of talent to choose from, as I'm sure you can guess. And…" she paused before another door. "Here we are: sorting."

We crossed through an antechamber that looked for all the world like an airlock, and after pressing a keypad combination into another door, we went through to emerge onto a platform, about three floors high.

It appeared exactly like an airline terminal, except I couldn't see the ceiling, the door we'd come through was a faint outline on a rock face, and instead of a few disconsolate passengers sitting around various seats with baggage, there were lines of people and beings I didn't recognize that seemed endless, some random creatures milling about, with an occasional isolated being here and there that seemed to…

"Is it crying?" I asked Devi as I pointed.

"Happens sometimes," Devi said as she spread her hands along the railing and gazed down. "For some, it's a genuine surprise that they end up here—and those ones, well, they're the hardest ones to cycle through and out."

"Cycle through?" I asked, as I popped a few shots with my phone. "Out? As in get out of Hell?"

"Yes." Devi faced me, her expression once more serious. "It's not about 'punishment' or 'reward'," she said, holding her hands out before as if balancing weights. "It's about learning—do you know *why* something is right, or something is wrong? Answer that question the correct way, and"—she pointed to way off into the distance, a seeming ten or more city blocks away, and at least another same amount above us to an opening that shone a pure white light that was unmistakable in the tawny atmosphere that surrounded us—"and you can go there, providing you pass the other levels, of course."

A loud shout cut through the background noise, and I looked back down to the ground level to see what appeared to be a human being, first small then swelling to incredible size, then back down again, over and over as he yelled. A security detail surrounded him as he heaved and bucked towards the gate they were guiding him to.

"Do you know who I am?" he bellowed. "I've killed"—

I leaned further over the railing for a better look and took a shot with my phone. He glanced up at and glared at me when I snapped.

"You're next!" he screamed.

Devi took my elbow to guide me back.

"I'm so sorry, that usually doesn't happen," she said in a low voice, her brow furrowed.

"Should I worry?" I asked and tried to laugh.

Devi forced a smile. "No, he's probably not going to re-enter the system, is all. He'll have a chance to redeem of course, but if he doesn't, well…" She gave an eloquent small shrug and made a moue.

"What *does* happen?"

Devi's eyes searched mine. "Do you know what happens to a candle when you blow it out?"

"Poof?" I asked, and snapped my fingers.

Devi flashed me a quick—and yes, wicked—grin. I liked it. "Exactly. So I wouldn't worry about him. The damage left behind… tsk, but that's what we're here for, to attempt to insure it doesn't happen again."

I stared at her in surprise. "Wait—are you saying that souls go back—incarnate again, I mean, and either get it right or…?"

Devi smiled wide as she nodded. "Yes—get it right, or eventually get gone. It's the ultimate energy recycling system."

❦

"Yes! Yes, yes, YES!!!" Sinestra yelled into her cell phone and to whomever at large as she charged through the Hall of the Fallen with Pablo and Minutae behind her—this was now happening—Itself and the human morsel had been forced into the abandoned torture chamber; the Legions of Pain would soon be under her command!

The thrill of impending victory and rule made an area somewhere in the middle of her chest feel tight, and she wondered for a moment if perhaps the not-quite-dead-yet smorelock, the part slug, part crab that she'd had for lunch, was trying to fight its way out.

Probably not, she thought.

"Keep Devi Morningstar with the mortal! I'll be right there!"

She clutched the dagger tightly in her fist. Funny how it fit so perfectly, she thought as she unfurled her wings and flew down the corridor.

If it got warmer in her grip, she didn't notice.

There they were—Devi and the mortal, pinned all around by Sinestra's own loyal henchmen, rock demons and fail-spirits all. Sinestra felt pride fill her, and her wings spread wider. Oh but it was hard to control the sheer excitement she felt seeing the angry red glow of Devi's eyes, the wide eyes of the mortal she shielded behind her.

"You do know that there's a price for this," Devi gazed up and said to her.

The feeling evaporated. "Of course there is," Sinestra said as she landed in front of her. She gripped the dagger even more tightly. "And you're the one to pay it. So hand over the mortal, and we can do this the easy way—well, easy for me," Sinestra told Devi as she gestured.

Those eyes were going to make the most incredible earrings—if she didn't eat them, first!

"This…" Devi began in her annoying calm voice. She placed herself firmly between Sinestra and the reporter. "It won't get you what you want."

"Oh… the things *you* don't know," Sinestra spat back.

"Getting into Heaven is easy," Devi continued mildly. "Getting out of Hell—now that's a challenge. Why do you think bureaucracy was invented? The Devil's in the details."

"Heaven?" Senestra sputtered angrily. Oh, Devi really did piss her off! "You think this is for Heaven?" She spat at Devi's well-booted foot. "That's what I think of Heaven—bind Morningstar," she ordered Pablo. "And the girl, too."

Sinestra didn't know what to make of the glance she saw pass between her soon-to-be-dead-former-boss and the bimbo, but she didn't care. She spat at Devi's face. "And that's what I think of *you*."

❦

Whatever was left inside of me that had once been a beating heart turned cold and sank. I knew what Sinestra had planned even before I'd seen the bone dagger in her hand. I'd known it since I'd had to continually guard Jessica from the rock demons and fail-spirits (well, if I actually let something *happen* to her, it would probably mean no band for at least another thousand years—and we did have that gig coming up), and the way they herded us towards the unused chamber.

Sacrifice an innocent, and use the power of the innocent blood on the knife to then to destroy Dark being—in this case, me.

And I had been truthful with Jessica. Yeah, sure, when I first became the head of this realm, I was a young hothead, made gorgeous and pure, with ideas of my own of how things should be done.

As rebellious as any teenager.

Only, since I'd been an angel, learning lessons from my rebellion took millennia instead of a decade or so. But I *had* learned, and I liked to think, I'd gotten smarter, too.

And as I'd grown, so had Hell, and the function it served.

Truth was, at the core of it all, I was still an angel. And I couldn't let this happen. And okay, not just because I didn't want to be confined nor have my instruments confiscated for some indeterminate time—Sinestra would destroy the work I'd created, and frankly, I actually found myself *liking* the brave reporter who dared Hell itself.

But again… I was still an angel, for Evil *or* Good. Which meant I couldn't interfere directly with what was happening, not too much, anyway.

It wasn't just rules, there were all sorts of energies at play that directly affected my ability.

But when they put Jessica on the table and she lay there, staring stoically up into the stalagmites, I knew I had to do something. I just didn't know what it would be exactly until I felt the bone go through my back all the way through to my chest.

Dammit.

I really liked this suit.

⚡

"Dammit, Devi!"

She didn't have to do that.

These immortals, or past mortals, or whatever they were. They hadn't seen past their own greater or other level powers. Just like the Valkyrie, I muttered to myself as they'd tied my hands together and hustled me to the table. So sure were they of their superiority to all things my dimension and mortal, they'd forgotten that us miserable monkeys had legends, we had lore—we knew how to deal with them. And they'd let me continue holding on to my bag, thinking I was a primate with a talisman.

"Exactly like Sword Time—Skalmöld," I corrected myself. Damn, but that Devi was infectious. Skalmöld had been a bit too... well, too anyway, and she'd backed down when I'd pulled Ehwaz, the rune of marriage, out.

Sigh.

Stupid non-mortals.

Just because I'd declared "atheist" on my intake form, it didn't mean I was a nihilist, obviously, nor that I had no moral compass. It merely meant that I had too much information to be a "believer" of any one thing—I was a seeker, instead.

I... was a journalist.

Which meant I had knowledge.

Which meant I did research.

Which meant that the water bottle in my bag—the same one I'd managed to tuck my tied hands into—held more in it than mere water. It had the energetic intention, the blessing of an old celibate man who followed the teachings of another man who had once, too, been sacrificed.

"I had this under control," I told Devi as she stumbled over me, and I pulled the bottle from the bag, splashing it on the bonds.

As the ancient priest had promised, they dissolved instantly, in seconds I was free.

"She was about to sacrifice you!" Devi choked.

The hench-demons or whatever they were seemed confused, and Sinestra's simian eyes had gone wide. She stared from the black dripping dagger in her hand, to me, to Devi.

"Can we get back to my being the Head of Hell, now?"

Devi laughed and seemed to recover. "Give me that," she said as she took the bottle from me. Strange lights began to weave back and forth between all of us, and the demons cowered in a corner.

"That was never going to happen," Devi told her, now seemingly fully recovered. All that was left was the scorch mark from the exit and entry points of the blade. She casually squirted the remains of the bottle upon Sinestra.

"Really? You're trying to melt me? I've still got the dagger, you know," Sinestra sputtered as she advanced.

"Does that even really work?" I asked Devi

"Wait for it," she said and cocked a grin at me. It was hard to tell, but in this weird fading and flickering light, it seemed the red gleam was slowly disappearing.

"Even now that you're mortal, you're *still* trying to give orders?" Sinestra asked and advanced. "Yeah, no. Not gonna happen. I'm the one with the—"

Her wings swelled to full, her hand swung up again, and Devi, one leg crossed over the other as she leaned casually against the stone slab watched as all that came down was… nothing.

Nothing but the stone blade.

Devi caught it as it fell.

Sinestra had disintegrated. The one remaining rock demon tore out of there, gibbering.

"Seriously? Is water the only thing that works on evil witches, demons, and—"

"Administrative assistants who think they're so much more? How do you think she got here in the first place?" Devi asked.

"Here," she said and tossed me the knife. I caught it in my right hand. It was surprisingly warm.

The flickering lights across her skin seemed to taper, to gather, to pour over mine. And I was fine with that. Despite being the target of a kidnap and attempted sacrifice, I felt just fine. I felt good, I felt strong… and a rush of heat powered through me, and I knew, I *knew*…

Devi watched my face.

"Yes, I'm mortal now."

I felt the warm thrill through me and I rounded a shoulder under my jacket. There was something… *new*… back there.

"And now I'm you?"

"Well, you're *you*," she told me and grinned. "You just have my position, now."

"Why me?" I really wanted to know.

She cocked her head and took a breath before she answered. "You managed to trick a group of demons and the Head of Hell itself. Not the work of an innocent." She grinned at me.

"Oh. So… what happens to *you*?"

"Oh. That's right." Devi's brow furrowed.

"What?" I was beginning to get a touch dizzy from the rush of power. I glanced down at my hands. My fingertips glowed red. "What's right?" I asked anyway.

"I need an apartment. I… I need a *job*! I don't even know how to put together a resume—how do I even start? And all those agencies—they're either purgatorial support or former Limbo babies…" She cocked her head and observed me. "Are you okay?"

"Yeah, sure. I'm fine. I started out a reporter and now I'm the Queen of Hell. I think I'm a little dizzy. I might be hungry. Are those wings growing out of my shoulders?"

Devi laughed again.

"Yeah, you've got a bit of adjusting to do. The wings are optional, you can think them in and out of existence, as it were. I will say this, though: they are pretty dang useful when you need to tour some of the really deeper levels."

I nodded. I was clearing, and getting used to the full warm rush that now filled me. I supposed it always would, from now on.

"I suppose…" I thought about what she'd said. "I suppose you could take my apartment—it's in Hell's Kitchen."

I laughed at what I'd just said. "You ever think that there really is some sort of plan to it all?" I asked Devi.

She shrugged elegantly. Even with the scorch marks from the dagger, she still was… yes, Devi was a handsome and charming devil. "So… where does the Queen of Hell get lunch around here?" I asked, glancing around the now-empty chamber.

"That's easy," Devi said. "Come with me." She held her arm out.

I took it.

We walked along crimson stone hallways. "It occurs to me, I need a new assistant, now that the last one disintegrated. Someone who knows the systems, the layout, someone who can explain the whole DAMN thing."

I stopped and took my arm from hers. "What do you think?"

Devi took a half step back and gave me a measured look.

"What'll it pay? I have an expensive apartment."

"We'll figure that out."

"Bennies? Perqs?"

"I'm not sure yet. You may have to handle some on the job leering from your boss, who will most likely insist you continue to keep that form and wear those suits, well at least ones without scorchmarks."

"Is that all?" Devi asked then smiled. "This *is* my form—I was *made* an angel, you know. And..." her grin grew wider. "I have centuries of suits to choose from—and we've got some of the best designers!"

"Perfect!" I agreed. I felt myself smile as a thought occurred to me. "One thing I can promise," I told her as this time I offered her my arm.

"Really? What's that?" she asked as she slid her arm through mine. It fit. It felt right. Even for this place.

I put my hand over hers and set my shoulders. "It's gonna be Hell."

GLITTER BOMB
Emily Kay Singer

Emily Singer began writing when she realized she didn't love math enough to become a paleontologist. When she's not writing or reading, she's likely at the comic shop, or studying world mythology. Then again, she might just be watching more *Elementary, Castle,* and *Firefly* than is probably healthy. Find her at emilykaysinger.com, on Twitter @emilyksinger, or on the *Beyond the Trope* podcast at beyondthetrope.com.

The public restroom in the capitol building wasn't exactly an ideal place to change into my super villain alter-ego. But if there was one thing I'd learned as the Scourge of Brighthaven, it's that you do what you have to do.

Faint music from the Governor's Ball filtered down the hallway. I banged my elbows and knees against the stall walls in perfect rhythm without even trying. Why the Villainess League insisted on spandex for everyone, I'll never know. Worst idea ever.

Stuffing the slinky dress I'd worn to the ball into my clutch—thank God for inter-dimensional warping algorithms—I finally left the stall. I fixed my powder blue eye-mask and took a moment to make sure the mandatory cleavage window sat right in the middle of my chest.

Satisfied that I looked appropriately sexy-evil, I opened the clutch again, shoved aside a forgotten bottle of my girlfriend's lavender-and-sugar-cookie perfume, and pulled out the squirt-gun-sized Rainbow Love Gun. I made a mental note to come up with a better name later and talk to Kat, my League henchwoman, about her excessive use of glitter on my super weapons. Especially the ones that were already small and unassuming.

Of course, the important part was that it worked. And it had done very well in the small-scale tests. The Governor's Ball would be the perfect place to unveil the RLG to the world.

After a quick check through my multi-dimensional clutch to make sure I didn't leave anything incriminating inside, I dumped the clutch under the counter and headed for the restroom door.

The door swung open before I reached it. Two young ladies walked in, their high heels clicking on the polished tile. They gossiped about some boy, until they caught sight of me. Then one of them screamed.

Just what I didn't need—people drawing attention to me before I was ready for my grand entrance.

I had to do something.

I flipped the RLG from "gayify" to "stun"—it was League protocol that all super weapons have some sort of stun feature, since some of us villainesses had a tendency to get trigger-happy—and zapped both of them. As they dropped to the floor, I heard footsteps and cursed under my breath. Of *course* someone would have heard that scream and come running. So much for strolling from the restroom to the ballroom, throwing open the double doors with an evil cackle, and relishing the looks of surprised terror on everyone's faces.

Then again, teleportation wasn't that bad an option, either. Except for the stupid flower petals that also appeared when I used my power. The League almost hadn't accepted me because of it—what kind of villainess appears and disappears in a flurry of heart-shaped petals? Me, apparently.

I flicked the RLG back to "gayify," held my breath, and popped out of the restroom, through whatever warped space let me jump from one piece of the universe to another.

The world bent around me, like a watercolor set had vomited everywhere, and I focused hard on the ballroom and the music and my goal. When reality solidified around me once more, I found myself hovering in the air above the DJ. Pink flower petals swirled around me and drifted down to the ground.

The music cut out with a shriek of feedback. Someone screamed, "It's Celestite!" Maybe my entrance hadn't been ruined after all.

I lifted the RLG to make sure everyone could see the light refracting off of it. "Good evening, everyone! I hope you're enjoying the ball. Didn't the governor tell you I was coming? No? Oh, I'm hurt."

Governor MacPhee pushed his way out of the crowd, his military medals gleaming on his tuxedo jacket. His big, black mustache looked like an angry caterpillar terrorizing his upper lip. "Security! Get her!"

"Oh, ho!" It was hilarious that "important" people thought they could just sic their security goons on me. Apparently they thought my teleportation only worked once or something. I pointed the Rainbow Love Gun at MacPhee. "You know what I want, Governor. Hand it over."

The squat little man drew himself up like it was supposed to intimidate me, even though I was still floating in midair. "I'll never give it to you."

"Then I guess I'll have to settle for your wife." I grinned and swung the RLG over to a plain woman in her sequined ball gown. Not my type at all, but she would be a great opening for the evening. I pulled the trigger.

A blinding blast of rainbow light shot from the muzzle. It practically sang as it zipped toward the governor's wife, like I had packed a hundred gay angels into the little gun.

Some dumb security goon jumped in front of her and took the blast. Rainbows slithered under his skin as he pulled himself back to his feet. He brushed himself off and looked around the room. Then he grabbed the nearest guy and kissed him full on the lips, smashing their bodies together. His hands instantly tried to worm their way into the other guy's pants, despite all the squirming and protests.

I made another mental note to re-calibrate the horniness factor in the RLG when this was over. I wanted to turn everyone gay, not into slobbering sex monsters. Oops.

A ball of water slammed into my shoulder, hard enough to make me tumble backwards through the air. My back hit the wall and it took me a second to be able to focus through the haze of the pain.

I looked down into the crowd. Water Witch—my weirdly silent nemesis—stood in a wide circle of open space, the well-dressed ball-goers having moved away to give her room. She didn't wear spandex—lucky bitch. Her costume was a beautiful turquoise Arabian-inspired getup, complete with headscarf and full mask; it offset her dark skin in a way I had always found alluring. But now wasn't the time to admire her. "Don't get in my way, Witch."

As usual, she said nothing, only lifted her hand. Water, wine, and punch snaked up out of glasses and serving bowls, flowing through the air toward her.

I wasn't about to give her another chance to kick my ass. Not if I could help it. As quick as I could, I braced myself against the wall and fired the RLG at her.

The rainbow light flickered through the ballroom. It dispersed the gathering liquid and hit Water Witch straight in the chest, but she barely staggered.

That wasn't good. That was really not good. Why wasn't she reacting? I shot her again. And again. Nothing. No slithery rainbows under her skin, no suddenly leaping at the nearest hot lady, no change whatsoever.

Was the gun malfunctioning already? I aimed it at a woman in an absurdly voluminous ball gown and fired. She had the same reaction as the security goon. The gun wasn't broken. Which meant Water Witch had to be…

Oh.

Well, that made things way more interesting. I flicked the RLG to "stun," just in case, and decided to have a little fun before she kicked me to Katmandu. "Hey, Witch, you got a girlfriend?"

The crowd muttered around her.

Water Witch didn't look fazed. She kicked off the floor and floated toward me. I didn't know she had levitation abilities. Shit. Why hadn't she ever used those before?

I aimed the RLG at her. "Stay back."

She held her hand out to me, palm up, waiting for me to give her the gun. She was close enough now that I could smell her perfume. The same kind my girlfriend wore. Weird.

"Like I'm going to just hand it over," I scoffed. But I didn't shoot. She might be my nemesis, but I didn't want to accidentally kill her if her powers cut out and she tumbled to the floor when she was unconscious. I was probably the only villainess in the League who didn't kill on a regular basis—mostly because I couldn't stand the blood and paperwork. There was no way I was going to slog through that bureaucratic hell just to get out of this situation. I was smarter than that.

Water Witch sighed—one of only a handful of sounds she ever made. She held her hand out again, more insistently.

Someone down below shouted for us to hurry it up. Someone else added that Water Witch should just kick my ass already. We both ignored them.

Water Witch moved closer, and I put my finger on the trigger of the RLG. "I told you to—"

Something soft, cool, and heavy smacked into my face, cutting off the rest of my warning. It wasn't until the thing slid off my cheek and hit the floor that I realized it was a large, ragged daisy.

Oh, crap. That meant Obnoxious Fanboy was here.

Water Witch's eyes looked as irritated as I felt.

"Who the hell are you?" Governor MacPhee's voice cut the sudden silence.

Both Witch and I turned toward the huge windows where the flower had come from.

Sure enough, Fanboy—or whatever the hell his real name was—perched awkwardly on the open windowsill. A black and red climbing harness bunched his cape up awkwardly around his thighs, but he didn't seem to care as he brandished a floppy, rubber knife in my direction. "Do it now, Water Witch! Take her out once and for all! I'll distract her for you!"

I wondered if he knew we could hear him without yelling like a bugle corps. Not that it mattered in the long run. I just wanted one fight with Witch that didn't end with my ears bleeding from his stupidity.

Much to my surprise, Water Witch reacted before I could find something appropriately annoyed to say. She zoomed toward him like she had kicked off a wall, even though she had been floating in empty space.

When she reached the open window, she took the young man by the shoulders and shoved.

Obnoxious Fanboy yelped as he tumbled out of the window. The crowd below us let out a collective gasp. His rappelling rope went taut and he started screaming something we could barely hear. Probably obscenities.

I suddenly had a newfound respect for my arch nemesis. Who would have thought the glorious defender of Brighthaven would shove a kid out a window? Totally impressive. And kind of incredibly hot. "That was awesome! You should join the Villainess League."

Water Witch turned toward me with a low growl. There was something stupidly sexy about that. Not for the first time, I wished the Heroines Guild would make her wear spandex like me, instead of letting her get away with that loose, flowing costume.

Before I could get my head back in the game, she lunged at me. I honestly didn't expect our fight to continue so quickly after the interruption. She hit me hard and we went tumbling. I guess I must have pulled the trigger on the RLG a couple times because rainbows flashed everywhere, giving our spin toward the wall a psychedelic rave vibe. Would have been kind of cool if it didn't end with my back slamming into stone. Not the worst pain she'd ever given me, but definitely not a party.

The people below us gasped and screamed. Some of them started cheering for Water Witch. Some of the smarter ones ran for the door. One or two threw silverware and shrimp at us.

I'd learned in previous fights that I was no match for Water Witch's physical strength. But I didn't have to be. After all, I had the best power for getting out of tight spaces.

I squeezed my eyes shut, held my breath, and teleported again. I hadn't meant to go far, just get behind Witch and out of her grasp, but I wound up outside. When I opened my eyes, my heart-shaped flower petals drifted down toward the dangling Fanboy, who seemed to be trying unsuccessfully to get himself out of his climbing harness. Oops.

Per League guidelines, I wasn't supposed to run from a fight with my designated Heroine unless it was part of a trap, my life was in danger, or I'd put more than forty hours into my weekly villainy. Evil didn't pay overtime.

Luckily, Water Witch didn't give me a chance to book it, accidentally or not. She appeared in the open window and found me in a heartbeat. Apparently, powder blue bodysuits aren't exactly the best camouflage. Go figure.

"Don't come any closer, or I'll shoot!" I pointed the RLG down at Obnoxious Fanboy. It was a weak play, but it was the only thing that came to mind.

"Please don't hurt me." Fanboy whimpered and squirmed on his rope.

Water Witch held out her hand. Droplets began to gather at her fingertips.

I pulled the trigger. Rainbows flashed again, painting the capitol grounds in sparkling colors.

Obnoxious Fanboy swayed on his rope, but seemed completely unchanged. Same as when I shot Water Witch—no slithery color under his skin, no sudden desire to find the nearest hot guy. Nada.

"Seriously? You, too?" I stared down at him. If the gun wasn't effective on him, he must already be at least a little gay. Given how he ogled Water Witch, I was betting pretty middle-of-the-road bi.

He shrugged as he swung back and forth.

Well, that sucked. This was really not my night.

Water Witch's ball of water slammed into my leg. Oh, screw this. If I couldn't follow through with my original plan, maybe I could at least work out some of my frustration with the fight.

I tucked the barrel of the RLG into my cleavage window to free my hands, made a mental note to petition the League for a costume change to include some sort of holster or utility belt, and turned to launch myself at my nemesis.

We collided and she shoved me backward.

I flipped head-over-heels toward Obnoxious Fanboy and smacked into his rappelling rope. Ouch. I could practically feel the bruises forming.

The capitol doors banged open below me and people flooded out into the night. Most of humanity had that weird, self-destructive habit of wanting to see a real super-powered fight, but not knowing how far away they should be for their own safety. The joke was on them—there was no safe distance.

Apparently, I didn't get a safe distance, either. I heard a familiar laugh from down below, followed by, "Sorry to interrupt your little shindig, Celestite, but you seem a little off your game tonight! You won't mind if I just take the key to the city, will you?"

"Shove it, Stretchy!" I shouted back. I didn't look at her, but I could tell it was Silver Snake, the only hyper-stretcher in the Villainess League. Bitch was always trailing me and taking credit for my best ideas. If she was here and announcing her presence, it was only a matter of time before her Heroine opponent—Ms. Amazing—showed up. That would be the most exciting thing since my computer died and took all my weapon schematics with it.

I turned to flip Snake off and barely managed to dodge a super-stretched hand reaching up to grab me.

Cloth ripped behind me, but I didn't turn to see what it was. Snake was giving me the perfect opportunity to hit her. I pulled the RLG back out of my cleavage window, realized that my boobs were now obnoxiously glitterfied, and fired at Silver Snake's elongated arm.

Rainbows slipped under her pale skin, radiating all the way down her rubbery arm. A super-powered lady the damn gun worked on! She stood completely still for a moment.

And then her giant hand grabbed me from behind, knocking the breath out of my lungs. She pulled me down toward her like a freight train. People were screaming again. I didn't really blame them this time; I wanted to scream, too. After all, I had expected Silver Snake to go looking for a woman within reach. Leave it to me to forget that practically everyone was in her reach, whether or not we were floating a full story over her head.

I tried to free one of my arms from her grip to flip the RLG to stun and shoot her again, but it didn't work. As a matter of fact, I somehow dropped the glittery gun instead. Then the best thing all night happened: it didn't break when it hit the ground.

I wasn't sure I could say the same about my knees. Silver Snake brought me down hard enough to rattle my teeth, then didn't give me any time to recover before she was all over me. Worst kiss of my life, too—like a tidal wave of spit and over-zealous tongue.

"Let her go, Snake." That was Ms. Amazing's voice, all patriotism and apple pie. The spice came from her next mutter, "I can't believe I'm defending a villain."

Silver Snake pulled back from the sloppy kiss and looked to the right.

I took that opportunity to teleport again. I really shouldn't have, since I'd teleported so much already, but I needed to get away from her before she started kissing and groping me again.

This time, I got myself back to the RLG and bent to pick it up. Except Water Witch beat me to it. A turquoise-gloved hand snatched it just before I could grab it.

Instead of lunging for the gun like an idiot, I looked up, ready to shout. My words stuck in my throat, and I'm pretty sure it wasn't because she tried to freeze all the water in my body again. Apparently, when Silver Snake had reached for me, she managed to rip Water Witch's headscarf, revealing a very familiar shade of dark blue hair.

Standing above me, with the RLG in hand, was my girlfriend, Jackie.

"Holy crap," I whispered. The perfume made sense now. "You're Water Witch?"

She smiled weakly. "Surprise?"

Questions tumbled through my mind, fighting to get out of my lips. Before I could actually ask any of them, something barreled into me and I went sprawling. Silver Snake was on top of me again, looking a bit worse for wear. Not that it stopped her from wriggling until she could grab my breast and start kissing me again. Gross. And in front of my girlfriend, too. Even worse.

I writhed and punched and squealed.

"Ms. Amazing told you to get off her," Water Witch said. Her blue boot came flying. Instead of hitting some part of Silver Snake, which I assumed was her intention, the boot buried itself in my side.

Really, really not my night.

"Crap! I'm sorry, Noelle!" At least Water Witch sounded apologetic. That made me feel slightly better. She'd never done that in costume before.

Through the pain-created stars floating through my vision, I saw Obnoxious Fanboy rocking back and forth on his climbing rope, like he was trying to start up a playground swing. What was wrong with this kid?

Ms. Amazing's yellow high heels appeared beside my head. "Why are you trying to help her, Water Witch? She's your Villainess."

I shoved at Silver Snake. Her wet kisses were starting to get suffocating. When she didn't budge, I bit her lip. That only seemed to make her kiss harder. Great.

"She's also a victim here," Water Witch said. "Which is a problem, regardless. Do you want to get yours off her or should I?"

Ms. Amazing huffed like Jackie had just told her Brightbucks was out of her favorite coffee syrup. But her stance changed and Silver Snake was lifted off me, kicking and squirming.

I rolled over and spit into the grass, pretty convinced her lip gloss was never going to come off.

Water Witch crouched beside me, one hand on my back. It was warm even through her gloves and my spandex. "You okay, babe?"

"Babe?" Ms. Amazing asked, her voice jumping up an octave. "Water Witch, you're not dating your villainess, are you?"

Both of us looked up. Oh, boy. Here came the fireworks. I leaned closer to Jackie and whispered, "Just say I shot you with the RLG. That'll get you out of violating the no-dating rule."

Instead of taking my advice, though, Jackie squared her shoulders and met Ms. Amazing's gaze. "Not that it's any of your business, Lisa, but I'm going to propose to her."

I don't know who was more shocked—Ms. Amazing or me—though I'm sure our reasons were completely different.

"Really?" I gasped when I got my voice back.

She looked at me with a sheepish smile. "I was going to when you got home from the ball tonight. Sorry to ruin the surprise."

"You can't do that," Ms. Amazing squeaked. She seemed completely oblivious to the fact that Silver Snake was doing her best to give her a great big hickey. "We can't date our villainesses. It's against the rules!"

Jackie sighed and stood up. She had dropped the RLG, but her hands were balled into sea foam-colored fists. "I know the Guild rules as well as you do, Lisa. But you can't help who you fall in love with. And it's a stupid rule, anyway."

Ms. Amazing stared.

I stared, too. But then I realized this was just the sort of distraction that could help me finally take over the city. If everyone was glued to two heroines facing off, they wouldn't notice little old me until I started my monologue. Perfect.

Quiet and quick as I could, I grabbed the RLG and crawled away from my girlfriend and her colleague. From the corner of my eye, I noticed that Fanboy was beginning to get a bit more height to his swings.

Someone in an expensive tuxedo and shiny shoes stepped in front of me. I looked up into Governor MacPhee's face. His mustache quivered. He looked like he was trying to be brave but wanted to go hide in a blanket fort until the world became a nicer place. His voice trembled when he said, "Give it up, Celestite. You're never going to win."

"Au contraire," I replied. I rolled to my feet and shoved the RLG into his chest. "With Water Witch occupied—and, apparently, about to propose to me—I can do exactly what I've been trying to do all night!"

He shook like a human-shaped blob of jelly. "I won't let you."

"Oh, please. You don't even know what my plan was." I tightened my finger on the trigger, mostly just for show. Sure, I was going to gayify the governor at some point, but I really wanted my monologue first. What good was playing the villain if I didn't get at least one good, old-fashioned monologue before the end of the night?

MacPhee just trembled and tried to look defiant. He didn't even play along, the jerk.

Well, fine. I didn't need him to ask; I could just monologue without prompting. I waved the RLG around to emphasize my words, glitter flying everywhere. It vibrated a little bit in my hands. "You've probably noticed by now that everyone I shoot with this gun turns gay. But it's more than that. I'm also upping their sex drives and Pride Protocols. Not only will everyone be hornier than rabbits, they'll also be driven to plan a zillion Pride parades, protests against heteronormativity, and all those other things that don't actually make much of a difference but take for-freaking-ever to plan! They'll be so distracted they won't even know when I take over. All I'll need to do is waltz in and proclaim myself Chief Lesbian and Brighthaven will be in the palm of my hand!"

Ms. Amazing laughed behind me. "Seriously? That's your plan?"

"So far, it's kind of working," I said over my shoulder. I pointed the RLG back at the governor. "All I really have to do is—"

"I won't let you." Water Witch stepped between me and MacPhee. She folded her arms and stared me down. "I might be in love with you, but I can't let you get away with this."

I whined like a puppy. That usually worked when we argued. "But, sweetie, it's just one itty bitty nasty ol' city. Pwease? It's not like they'll be too upset with their new lovers and their sweet parades."

Water Witch shook her head. "I'm sorry, Noelle; I can't let you do this."

"But you wuv me!" I don't know where the stupid baby-voice came from, but I could tell it was having an effect on her. She looked at Ms. Amazing like she was looking for support. So kicked-puppy whining, baby voice, and a kiss would probably seal it. I stepped forward.

"Don't," Water Witch muttered. She took a step back, into MacPhee's flab. The Governor practically tumbled backward, but she didn't notice. "Please, babe. Listen. I can't let you do this. You can't just run around messing with peoples' sexuality to take over a city. It's not right!"

"Sweetie, I'm a villain. Moral's not exactly my forte."

She tilted her head to the side at just the right angle for her disappointed expression. "If you go through with this, we're going to need to have a serious talk."

Well, this sucked. Hard. "Serious talks" with Jackie were never a good thing. They meant I'd royally screwed up and, with something this big, I didn't know if she'd ever really forgive me.

Which was I more afraid of losing—a job I adored or the woman I loved?

Sirens blared in the distance. The cops were finally on their way. Crappy response time tonight, apparently. Not that I was complaining. The longer they took to get to the capitol, the longer I had to decide.

Water Witch held her hand out to me. "Give me the gun, babe."

"I spent months perfecting it," I whined.

She didn't look impressed.

"It's not actually hurting anyone," I insisted.

She just kept her hand out, waiting for me to put the RLG in it. She gave me her "you're being a child" look. That look always made me feel so *irritated*. But I couldn't let my frustration get in the way—not if I wanted to avoid metaphorically shooting myself in the foot tonight.

Just as I was about to completely give in for the sake of keeping my girlfriend, someone snatched the gun out of my hand.

"What the hell?" I turned, reaching to get it back.

Obnoxious Fanboy crowed triumphantly, waving the gun above his head. Some of the glitter sprinkled onto his cat-eye mask. It made him look like some sort of deranged anime hero. He swung on the climbing rope in a big arc, like a yo-yo in a cape. "I got it! I saved Water Witch!"

I really had no idea what to do with that. How the hell had he managed to swing that hard that fast?

He pointed the RLG directly at me. Which wouldn't have been much of a problem except that he found the trigger. The light hit me in the chest and, for a moment, I wondered what might happen. Turned out, I didn't need to be concerned at all. It felt pleasantly warm for a couple seconds, and disappeared.

Once the fuzzy, multi-colored light dissipated, I could see the RLG shaking in his otherwise-still hands. It squealed again and glitter puffed off the barrel like a cloud of sparkling steam. I didn't know exactly what was going on—I'd never encountered this, even in testing—but I could tell it wasn't good.

"Put the gun down," I said. "Now."

He laughed as he swung back toward us. "No. Tonight's the end of your reign of terror, Celestite! I won't let you get away again!"

Water Witch stepped forward. "Put it down, kid. For your own good."

"She's infected you," Fanboy hissed. He seemed to have a harder time keeping the RLG steadily pointed at me. It looked like it wanted to jump right out of his hands. And I was pretty sure it wasn't just an effect of his flying through the air.

"I haven't infected anyone, man. Well, no, wait. Just a few people. But not Jackie. Not you. Come on. Don't be an idiot."

Despite his show of bravery, it looked like he was terrified of my approach. He squirmed in his harness, apparently trying to slow down his momentum. The RLG was whining almost constantly, making his arms tremble as he struggled to keep a hold of it.

He pulled the trigger.

The RLG's keening jumped up an octave. Rainbows leaked from the place where the barrel met the grip. Glitter tumbled to the ground in clumps and showers. And then it exploded.

Multi-colored light painted the capitol building and lawn. People screamed. The weirdly delicious smell of smoke and strawberries filled my nose. When I could see again, it looked like a giant had sneezed glitter and bits of metal across the entire lawn. Everything sparkled. People had already started kissing and humping each other. Even the governor seemed to have a newfound interest in his security team. It was almost cute, except for the fact that MacPhee was a mustachioed perv with a physique I really didn't want to see out of his business suits.

Obnoxious Fanboy hung limply in his harness, unconscious.

"You are so getting kicked out of the Guild," Ms. Amazing said from behind me.

Both Water Witch and I turned toward her. She stood right where we had left her, but she was now holding Silver Snake at arm's length instead of letting the other woman crawl over her. Mental note: Ms. Amazing was already batting for our team. I could probably use that in the future.

Water Witch squared her shoulders and propped her hands on her hips. "Why's that?"

Ms. Amazing rolled her eyes over her yellow mask. "You're dating your villainess and you failed to stop her from fulfilling her plan. No way they'll let you stay. I'll finally be the Savior of Brighthaven."

Guilt wormed its way into my stomach, like a slimy little slug. I had ruined Water Witch's standing with the Heroine's Guild, which meant I had probably crushed her dreams. If she had wanted to be part of the Guild as much as I had wanted to be part of the Villainess League, I might have been the best villainess in the world at the moment. "Jackie…"

She didn't look at me.

"I'm sorry," I whispered. I would have shouted it to the sky if she wanted, but with so many people around and my reputation as a villain to uphold, I didn't exactly want to start there. I swallowed hard and stepped forward, but I couldn't bring myself to touch her like I wanted to. "The gun must have gotten damaged when it fell. I didn't mean to do this. Really. And I never wanted to get you kicked out of the Guild."

"Stop talking." Her voice was soft and hoarse. I wondered if she was crying. I really hoped not; I felt bad enough already.

Ms. Amazing moved to throw Silver Snake over her shoulder. Silver Snake didn't seem to mind. The heroine looked at Jackie and me for a moment before shaking her head. "I'll see you back at HQ, Water Witch."

Jackie didn't seem to react.

Ms. Amazing shook her head again and jumped up into the air, disappearing into the night.

After a long moment of watching the beginnings of an orgy the explosion had caused, I muttered to Jackie, "Maybe stopping the governor from screwing his chief of security would help you stay in the Guild?"

Jackie snorted in that way that meant she was trying not to laugh out loud. "Nothing's going to keep me in the Guild now. Ms. Amazing's been trying to get promoted for ages and now she finally has an opening to take over my position. She won't stand to see me stay, even if I hadn't violated several Guild guidelines."

I shifted my weight from one foot to the other. "So… what are you going to do, then?"

She finally turned toward me. Her beautiful brown eyes were watery, but they crinkled at the corners like she was smiling, or at least trying to. "I was thinking maybe we should get out of here before the cops show up."

"Yeah." I smiled weakly, hoping that meant we could go home and snuggle. "Sorry about the Guild, though. Really."

"I was thinking about retiring at some point soon anyway. Just happened earlier than I thought." She stepped forward and threaded her gloved fingers through mine.

"You could join the Villainess League," I suggested before I realized what had come out of my mouth.

She chuckled weakly.

"I'm serious. Think about it—we'd make one hell of a team."

One of Jackie's eyebrows lifted a fraction of an inch.

Her curious gaze made me feel like I'd strapped myself to the front of a freight train without realizing it, which only made my mouth run faster. "We've got an opening, if Silver Snake's down for the count, and you could get revenge on Ms. Amazing for ruining your Guild career, and you just know being evil is way more fun anyway. Come on, sweetie. Think about it."

The sirens were getting closer. Police began to shove their way through the writhing mass of sex fiends on the lawn.

"I'll think about it." Water Witch leaned closer and pressed her forehead against mine. Her whisper made me grin. "But for now, let's go home. I have a not-so-surprising-question for you."

My smile widened. "For what it's worth, Jackie, the answer might be almost-exactly-a-yes."

Before she could respond, I leaned forward, lifted her mask, and kissed her. I tapped into the last of my teleportation powers to get us home ASAP. For once, it felt completely fitting that we disappeared in a shower of heart-shaped flower petals.

FOR WANT OF A HEART
A. Merc Rustad

A. Merc Rustad is a queer, non-binary author and filmmaker living in the Midwest U.S. Their stories have appeared or are forthcoming in *Lightspeed, Fireside Fiction, Daily Science Fiction, Escape Pod, Inscription Magazine* and *Scigentasy,* as well as the anthology *The Best American Science Fiction and Fantasy 2015* (ed. John Joseph Adams and Joe Hill). You can find Merc on Twitter @Merc_Rustad or their website: amercrustad.com.

Glossy. That's Mirdonna.

Glossy: from the tips of her supple thigh-high leather boots with heels as thin and sharp as cobra fangs, to the deep orange corset laced with ivory threads. Her eyes are painted radiant poison-green. It's her smile, though, that captures everyone's attention. Her thick lips are glazed in brilliant umber; the tip of a red tongue pokes between her teeth.

"If I asked," she murmurs, her voice like molten honey, "would you give me your heart?"

I swallow. "Literally or figuratively?"

We're in my flat, which feels dim and desaturated now, with its nicotine-stained walls, frayed couch covers, ceiling paint peeling. The windows rattle in the storm. Sleet pecks the panes, and the chill digs through the worn weather sealing.

"A little of both." That hypnotic smile widens. Mirdonna stretches out one smooth hand. Her short nails gleam like frost etched in hypothermia-blue. "If you're still desperate."

Desperate? If I don't find a way to repay my debts, there won't be enough of me to write an epigraph on a tombstone I can't afford.

I know how deals with the devil end, but when she's handsomer than any devil you can imagine, is it really so bad?

I take Mirdonna's hand. She lifts it and kisses my knuckles. Her chill breath burns my skin and I shiver. It's not unpleasant, this pain.

"Ask and you shall receive," I tell her.

"Oh, I will."

Glossy. And cold—but that's a given for the Winter Lady.

Two days before, I met Mirdonna. I was bar-tending for Madam Eve.

Summer incarnate, that was Madam Eve. Long, marbled gold and red hair, eyes so blue they burned her lashes umber, her smile non-existent. She wore skin-tight lace, rosebud pink and mossy green, patterned like ferns and leaves. It clung to her skin, restless, always a breath shy of sloughing off and flying free.

I pulled taps for the regulars, all women. I stocked the bar, counted the till, and always behind the counter. That was her rule. Know your place.

Madam Eve lounged beside the stage. Her chair was spread with spotted fawn hides and decorated with antlers too big to be real—which were, nevertheless. A pair of great wolfhounds, reddish fur combed and oiled to gleaming, lay by her feet. I remember the women they used to be: lucky twins who'd run up gambling debts at Madam Eve's tables in back. They'd accepted her leash; in exchange, she'd forgiven their debts.

I felt my name, like an itch, on the ledgers she kept of who owed her what, and how, and for how long.

Every night after work, I swore to myself I wouldn't slide through the frosted glass doors and into the velvet-walled parlor. I wouldn't pick up the dice. I wouldn't push chips stamped with her face onto the felt tabletops.

But I was hooked on the perfume the dealers wore, their easy smiles, the wins just often enough to make me hope.

I knew how it worked. The cycles. The addiction. But I just couldn't make myself stop. Part of me wondered: what was the point? What was left?

My brother was financially secure. He had a two-bedroom apartment with his wife in uptown. A steady job. Good benefits. He didn't need my support any longer, and I refused his charity. I didn't want to drag him into my pit.

Friends are hard to keep when you always push everyone away to stop them from hurting, or hurting you in turn.

That night, Mirdonna swept in the front doors in a swirl of icy wind and snowflakes sharp as razors. She nodded once to Madam Eve, who inclined her chin in turn.

The air in the bar seemed to split, about to explode in lightning from hot and cold now meeting.

"Sister," Madam Eve said in her slow, elagant drawl. "How good of you to visit."

"Darling," the Winter Lady replied with a smile that would have turned anyone else into an ice sculpture. "Is my money good here?"

"Always," Madam Eve said, laying a hand on one of the wolfhounds. "Jordan, dear, a drink for my sister on the house."

I nodded, heart pounding.

"Unsweetened cider," the Winter Lady said as she sashayed to the bar. "Hot."

The apples were picked from the indoor hydroponic garden, huge golden fruits with skin as soft as a newborn's skull and pomegranate-red flesh. These apples only the Summer Lady could grow.

Her cider was the strongest drink the bar served. It tasted, I was told, of breezes across a wild meadow, the screams of mice caught by hawks, the musk of rutting deer, and the burn of fires engulfing pine forests and everything that lived within.

I pulled on heavy leather gloves, then took the slim bottle of cider from the shelf.

The Winter Lady leaned one elbow on the rosewood, with the look of wild cats tearing apart rabbits. "You're new here, aren't you, miss…?"

"Cashier. Jordan Cashier." I licked my lips, wishing I had a moment to pop my chapstick from my purse. "I've been here about a year."

She smiled again. The ice from her skin had fogged the bar counter. "Eve's staff does have a rather… high turnover."

I shrugged. Careful to watch my hands and the red, red juice, I poured the cider into a steamed mug and set it across from her.

"My sister and I have always had an affinity for sensing the lost," she said.

I grabbed a cloth to wipe the bar, even though it was spotless. I'd usually make small talk, play sympathetic ear, or flirt with the customers. But if I looked at the Winter Lady too long, I thought those brilliant eyes would absorb me and leave nothing left.

"Let me know if I can get you a refill," I said, and sidled down to check on my other regulars.

Sweat dripped down my neck. I ignored Jasmine's usual come-ons and told Laretta her she'd reached her limit. The Winter Lady hadn't moved.

Finally, unable to ignore her, I looked back.

"If you find yourself in a bind…" One lacquered nail slid a business card towards me. "My number."

I looked at the card: crisp white stock with silver lettering. It said, simply, MIRDONNA. There was a phone number on the back. I tucked it in my pocket.

Then she glided out. She hadn't taken one sip of her cider.

✺

She wants to rule the world. Don't we all?

✺

"Not rule, honey," she says as we sip mocha lattes in her laboratory. "I intend to correct the world."

Mirdonna's lab is ensconced in a tower, a time-warped fairy tale planted in the middle of the arctic. It's all polished steel and sparkling glass and burnished wires.

I'm not much of anything by trade—bartender, cabbie, retail cog, gambler—so I can't name half the things lining the walls.

She whisked me here in a sleek chopper painted with snow camo pattern. Eerily silent rotors spun wind.

For my safety, she said, but I've been trapped in enough dead-end jobs and relationships to know what a prison's like. It's okay. I'm safer here than back in the city, where Madam Eve's huntresses are on the prowl.

"Correct it how?" I ask. The coffee is burnt, the foam too sweet. It's keeping me awake though. Going on thirty-six hours without a nap, I'll take whatever I can get.

"Look at you." Mirdonna sets down her mug. There's frost patterns along the lip of ceramic. "A woman down on her luck. Perhaps it's bad decisions, but we all make those. And why should those bad choices result in pain?"

I fiddle with my mug, now empty but for the film of steamed milk on the inside curve. "Isn't that how it works?" I laugh, cough, then swallow back the bitterness knotted deep in my chest. "You fuck up, someone fucks you up in return."

"Exactly." Mirdonna's voice is a low purr. Her fingertips brush mine, and an electric chill makes my skin prickle. "And why should we let this destructive pattern continue?"

I squint at her. "So you *don't* want to rule the world and bend it to your will? You told me—"

"I told you I want to make the world better," she says, "and under my guidance, it will be."

"I'm here, aren't I?" I nod at the laboratory. It's all business: mechanical efficacy, charts on the walls, computer screens humming with equations and weather patterns. "You keep me from ending up in the river as a fishy consort and I…"

I'm still not sure how literal she's being when she says she wants my heart. You can survive with artificial recreations of the organ, but she doesn't strike me as a surgeon.

"You help me change the world," she says, and her hand encloses mine.

Her touch isn't as cold as I remember. She pulls me closer, her lips a fraction from mine, and when she kisses me, all I can feel is heat.

My brother calls my cell phone again. This time I answer.

"Jordan?" His smoke-husked voice is a welcome, familiar sound.

"Yeah, it's me."

"Thank god." He's the nicest man I've ever met. He recently married and his wife is pregnant with their first kid. Jacob has always worried about me. He's younger, but when we were children, he felt it his duty to watch my back while I tried to scrape by with part-time jobs after school. "I stopped by to bring back your crockpot, but all I found was a pile of newspapers on your mailbox and your neighbor said you haven't been home in over a week."

"Yeah, I'm fine. I got a job that's out of town. Short notice."

I tighten lug nuts on the glass octagonal containment chamber. I'm good at mechanical jobs: I can work with my hands, and follow instructions. Mirdonna has given me a few tasks to keep me from worrying.

"You're… not in trouble, are you?"

I imagine him biting his lip or sucking on a lollipop—his two tactics for when he quit smoking.

"No," I tell him. "I'm just fine. The job pays well, but it's up north."

The wrench is cold and heavy in my gloved hand. Like the lies.

"That's good." He clears his throat. "Carol wants to know if you'd like to come over for dinner sometime this week."

I tighten the next bolt; metal whines.

"I don't think I can."

"Oh, okay." A long pause, just our breathing and the crackle of bad signal. "Well, respond to my texts a little sooner, would you?"

I try to laugh, but it sticks in my throat. I can't tell him I deleted them all without reading. If I read them, I'll have second thoughts. I'll remember where I am.

Jacob says, "I was afraid you'd gone off into a ditch. Roads are slippery. And I bet you haven't gotten winter tires, have you?"

"I'll get to it." On the phone, it doesn't matter if I cross my fingers or not. "And I'll drive safe."

"Promise, sis?"

"Always."

I hang up before Jacob can drag out goodbyes and make them hurt more than ever.

❦

Mirdonna's machine is like a cocooned butterfly. A network of membranous arrays will fold out from the tower into modified satellite dishes. Inside, like the unsettled bio-mass, lie the containment tanks and the mechanic nervous system that powers them.

Each tank holds a person, comatose, strapped into nutrient fluids that look as cold as the winter sea.

"What does it do?" I asked her when she first showed me the control room: a dozen security camera screens, inside and out, and a slim panel with only two buttons—one blue, one white.

"I call it Empathy," she said. "It's based in sympathetic magic—emotions distilled from love, compassion, kindness, joy. The energies will be conducted into the biological equivalent of an EMP." Her finger hovered over the blue button. "When I press this, the world changes."

"How?"

"It will eradicate the human desire to harm," she said. "No one will crave violence, feel anger, or seek to hurt another."

"You're taking away people's free will?"

"What use is it if they cannot control it?" Mirdonna smiled. "Relax, darling. I'm not taking everything. Think of it as neutering. Everyone will still feel happiness and satisfaction. It will not change who you love, or sleep with, or build your life with. It simply removes the baser elements from the human equation. We've wasted millions of years and humans still can't control their baser urges. I'm tired of waiting."

I shivered. "It will affect everyone?"

"Yes." Her eyes gleamed like new ice. "Can you imagine a world without pain, Jordan?"

"No."

Her finger brushed my lips. "Not yet."

❧

The next text I get is from Madam Eve herself.

Darling, I'd rather not send my pets to sniff out your poor dear mother. She's hardly got your vigor and charm. But even an old dog can beg if taught.

Come visit, honey, and make this easy on yourself and your dam.

I drop the phone, shaking.

When I catch my breath, I try calling Mom.

There's no answer.

❧

I was just getting off shift at midnight. I handed over the new till to Kelsey, a cute transgender woman who always wore iconic rock band shirts. I pocketed my tips.

"Jordan, dear, I'd like to speak with you a moment," Madam Eve said.

My fingers itched to grab my lighter. I craved a smoke. The ivory case engraved with my dad's initials was more than just a light. It was my protection; he hadn't been carrying it—he'd quit on my birthday—when he died. I thought that if he had, he'd have come home.

I knew I was screwed, but I kept my smile fixed as I stepped around her wolfhounds and stopped by her throne. "Madam?"

Her hand stroked the bigger dog's head. The hound shivered under her touch, its tail tucked beneath its haunches. "Genevieve tells me you haven't been paying back your… tab."

I tugged my button-up shirt collar. *Fuck.* "Money's a little tight right now, Madam." I tried to laugh. It failed. "What with—"

She lifted an index finger, and the entire bar went silent. The air was hot, thick, like a living thing that coiled around my throat.

I struggled to breathe and not panic.

"My dear, I'm a lenient woman." Madam Eve indulged me with a raised eyebrow. It made my stomach cramp. "Tell me, can you have your payments made by dawn?"

No. I was broke. I'd used my paycheck to scrape by on rent and groceries, sending my mom a tiny stipend via her bank account as I did every month to help her out, and… the rest went to the house's coffers. A hole that got ever deeper.

My brother didn't know Mom was struggling. She'd demanded I not tell him. He had his own family now. We could get by. We always had.

"Of course, Madam."

Her nod was nearly imperceptible. She sipped lies like fine champagne. "Marvelous, my dear. Come back in six hours, then, and we'll settle the books. I do like to make my ledgers neat before the solstice."

I nodded, jerky as a broken marionette.

Everyone in the bar who knew me—most of the regulars, Kelsey, the bouncer (and ex-girlfriend) Carlotta, the hounds who I'd known once upon a time as Meryl and Mara—averted their eyes. Everyone knew.

I couldn't repay what I owed. And I couldn't run—where do you go in a world where there's nowhere to hide?

By dawn, I'd be either dead or transformed into one of Madam Eve's pets. Everyone knew. Especially the Summer Lady herself.

Outside, hands shaking as I lit my last cigarette, I remembered Mirdonna's business card in my back pocket.

"If it's fueled by sympathetic magic," I asked her over dinner (smoked salmon with roasted asparagus and on a bed of jasmine rice), "Where does the energy come from?"

"People," Mirdonna said, as if it was the most obvious thing in the world. I chased my food down with a delicate white wine. "You mean... me?"

"No. One is not enough. Not even two." She sighed. We sat across from each other in her parlor.

Outside, the wind raged and hurled snow in blistering curtains against unbreakable glass. "I tried that, in the beginning. I thought two who loved me would suffice. But they did not, in the end, truly love me. So I've gathered others. The desperate, the altruistic. They must come willingly, and when I ask, give me what I need."

I lit up. She didn't care if I smoked. It wasn't my health that she needed.

She smiled, but it had a shadow of sadness—the first regret I had seen in her. "It won't hurt. I can ensure that much."

I nodded. "How soon is it operational?"

"When the last of my hearts is ready," she said.

In the end, wasn't it better to die knowing I might have changed the world?

❧

Mirdonna's machine isn't ready.

I don't know where she's gone. No one else but me here in the tower, except for the containment pods.

I need something to bargain with, to pay off my debts, or my mother will become collateral.

Shit.

There's a cot, a space heater, and an electric kettle and microwave atop a small fridge in one corner of the lab. Food, instant cocoa, tea bags, coffee. The bathroom is across the short hall, buttoned by featureless steel doors.

I have a proper bedroom—lush, maroon and orange curtains across unopening windows, a vaulted ceiling, a rosewood armoire, a king sized bed so soft I thought I might melt if I touch it. Plenty of outlets for charging my laptop and phone. No internet, though the cell reception is excellent for being in the middle of the arctic.

Mirdonna doesn't answer her cell.

"Shit."

I almost call Jacob, but I've deleted his contact from my phone. I know the number. It hasn't changed in years. I don't want him involved. He deserves his happiness. He can't help me or Mom anyway.

There's one room I'm not allowed inside: Mirdonna's private office.

We've fucked in her bedroom, all plain white velvet and therapeutic pillows and the walls decorated only with a single painting of Madam Eve. There's nothing in there, beyond her scent and the memory of orgasms.

The office isn't locked.

She simply told me, "Don't," pointed at the door, and strode past it when she gave me the initial tour.

I look for cameras, any sigils on the threshold that spells death to anyone who opens that white oak door.

Will she be angry? What can she do that Madam Eve won't?

I've already promised her my heart.

Fuck the rules.

I open the door and step inside.

There's nothing in the circular room except a pedestal with three crystal globes.

Inside each is a slow-beating heart.

I suck in my breath. The room is like ice. The air burns my skin. I take a step, and frost crunches under my foot. The carpet is frozen chenille.

"Have you no respect?" Mirdonna says behind me.

I whirl around. "You—"

"You are not supposed to come here." Her eyes are flecked with winter lightning. "Do you think you're the only one I need? I should destroy you."

I glare at her, sudden fury overwhelming me. "So what's to fucking stop you? You could have anyone you want. Anyone in the world! Why me?"

"Because you belonged to my sister," Mirdonna says.

"Yeah, and I will again if I don't pay her off. She's coming after my mother."

"And what, darling, do you think would happen if you gave her back our brothers or myself?" She sweeps past me and lays a finger on the center crystal. "She will just let your mother return to whatever squalor she lives in? That the Summer Lady will not simply take you and make you *watch* what she does to your family?"

Panic settles sour in my gut. I crave a smoke but I'm out. My lighter's all that's left in my pocket.

She's right. I know it like I know how much I've fucked up.

"Then what do I do?"

❧

When the Winter Lady left the bar, I dumped her untouched cider into the carefully marked drain that went back to the garden.

Even if it wouldn't have cost me my job, I didn't dare contaminate the municipal drainage. Who knew what would grow from the pipes if I did?

"If they're sisters," I said to Desmondelda, one of the regulars who was freer with her words than most, "where's spring and autumn?" I meant it half as a joke. Elements like Mirdonna and Eve were never isolated.

Desmondelda chuckled. Her nails tatted against the polished counter. "Those boys? Pretty sure Madam Eve and Lady Winter skinned them and used them for rugs long ago. No one's ever seen 'em."

I laughed, as was expected, and refilled Des's beer.

❧

"Finish what we've begun," Mirdonna says. "Your mother's fate is decided regardless."

My knees wobble and I sink to the floor. I can't feel anything.

I know. I *know*. As soon as I got that text, I understood.

I'm a fool if I pretend there's hope left.

"I thought they would be enough." Mirdonna lifts the two crystals, turning them in her hands, then flings them to the floor. "But no. My brothers have never loved me. They tried to take my power when I told them my plan. So I took theirs instead."

I laugh, bitter. "So you already failed once."

Ice flares along her skin until it becomes long talons on her nails. Her hand hesitates just shy of seizing my throat.

"Do you dare accuse me?"

"It's true, isn't it?" Numb, I get to my feet. I brush her hand aside, incautious. "Is the third one yours?" I nod at the crystal heart still on the pedestal.

She sighs, but the ice fades from her hand. "It is."

I want to pull her close, tell her I'm sorry for what she endured.

But she wants no pity, and I'm so tired I don't know how much more I want to feel.

I look up into her eyes. "Tell me one thing. The people who offered to help. Do you feel anything for them?"

Can you still love?

She looks away, her jaw muscles bunching. "It's not necessary. Their devotion is all that matters."

"Magic is a conduit. It flows both ways. If you don't care about them— hell, maybe it only takes one to spark the spell, like a fuse. But if you don't love any of them in return, it won't work."

Her rage dims. Her flesh isn't as cold as I once thought.

"And you, Jordan? Do you love me?"

"No."

She tilts her head back, slow, as if the bones in her neck are melting snow.

"Fear you, respect you, desire you, sure." I won't lie. "But I don't love you. Not yet."

She crosses her arms, pushing me back a step. "My sister is coming for you, and she will learn what I have created. She will want to destroy my work."

Figures.

I wish I had told my mother goodbye before I followed Mirdonna. I wish I had the backbone to stay, to face Madam Eve alone.

I'm so sorry, Mom.

I shut my eyes against burning tears.

"Is my mom dead?"

"Not yet." Her tone is cool, clipped. "My sister will not waste her so easily."

I nod. I've wondered, since I came here, why there is no one else in the tower not enclosed in glass. Is it because Mirdonna has put all her power, all her skill and magic and will into the machine? She has no soldiers left. She has no army to combat her sister.

She cannot save my mother—but perhaps I can.

I take a deep breath.

"I have an idea."

❦

There's a winding catwalk that connects all the containment chambers. Each has a name.

I look into each tank, into each face. None of the sacrifices see me. But I study them. I memorize their names.

I wonder who they are. Who they love, what they are giving up. What they want. What regrets they still have.

I make myself watch them until I'm raw, devastated. They're all going to die.

Ninety-nine human beings out of billions. Each an individual. Each a universe—starstuff, souls, history, memory, passion, dreams. I still have enough of a heart to mourn them. To feel empathy.

That is the purpose of the machine, after all.

❦

"Jacob, it's me. Yeah. Is that dinner invitation still open?"

❦

Jacob looks at me through the anesthetic haze. His mouth forms sound-less words inside the containment tank.

"Hi, little brother." I speak into the mic from the control room.

He'll hear. The containment tank is equipped with speakers that have, until now, played soft, soothing playlists of spring rain and loons, water lapping against sandy shores, delicate wind instruments guiding thoughts through peaceful melodies.

"I wanted to tell you Carol's just fine. Your baby's healthy and due to be born next week, right on schedule."

Jacob's eyes focus. He's suspended at the top of the pyramid of bodies. I only want him to see my face, in the end.

Below him are the ninety-nine who've offered their hearts to Mirdonna. Interlinked with needles and tubes, electric primers strapped over ribcages. Dreaming, I hope, of a new world.

"Dinner was nice," I continue. "I'm glad we had a chance to get together." Carol told me they were having a baby girl. The name they'd picked out: Jaclyn Rose.

"Pretty," I said.

Carol laughed. "Your mom's name and mine combined. I think it's perfect."

I'd brought a bottle of Mirdonna's favorite vintage wine. As soon as Jacob passed out, while Carol was in the bathroom, I carried him out to the chopper.

I'm stronger than I look.

Jacob blinks, now, focusing on my voice.

"Remember that time we built a snow fort on Mrs. Kelroy's vegetable garden to protect it from invading lava monsters?" I ask. "Mom got so mad, even if Mrs. Kelroy thought it was hilarious and brought us hot chocolate with marshmallows to drink in our fort."

Tears drip down his face. He mouths words again, but I can't hear.

"It's one of the few good memories I still have, Jake."

Outside, in the wild arctic, I hear Madam Eve's huntresses.

I see them on the security cams: They've shifted into bears, foxes, wolves, elk. Some of the women ride snowmobiles, winter coats flapping about their shoulders like capes. Madam Eve is with them, running bare-legged across the snow like a living flame. A stream of boiling water flows behind her steps.

Mirdonna is on the roof, shaping the last threads of steel and living membrane to carry the Empathy across the world.

"It was the day Dad…" I take a breath. "The day he was murdered. I know Mom told us it was an accident. Christmas Eve, and some asshole just walked up to him in the street, high as fuck, and shot him for kicks."

Jacob shuts his eyes.

"That's the kind of world we have right now. Random violence. Grief. And I know. I know. I'm taking you away from Carol and your daughter. I'm sorry,

Jacob. But they'll be okay. Because tomorrow… no one will want to kill. No one will want to hurt each other."

Mom will live. She'll walk away from Madam Eve. Everyone who's bound to the Summer Lady will be free.

"We'll be okay. Your baby's going to grow up not having to be terrified that if she looks at a guy wrong, he'll kill her. Your wife won't have to get catcalled and harassed on her way to work or out for a jog. Mom won't get her teeth knocked out by a drunk boyfriend."

I turn off the security feeds.

Madam Eve and her huntresses won't get here in time. And if they do… it won't matter.

"I couldn't have done this without your help, Jake. Goodbye," I tell my brother. "I love you."

❄

Inside the control room, it's dim and cold. Snow flurries buzz down from the opened roof. The flowering antenna and dishes are positioned. Mirdonna glides down the ladder and stands next to me.

"I don't know what to do when this is over," Mirdonna says, her fingers poised above the launch button.

When she presses it, all the empathy and life force will multiply and bloom like a great tidal wave. It will ripple through the atmosphere, airborne, and infect everyone who breathes.

We don't know if it will change the unborn—like Carol's daughter—but we can hope. Perhaps, if brought up in a world where pain and hurt are not necessary, children will learn without being neutered by the machine.

"We'll figure it out," I say, and she smiles.

The countdown begins: ten, nine, eight…

Engines hum. Power floods the circuitry and the transmitters begin to glow.

The ninety-nine bodies convulse as needles pierce their hearts, leeching out life energy and blood into the tubes winding into the converters.

Seven, six, five.

Mirdonna takes a breath. She looks up at the stormy sky, the snow crusting her lashes.

"Tomorrow," she says. "Tomorrow…"

Four.

I grab her wrist. Mirdonna turns her head, slow, predatory. Her eyes meet mine.

Three.

The needles pierce Jacob's heart.

The status bar on our screen is at ninety-nine percent.

"He's my brother."

She nods.

Two.

Mirdonna pulls her arm back; I let her go.

One.

Jacob's eyes close for the last time.

One-hundred percent.

I press the button for a new world.

ABSOLUTION
Claire Monserrat Jackson

Claire Monserrat Jackson has been writing since she learned to put the pointy end of the pencil to the paper. A published poet, novelist, and illustrator with a deep commitment to LGBT equality and trans* rights (and a slight obsession with gaming and general geekery), Claire is usually either writing or asleep. On occasion, she can be found scouring local book stalls, planning her latest expedition, or stomping around the woods near her Ohio home, startling the wildlife. She can be found online at ClaireDeLunacy.com or on Twitter as @LaBarceloneta.

It was an okay day, right up to the minute the witch shot me in the face.

I suppose that requires a little bit of explanation. So let me lay it out for you. I'm what you call a problem solver. Not in the algebra/think tank/Millenium Prize way, mind—my methods are a bit more… direct.

It's a tough old world out there, and people have all kinds of problems. Debt problems. Blackmail problems. Eldritch-horror-from-beyond-the-Nth-dimension problems. But whatever their problem, the solution always seems to be the same: a dirt nap for somebody else. And in my little corner of the world, I'm Mr. Sandman. Well, Ms. Sandman. Semantics don't matter to the dead.

It had been a busy Spring for me. I'd spent most of it recovering after my last case, an unholy shitstorm that left me with a limp on rainy days and a lot of very bad people dead inside a mountain. And also on it. And near it.

Again—semantics.

That case was meant to make my fortune. Instead, I ended up giving most of my take to a bunch of orphans. Orphans! I must be getting soft in my old age. Little bastards.

Even though I was broke as the proverbial joke, gimping around for most of the rainy season meant my caseload was a bit more sedate than usual. I was starting to get tired of chasing down wayward husbands and petty thieves and mostly harmless creepy-crawlies from whatever bit of the Fae had bubbled up near the local yokels.

The Fae—if you've been living under a rock, that's the fairy-land that started busting through as soon as people started dying off in significant numbers, back during the Malthusian Wars—kept me and my team busy enough, I suppose, although I missed doing things that *mattered*. Chasing down the goblin equivalent of teenagers in order to get rid of the tail they'd given the mayor's kid was not my idea of Fighting the Good Fight.

To make matters worse, I'd broken things off with my girlfriend, Lara. She couldn't handle my job (the number one killer of my relationships since… well, when did the Earth cool?) She gave back her key, I gave her the half-dozen bags of crap she brought with her. I thought we parted amicably, but then I discovered the scheming little brat had taken my record player with her.

Given that the last electronics store went up with the rest of New Chicago, back in 2140, I can't exactly pop 'round to the shop and grab another.

The part that really burns? She left the records. Just to taunt me.

All of this added up to create the exquisitely piss-poor mood I was in on the morning Tommy O'Shea came stumping into my office and plopped his dusty ass into my one good guest chair. He was clad, as always, in a worn but mostly clean jumpsuit.

"Make yourself at home, Tommy," I sighed, waving aside the cloud of dust and smoke that surrounded my best friend like a pocket atmosphere. "What's up?"

The man sitting across from me would probably be mistaken for a corpse by most folks. His desiccated flesh clung to his wasted frame, the stringy tendons visible beneath the leathery hide giving him the look of a discarded puppet from hell's toyshop. Tommy's an Afterlifer; one of a few thousand (we think) folks who didn't survive the war, but walked home anyway.

"Well, my darlin' Cuicatl, it's a job o' work." He leaned forward and fixed me with his good eye ("good" being a relative term when you're talking about an Afterlifer) and winked. I did my best to keep my breakfast from making a break for it and tried not to think about Tommy as he'd been when we'd met, all those years ago. He was a wreck now, but his eyes were still green as an Irish hillside. It's funny, the little things that stay when everything else has gone.

I narrowed my eyes. "Oh? Something really exciting, I suppose. Did a chimera steal somebody's horse again? They're not getting that back, except as burgers." I should've been more grateful, I know. Despite being technically dead, Tommy's a good guy to know. Cheap as chips, and never one to stand a round down the pub, but a fast friend—and one hell of a surgeon with a shotgun.

Tommy shook his head. He used the butt of his cigarette to light a fresh one, then ground the expired coffin nail into the ashtray I kept on my desk for his exclusive use. He took a deep drag on the cigarette, smiling in satisfaction. I watched a few streams of smoke escape through the tears in Tommy's neck, then said, "No? So what, then? Oh, God, Steven's not stepping out on Charlie, is he?"

Tommy tilted his head back and coughed, the creaky rustle that passed for laughter among Afterlifers filling the air along with a cloud of smoke and a disconcerting miasma of tiny brown flakes. "Are ye mad? She'd have his balls for breakfast. No, girl, this is something *real*."

He took another drag on his cigarette and leaned back, draping one arm across the worn wood. "Question is, are ye up for it? How's the bum flipper? Still gimpy?"

I leaned back in my own chair, crossing my legs as I plopped my booted feet on the scarred mahogany. "Fit enough to run circles around you. Didn't your mother ever teach you it's rude to tease?"

He laughed again and set his cigarette on the edge of the ashtray. Reaching into the breast pocket of his jumpsuit, he pulled out a NanoSSD, along with a crumpled photo. "Latch yer peepers onto this, and tell me if it's not a long sight better than chasing lost horses and idiot husbands."

I took a quick look at the photo. Some flyspeck town at the edge of the sea. A woman—pretty, mid-30s, maybe, with a cloud of ash-blonde hair surrounding her heart-shaped face—stood on... no, in... the sand, up to her waist, her hands bound behind her. Her black dress was torn in several places, the bruised flesh clearly visible through the rends in the fabric.

The tide was coming in, and the verdigris water was already foaming around her. A crowd of people were gathered on the beach behind the woman; some with solemn eyes, some with faces darkened by rage.

The woman's own face, I noted with interest, was serene.

I slid the tiny drive into the slot on the side of my cranial implant. I heard a click, and a short video began to play, floating in the air about six feet in front of me. The sound was tinny, but I could still make out the narrator as the camera opened on the same stretch of beach depicted in the photo.

"I am not given to understanding the Urbanite devices, but my youngest, Matthias, did set up this camera for me so I might send a message with greater speed than by horse. I am Hiram Jacobson, Third of My Name, and Pater of the Five Families in the Lakeland."

"The Lakeland?" I said, raising an eyebrow. "Neo-Amish," answered Tommy. "He and his folk have the farming rights for most of the coastal agrarian areas up past the Chicago Territory. If it's between Lake Jefferson and the Greats, chances are they farm it. They call the Minnekotasin Territory 'The Lakeland.'"

"Hmm. Interesting." I resumed the video.

"In the year of our Lord 2187, the witch Samantha Corvus did come to one of our young women, promising pleasures of the flesh in exchange for certain favors. The young woman, Lucretia Schultze, was naive and foolish, and given to sins of perversity born to Man by the poetess of Greece."

I rolled my eyes and paused the vid again. "Sins of perversity? Tommy, is this a joke?"

He shook his ragged head solemnly. "Just watch, Cuicatl."

I sighed and tapped my implant. "Lucretia opened herself to the Corvus woman and used the craft she learned at her altar to entice other young women to the witch's service," said Hiram, his voice quivering slightly. "By the time we did discover their secret, the witch had built a coven of our youth and was working her wroth against the Families, plotting their destruction."

I suppressed another eye-roll as the camera moved closer.

The camera zoomed in, showing a ring of black, blasted glass set into the sand. Despite the wind driving both sand and surf across the beach, neither a single grain nor the smallest drop of seawater marred the glossy surface. "And so it was that my great-grandfather, Josiah Jacobson, and twelve strong men of faith, rose up against their wickedness and smote the witch in the name of the Lord."

"Oh, HELL no." I looked at Tommy. "I'm sorry, are these the people I'm supposed to be *helping?*" Tommy shushed me and gestured to my implant with his cigarette.

"But the witch was canny, and even in defeat did scheme against us. We gave her to the sea, so that salt and sand would scrub her from the Earth she sinned against; but at her death, the witch called upon dark forces, and in her dying, did slay many members of the Five Families, throwing all into disarray and nearly unmaking the oldest of Covenants. This scar on the Earth is a reminder of the horror visited upon us."

"I notice grandpa Joe apparently escaped the big boom," I muttered darkly.

"It has taken us many seasons to recover from the loss of our beloveds, and only faith in the Lord and in *ordnung* has preserved our folk on this sorry, sinful Earth." Hiram's voice grew muffled as he turned away to consult with someone out of mic range—presumably the techno-savvy son, Matthias—and then grew clear again. "We thought the blood price we paid that dark day was our punishment from the Lord, for surely were we blinded in forgetting vengeance is for the Lord alone. But... but..." The man's voice broke, and for the first time I felt a tinge of pity. Even bigots can be scared shitless, I reminded myself.

Hiram's voice firmed. "But now, the sins of the father are indeed repaid upon the son, because Samantha Corvus has returned—a shadow in the night passes over us, bringing death. And our women... they are mad. Mad! My own lady wife did try to murder me in our marriage bed, not a fortnight gone."

So what's the big deal? I wondered, feeling only slightly uncharitable.

"We have, with grief in our hearts, locked all of our women who have had the blood in our largest barn. They wail and rage, day and night, seeking to smite us in the Corvus woman's name. We dare not strike them down, and risk aggravating the Lord further, even if it would free them from the demon's curse." He was sniffling, now, and paused to blow his nose. I winced at the honk and shook my head. "Miss Cruz, we have your name by way of our cousin, Tobias, who although he is a sinning Urbanite does still hold to some of the old ways. You came to him in his hour of need, and we would ask you do the same for us. Free us from this curse and we will gladly compensate you in whatever form you deem appropriate, except that which would imperil our souls further."

The video ended, and the NanoSSD uploaded coordinates into my GPS. I tapped the implant on the side of my head and leaned back in my chair, closing my eyes.

After a long moment, I said, "So... let me get this straight: I helped Toby 'The Thumb' Fenstermacher get out of a deal with a particularly stupid demon, and now I'm on the hook to save the Mennonite Moral Majority from some bullshit their own bigoted ancestors brought down on them?"

Tommy was lighting yet another cigarette. "Well, now, Cuicatl, I've got two things to say to that: Firstly, even a Catholic heathen sort such as yerself knows the Mennonites and the Amish are two different tribes."

He exhaled slowly, and I sang a few bars of *Summer Wind* to push away the smoke. He smirked and fanned a little of the cloud toward the window.

"Second, ye need to get back out in the field. Yer not cut out for this penny-ante malarkey. Christ, girl, I watched you tear the beating heart out of that… what was it, a monkey-god?… down in Mexico. You sang that bear fellow back into his own skin. And as for Silver… well, that mountain of his is more of a molehill now, wouldn't you say?"

I looked away, chewing on my thumbnail and trying not to rub my leg.

Tommy snapped his fingers at me, drawing my eyes back to his. "And now you're, what, sniffing around after Johnny Jerk-Off because he can't keep it in his pants? It's embarrassing. For both of us. But especially you."

He fixed me with a gimlet glare before ruining the effect by bursting into a fit of hacking. "I'm not… *cough*… used to… *cough*… flappin' me gums so much… *cough*… anymore," he said, trying not to deposit any more flakes on my desk than was absolutely necessary.

"You flap 'em enough, you dime-store fossil," I said, trying and failing to conceal my grin.

"Well, what do you say? Are we bringing our sinful ways to God's own country?"

I looked at the pile of cases on my desk. Three suspected cheaters. One missing llama. A husband whose wife insisted he had been replaced by a changeling. A possible infestation of brownies at the Wilcombe farm.

With a flourish, I swept the lot into the trash can next to my desk. "Fuck it. I need some fudge anyway."

"That's my girl!" Tommy cried, jumping to his feet and embracing me.

"Gah, I'm gonna smell like a bowling alley. Get off, Tommy!" He released me and I fanned the air for a moment before grabbing my keys from the desktop.

Three keys and a simple song later, I unlocked my safe and pulled out my gun, Lady Midnight, then slipped her into the modified holster I wore under my jacket. I grabbed a few other bibs and bobs from the safe—travel essentials like metal currency and my 'pothecary kit—and then slammed the door.

I turned back to Tommy. "Come on, King Tut. Let's go save some homophobes."

◆

The quantum transport we picked up at the nearest NaviPort dumped us out in a little village called Mason's Briar, on the south-eastern point of the Lakelands, just over three hours later. I say 'dumped' because I'd foolishly left it to Tommy to get the tickets, and he'd (naturally) chosen a package one step up from being shoved in an old bucket and chucked 900 miles by catapult.

"Only you, Thomas," I said, rubbing my tailbone, "Could find a way to make the miracle of quantum displacement into a jalopy ride."

"Ease your hurts with all the extra Credz in yer account, dear heart. Passage was practically free after I told that old gaffer working the freight docks we needed to get home to visit your poor sick aunt."

I leveled my best death glare at the man who'd been my professional partner and best friend for the better part of three centuries. As usual, it slid off, along with the smoke from Tommy's first post-pod coffin nail.

"Yeah, well, you get what you pay for." I looked around the humble, if tidy, WayStation. Situated on a small, wooded hill overlooking a slow-flowing, picturesque river, both the WayStation and its utility shed were painted barn red with white trim, nestled amid a variety of fruit and nut trees planted (by the Neo-Ams, no doubt) for the refreshment of weary travelers. A small bubbling spring, fed by the river or some inverted Artesian sorcery I didn't really care to investigate, completed the look.

The WayStation was deserted. No surprise there; the Neo-Amish didn't exactly have a bustling travel trade to the cities. Most of the traffic into Neo-Am territory was one-way: Urbanites looking for hand-crafted furniture and a chance to ask Jeroboam if he'd ever seen a zipper before they hightailed it out to either the Greats or the inland sea now known as Lake Jefferson.

At least I didn't have to bother with baggage claim.

"So where is Jacobson?" I asked, scowling. "I thought you called. Sent a pigeon. Whatever method is appropriate to the century these people are living in." I walked over to a wooden bench thoughtfully placed in the shade of an enormous elm tree and sat down. Gently.

Sick aunt, indeed.

"He'll be along presently, I imagine," Tommy began, when a voice called out, "Nay, he is already here!"

I stood up, one hand dropping casually to my hip. Out of the corner of my eye, I watched Tommy back up, pulling his shotgun from his shoulder holster with practiced ease, ready to provide cover if necessary. It was an old dance, and we did it automatically in most situations.

The owner of the voice came into view on a narrow path that rose from the road below, black hat firmly planted on his greying head. He was stocky, but not fat, and like the WayStation, plainly but proudly dressed. The most striking thing about him was not his neatly trimmed beard, but the penetrating blue eyes that peeked out of the shadows between his Roman nose and the brim of his hat.

"Be you the English?" he said cautiously. "My brother, Rowan, has the watch, and said he did see the blue lights of your... pod."

"Aye," said Thomas, holstering his shotgun and stepping out of the shadows of the elm. "I'm Thomas O'Shea, and this dark-eyed beauty is none other than Cuicatl Cruz. And you must be Mr. Jacobson, yes?" Tommy extended one decrepit hand, discretely gloved for the occasion.

Jacobson, who'd taken one look at Tommy and turned seven shades of green, declined to shake. After a moment, Tommy lowered his hand and stepped back. "Ah. I thought you'd be familiar with my condition, since we're all such *great pals* with yer cousin Toby."

"I... I did not know my cousin was so lost as to treat with the Walking Damned," said Jacobson, shivering despite the warmth of the sun. He looked at me warily. "And you? What manner of dark powers are at your command that you would so casually take on the very bride of Satan himself?"

I looked at Tommy for a moment, then turned back to Jacobson, choosing my words carefully. I slid back the flap of my jacket and let my hand rest on the butt of my revolver.

"OK, Mr. Jacobson. This is how things are going to play out. I'm here to solve your problem. I'll deal with this ghost, or demon, or whatever the hell it is, and in return you will do two things. One, you will pay me the sum of

640 ounces, solid platinum. No Credz, Territorial Vouchers, or Neo-Amish apple butter."

Jacobson frowned and drew himself up. "Now, see you here, I will not..."

"AND TWO," I continued with a glare that shut his bearded mouth with an audible click, "you will treat my very talented, and very charming, partner here with the same respect you'd give J.C. and the Boys if they came strolling through here on a Sunday morning." I was struggling to keep my temper, and although I had a tight leash on my aspect, the music of the world swelled in my head, making it hard to focus.

Tommy, as usual, saved me.

"Cuicatl. Come on. It's not... you know how it is. Let it be, girl." He smiled his sad, ragged smile at me, and I forced myself to take a deep breath. The melodies faded.

"My... my apologies, Mr. Jacobson. As you and your tribe know, the world is not a kind place to anyone who fails to fit its limited expectations, yes?" I let my jacket fall over Lady Midnight and walked to the bench. I took a seat, crossing my legs, and looked at Jacobson expectantly.

For a moment, it seemed Jacobson might regain his own misplaced anger, but then his weariness and fear got the better of him. "No offense meant to you, of course, good sir," he said to Tommy after a beat. "If you helped our cousin, well, there's an act of Christian charity if ever I heard one."

Tommy nodded, far more graciously than I would have, and walked away to see if cigarettes had suddenly developed any exciting new flavors or aromas. Jacobson sat down on the far end of the bench, his face pinched by too little sleep and too many worries. I felt another momentary pang of sympathy and wondered if I really was losing my edge.

"Payment is of no concern," he said slowly. "We are also fond of hard currency, not being given to using the Dev... the HoloNet."

"Excellent. So, give me the details, please. Where are the women you say are possessed?"

"The women folk are locked up in the largest barn. We've had to move all the cattle to my brother Stephen's farm, down the valley." He said this in a tone that suggested I should be picturing every cow, and its journey, with him. "Girls not yet come to womanhood are unaffected, but Rowan and I thought it wise to relocate them as well. Until the demon is purged. So they've gone to my cousin Mordecai's farm, up Kleinhaus way."

I nodded. "And this demon? The ghost of the Corvus woman? What's become of her?"

Jacobson shivered again. "Every night she comes, howling and cursing our names, demanding absolution. She brings in her wake unclean things; walking corpses, ripe with corruption."

I sat back, considering. "And has she been *specific* in her demands? In my experience, ghosts only hang around for one thing, and that's unfinished business. So what does she ask for, when she and her crew aren't, you know, wrecking the family farm?"

Jacobson's piercing blue eyes fell away from mine, and he twisted the hem of his vest fitfully in his big, sweaty hands. "She... she speaks lies on the wind. Seeking to divide us."

Paydirt. I knew this guy was shady.

"I see. And what sort of... *lies*... is she spouting, exactly? The sky is green, cows are awesome, that sort of thing?"

Jacobson's frown returned. "You make sport of me." He was, I noted with surprise, near to tears.

I tried a different tack. "Mr. Jacobson—Hiram—you've got to tell me everything if you want me to solve your problem," I said gently, letting my hand drift onto one of his. He started, then let it stay, relief warring with fear and regret on his craggy face. "If I don't know what I need to do, I can't do it, now can I?"

He took a deep breath, leaning back against the sturdy wood of the bench. "My great-grandfather built this bench, you know. He gave it as his tribute, to the Urbanite governors who demanded we build this station for their... *Blitzschpielsache*. And now, I sit on it, and am forced to tell a stranger shameful things that would make him weep to hear."

I'll bet, I thought. *But not for the reasons you think.*

"Hiram, please."

"Very well. The demon claims my ancestor did conspire with the other Elders to murder this woman, to prevent her from pressing her claim upon Lucretia, who was not, as the records say, a Schultze, but a Jacobson herself.

His daughter, my own blood, fallen to sin during *Rumspringa*. She gave her heart to the Corvus woman in the Urbanite city. The spirit says Josiah and the Elders murdered Lucretia and blamed Samantha Corvus, to... to cover their sin."

Holy shit, I thought, trying not to let the shock creep onto my face. *Did I just walk into Salem?*

"That's... that's a lot to take in, Hiram," I said carefully. "Is there anything else? You said the spirit demands 'absolution.' What does that mean?"

Hiram tore off his hat and pulled his hand free of mine, then ran it through his thick locks. "Ah, God, You have seen fit to test us mightily in your wisdom," he muttered. He put the hat back on his head and said, "When Samantha Corvus... when the explosion happened, all the Elders and their brides were gathered on Widow's Beach. All but... all but my great-grandfather, Josiah, and his lady wife, Catherine. Josiah had fallen ill, it is said, and could not come, and with the death of their daughter at the witch's hand, Catherine could not bring herself to..." He trailed off, hearing the story the way I was hearing it. I saw fearful recognition dawning in those blue eyes.

I knew what was coming, but I didn't say anything. Some things can't be pulled out. They have to be pushed clear from inside.

"She wants my blood, Ms. Cruz," he said, choking back a sob. "She wants *my life*." He jerked to his feet, swaying, and I drew back, startled. "And God help me, I think she may deserve it."

⚡

It took me half an hour to get Hiram back to his stoic self. Tommy stayed in the background the whole time, chain-smoking and taking mental notes.

It was nearly sundown by the time I convinced Hiram to head back to Mason's Briar and settle in for the night. They were holed up in one of the family's enormous farmhouses, well supplied with candles and food and, I assumed, old-fashioned frontier grit. I told Hiram and his boys to stay put, out of sight, no matter what they heard or felt or thought they saw.

Perhaps unsurprisingly, it took very little convincing.

After Jacobson left, Tommy came over and sat down beside me.

"Welladay, Cuicatl. It seems I'm not the only dead duck who's still got some flap left in the old wings." He smiled to show he was joking, but I just shook my head.

"What do you think, Tommy? Why now? Why wait more than a century to come back for vengeance, long after the man who bumped her off is worm food? It doesn't make any goddamned sense."

Tommy took a pull on his ubiquitous coffin nail and exhaled slowly, the fading rays of the setting sun turning the smoke into a light show. "I don't know, m'dear. I don't know. But I think we're likely to find out. Shall we trot down the lane?"

I nodded, hugging myself as a cool breeze raced up the hill. "No time like the present," I said, hoping that was true. "But then again, it's not the present we have to worry about, is it?

❧

The last beams of the setting sun were vanishing when Tommy and I arrived at the barn Hiram had indicated. The barn was a fair distance from the farmhouse, and other than the wind and the distant howls of what I hoped were plain old, non-lycanthropic wolves, everything was quiet.

"So what do we do, Cuicatl? I don't think it'd be smart to go poking our heads in there without having a bit of recon."

I started humming, low, under my breath. It was a simple song, one I'd been singing since I *could* sing. A song of me, to ground myself before I opened my awareness to the other songs around me. Colors grew clearer; details grew sharper; and as always, the smell of *huele de noche*, night jasmine, filled the air.

I opened up the song, introducing new melodies. *The air, it is my breath; the earth, it is my flesh. Ay-ya, we are one.*

The barn faded away, even as it grew sharper in my vision; the hard lines of wood and metal were replaced by fire-bright phantoms I knew to be the very essence of *wood* and *strong* and *hay* and *safety*.

Beyond these simple forms, huge bonfires of color and sound capered, shimmering like diamonds one moment, and smoldering like coals the next. Inside each were smaller, if just as vibrant, forms, their planes and lines painted the sickly yellow of fear and splattered with the madder tones of disgust, confusion, and rage.

Demons. And, trapped inside their songs, the women they'd possessed.

I continued to sway, tapping out the beat. "Tommy," I whispered. "We've got company."

"So I thought. How many?" He was all business now. His music, full of pipes and peat fires and deep, inchoate longing for some green place I couldn't quite understand, brushed against my own.

"At least a dozen. Maybe more. And they're all mad as hell. If you'll pardon the pun."

"Can you sing them down?"

"I don't know. They're strong. Something, or someone, else is feeding them. They didn't just show up; they were paged. All their songs are just snatches of a larger melody. One coming from somewhere nearby. Beyond the hill. Toward the sea."

"The Corvus woman, then."

"Perhaps. We'll know shortly. She's—"

"Look out, English!"

A girl's voice, sharp as glass in my heightened state, cut deep into my focus. *Where the hell did she come from? Why didn't I hear her song when I…*

The first shot took me in the chin, spinning me around and shattering my cantrip. The music of the world fell away, replaced by white-hot pain. *Fuck, that almost took my jaw off.*

I sat up, blearily, my hands flying to my face, trying to assess the damage. I was barely upright before another two shots took me in the shoulder and the chest, slamming me into the wall of the barn.

Ow.

Through the haze of pain, I could hear the thunder of Tommy's shotgun, followed by angry cries and the wet spatter of gore.

At least we're giving as good as we're getting. I hope.

"WHAT MANNER OF WITCH IS THIS," roared an inhuman voice, "WHO COMES TO CHALLENGE MY CLAIM? ARE YOU IN LEAGUE WITH THESE MURDERERS? THESE WOLVES WHO CALL THEMSELVES SHEEP?" The owner of the voice was a massive shadow, blotting out the new-risen stars, drinking in all the light until only two red, glowing eyes were visible.

I fumbled at my belt, jamming my hand into my apothecary pouch, and took out a Memestone. There was no time for finesse; this bitch was killing me, and not waiting around for answers. I slammed the stone into the dust, then into the flesh of my thigh, biting off a scream as the creamy quartz pierced fabric and skin.

Time rolled back in its rut, making the world around me shudder and jerk. I felt the wounds unmake themselves as my body reverted to the state it had been in while Tommy and I were still safe and sound in my office. The 'stone dissolved, and I pushed myself to my feet, singing a song of shelter, weaving multiple melodies until the air in front of me grew hazy.

"Please don't do that again," I said, peering through the frost of my song at the woman hovering roughly twenty feet off the ground in front of me. A row of corpses lay scattered at her feet, most in extremely messy pieces. I could hear Tommy swearing quietly as he crouched behind a nearby tractor, reloading.

"For what it's worth, I'm not a witch." *And I don't think you are, either.*

"LIES."

Another barrage of magic flew toward me, but my song was strong. Wrapped in the song, I could see they weren't really magic, just telekinetic energy wrapped around…

Rocks. The big scary demon was trying to kill me with rocks.

"I think it's time you and I had a talk, sister." Another barrage crumbled to dust as I listened to the rhythms flowing out of my attacker. I waited for the dust to clear, then sang a counter-melody, working it into a round with my song of shelter. *Be as you are, not as you seem. Rage fades, now comes calm, sweet and serene.*"

Samantha Corvus decided her rage was better spent reanimating her dead helpers than trying to shoot me, so her back was to me when my song struck her, full-force. The shadow fell away, along with all the dime-store theatrics. I watched her shade drop toward the earth and then stop, hovering about a foot in the air. Inside the transparent form of Samantha was a young woman in her early 20s, dark of hair and eye, the Jacobson nose aquiline rather than brutal on her pretty face.

Fathers and daughters. Sinners and saints. Lord have mercy.

"What... what the fuck did you just do?" Samantha said, speaking in unison with her host.

I let go of my song of shelter and raised my hands, walking toward her. "Samantha? Samantha Corvus?"

"How do you know my name? You're... you're not one of them. Your clothing..." She seemed momentarily captivated by the cut of my jacket, and the used the girl inside her to reach out, caressing the fabric. "Has it been so long, then? I was dreaming about Luci... then the girl came. She had the sight, like Luci. My sweet Luci." A flash of grief, discordant and red as flame, rippled through her.

I hummed a little louder. The girl inside the ghost blinked and whispered "English—help me, English."

Then Samantha took control once more. "She... she is my conduit. She came to me, seeking comfort. The sight is not the only thing that runs in the family, it seems." The ghost laughed, but its mirth never touched the terrified girl it was riding. "I pulled them all from their beds in the ground," she said, gesturing at the recently re-murdered corpses scattered at our feet. "They dance to my tune. Or did."

"Samantha, I know what those men did to you, and to Luci, was monstrous. Horrible. But they're all dead. Even Josiah. And the people you're hurting now, they're... they want to be better."

Another ripple of red; a dark hint of shadows. "Even the spawn of that demon, Jacobson? He was the worst of them. Luci tried to tell me, tried to warn me. She saw it. She saw it all. I didn't believe her. I didn't think a father could... would..."

Samantha shivered, and the girl inside her slid an inch or two toward the ground. "He destroyed us both, because she loved me. And I dared to love her, right out in the open." She lowered her head. The girl slipped another inch. "We were going to go away, you know. A fresh start." She pulsed with yellow and orange and grey, now. Rue. Regret. Loss.

Another few inches, and I could sing up a shelter against spirits. Much easier than trying to sing her out of Samantha. I just had to...

"HANNAH! NOOOOO!" roared a voice, ragged with fear and hate. A squat, bearded figure tore up the path toward us.

Hiram Jacobson.

"Goddamnit, Hiram, I told you to stay put! Samantha, please, just wait, you don't have to..."

Naturally, everyone ignored me. What else is new?

"NO! SHE IS MINE, YOU BASTARD!" Shadows began to coalesce around Samantha and the girl once more. Behind her, the barn door burst open, and monstrous forms, each surrounding a helpless, struggling woman, surged forth, claws sharp and fangs gleaming.

I cast a desperate glance at Tommy. "OK, so we do this the hard way."

"When have we ever done it any other way, Cuicatl?" He laughed and cocked his shotgun, turning to face the horde.

"Let her go!" It was the same voice that had tried to warn me about Samantha's attack. It belonged, I discovered, to a young woman with red hair and nut-brown eyes, who skipped out of the shadows behind the barn's silo and stood defiantly in front of Samantha. She was wearing the same sort of homespun shift as Hannah.

For a moment, everything froze. Hiram came running up and thudded to a halt next to Tommy, panting like a racehorse. He opened his mouth to speak, and my glare slammed it shut. All eyes were on the girl who'd appeared from the shadows.

Isabelle, breathed Hannah, reaching out toward the girl. The shadows began to diminish.

"Hannah. My love." She smiled up at the captive girl, and I saw, rather than heard, Samantha's music shift. The red was leaching out, fading to a warm rose.

"She's wrong, you know," said Isabelle, pushing past the demons. "You're not hers. You're *mine.*" She reached up and took her lover's hand, pulling gently. Samantha sighed, and let her go.

Hannah collapsed into Isabelle's arms, weeping. Hiram moved to grab his daughter, then stopped as Isabelle raised her head, her brown eyes defiant.

His brows knitted, and, still not quite sure what was happening, I sang a little song under my breath. A song of clarity. Of open heart, and good intentions.

Hiram stopped in his tracks, staring at his daughter and the woman holding her tight. "Oh, my holy God, I am Your greatest fool," he muttered, then burst into tears and ran back toward the farm house. Nobody even tried to stop him.

A series of thuds behind me pulled my attention from Hiram's retreat. The demons were streaming away into the night air, losing their coherence—and dropping their victims into the dirt. I turned to Samantha and saw she was joining the rainbow of ectoplasm streaming toward the beach.

Her eyes were kind as they met mine. "Ah. Not a witch at all, then," she said gently. "Something more. Something less. Just like my Luci." She laughed, her eyes sparkling, and I spared a moment to wish Josiah Jacobson an especially roasty seat in hell.

"I've been a fool. I let them have her without realizing they couldn't take her from me." She was a vision from a half-remembered dream. Her song, freed from rage and regret, was sweet as a samba.

"I'm glad I met you, singer. I wonder, will you sing me a little traveling music? Someone's waiting for me, and I've kept her waiting far too long."

The tears in my own eyes and throat made my voice uneven, but I still managed to make it through *Tanto Tempo* three times before the last of Samantha's music vanished into the ether.

In the distance, the Widow's Beach threw shades of rose and gold into the night.

✺

It turned out that the damage to the farms was pretty substantial. Substantial enough that the fine folks of the Five Families were going to have a hard time coming up with the extra platinum to pay me anytime soon.

But hey, free apple butter for life is nothing to sneeze at.

"Yeah, yeah. Blessings upon you, *et hoc genus omne*," I said, hugging my umpteenth bonneted housewife. "Remind me why I do this again, Tommy?"

He blew out a cloud of smoke and then kissed me on the cheek. "Because you're your father's sun, but your mother's daughter. I'll be outside." I watched him walk past the beaming Neo-Amish women, all glad hands and ready smiles, wondering how a man so dead could flirt so shamelessly.

"Miss Cruz?"

I turned around to find Hannah pulling a wooden cart she'd covered with a scrap of burlap. "Hannah? Are you okay, honey?"

"I am. Thanks to you. Father says Isabelle… we may court. He says that the greatest of all things is love." She blushed prettily, and I felt a momentary pang of envy for Isabelle.

"Also," she said hurriedly, changing the subject. "I have these things, from my great-great-aunt Luci. From her *Rumspringa*. I think she would be most pleased if I gave them to you. It would be like a part of her…" Tears sprang into her eyes, and she lowered her head as she pulled the cloth free.

"Oh, sweetie, that is so kind, but I don't think I could possibly…"

And then, among the assorted posters for long-dead bands and ridiculous clothes, I saw it.

An honest-to-God Music Hall MMF-5.3se turntable. Complete with dust cover and one—no, *two*—extra Blue-Point cartridges.

Hannah looked at me expectantly, unsure how to react to the sight of a grown woman weeping into a Duran-Duran sweatshirt.

"Now that I think about it, it's probably what Luci would want."

✼

Dawn rolled around a few hours later. I sat on the sand next to now-unblemished grave, waiting for the green flash that always precedes true sunrise, and thought about Samantha Corvus. What would've happened, I wondered, if she and Lucretia had simply been allowed to leave? Certainly, none of the people who'd gone up like Roman Candles on this beach a century hence would have met their ends in such a grisly fashion—not to mention being reanimated by the woman they'd tried to murder so long ago.

And all because one old man couldn't handle change, or follow his own rules. Or love his daughter enough to do either. Hopefully, Hiram could manage what his great-grandaddy couldn't. There's room at the table of absolution for just about everyone, I think.

There. The green flash shot across the horizon, bisecting the heavens and the earth for the briefest moment before giving way to the fiery glow of the sun breaking the waves. For a moment, I thought I saw a pair of figures, holding hands and illuminated against the sky in that verdant glow; one short and dark, the other tall and fair. Probably just my imagination.

The tide was coming in now, and as I gathered up my phonograph and the rest of my payment, I heard Tommy's raspy voice call, "Come on, dear girl! The pod's a-waitin'!" I took a few steps up the beach, then turned around, searching the sand.

I could just make out a divot under the foam, a slight depression in the sand. I wondered if I'd be able to find it again, if I wanted to visit. But whatever magic it held was gone; it was just a hole now. A scar, waiting to heal. Another wave rolled in, smoothing the sand, and by the time I reached the road, I knew, the wound would be gone.

SO MANY THINGS SEEM FILLED WITH THE INTENT
Jude McLaughlin

Jude McLaughlin is an author of speculative fiction web serials, novels, and short fiction who lives and writes in Massachusetts. Her work includes the Lambda Literary Award finalist *Wonder City Stories* and its sequel *Ephemera*. In addition to her fiction writing, she is a technical, medical, and science writer, and her work has also been known to appear in tabletop roleplaying game books from White Wolf Studios and Guardians of Order, as well as videogames published by Electronic Arts.

Nereid looked around the rolling green Canadian field as she and Sophie carefully climbed over the electric fence. She saw a sea of tiny yellow and white flowers, lush grasses, and hills beyond this one. Sophie was wearing one of her vests of many pockets over a band t-shirt, faded jeans, and work boots. Her glasses, with their many little lenses on many little movable arms, perched precariously on her aquiline nose.

"Watch your step," Sophie said, pointing downward. "No cows here right now, but they've been here."

Nereid danced awkwardly around a cow pat and followed her girlfriend up the slope. Sophie shifted one of the lenses in front of her left eye and squinted through it at a device in her hand. After three more steps, she said, with finality, "Okay."

Nereid stopped, one foot half-raised. "Okay?"

"Right here," Sophie said. She slid her slim black leather backpack off and gently set it on the ground.

"Oh. Oh!" Nereid recalled that Sophie had been given very precise global coordinates. She watched Sophie pull several things out of the backpack: a low, flat, plastic and metal device; a metallic cylinder; and several cables. Nereid, as was her wont in Sophie's laboratory, took up the cables and untangled them.

Sophie assembled her gizmo so fast Nereid really didn't have a chance to see what cables went where. The flat device was hooked into the cylinder, and the cylinder began to growl somewhere down at the lowest edges of Nereid's hearing. The device lit up and Sophie sat back on her heels. "Well, that's it, now we wait," she said.

"For what?" Nereid said, sitting down in the grass after making sure there was no immediate evidence of bovine habitation. She was glad she was wearing her jeans instead of her superheroing costume; the costume fabric was a pain to get grass stains out of, as she'd learned the last time a villain had flung her like a football down the playing field of one of Wonder City's high schools.

"For it to print whatever it's going to print," Sophie said, throwing herself down next to Nereid and laying back in the grass. "Prudence sent me very specific parameters for a 3-D printer. Not something that's commercially available, mind. The whole thing is a test."

Nereid rested a hand on her girlfriend's thigh. "Do you guys do this all the time?"

"Do what all the time?" Sophie asked. She had pushed her glasses up into her short, dark hair and had an arm over her face.

"Test each other," Nereid said, twisting her own rather less dark hair around a finger. "I mean, for the rest of us—superheroes and supervillains— it's all about powers, or detective skills, or whatever. But you guys..."

"You mean *mad scientists*, when you say 'you guys,' right?" Sophie said, her tone light, but Nereid knew her well enough to hear the edge there.

"Yes, that's what I mean," Nereid said, letting go of her hair and Sophie's leg, and wrapping her arms around her knees. "Sorry. It just seems like you *expect* her to poke you like this."

The printer hummed to life and began to make the grinding noise Nereid associated with actual printing. Sophie didn't look over at it.

"Yeah," Sophie said after a few moments. "We *do* test each other all the time. Even when we're technically on the same side. We keep trying to one-up each other with our inventions. Mom pointed out, once, that I mostly helped my friend Gogo get started in a lab and on her music production because I wanted someone I could compete with."

Nereid made a noise of acknowledgement and wondered idly about her own parents. *I really haven't felt like I could... hang out at home since... everything happened.* "Everything" included killing a major supervillain (mostly by accident), besides getting herself into a really *bad* relationship while Sophie was missing and their relationship status was... uncertain. While her apartment at the Young Cosmics' superhero compound was not exactly welcoming, thanks to memories from said bad relationship, it was better than her parents' disapproval. *Mom and Dad are such decent people. I can't imagine what they'd think of me if they knew about the... killing part. It was embarrassing enough that they knew about... and helped get rid of... that guy who I'm trying not to think about.*

The printer beeped gently. Sophie sat up, pulled her glasses back down onto her nose, and opened the lid. There was a pause, then she said, "Huh."

Nereid peered over her shoulder. Sophie held something that looked like a thick plastic business card.

Sophie turned it over, then again said, "Huh."

There was some writing in a bold script font on both sides. Nereid read aloud, "Professor Prudence Pleasant. Practically perfect and perfectly pleasant. What... huh?"

In response to her words, the card began to change in a kind of contortionist origami way. Sophie dropped it into the grass as it did so. "Sharp edges," she said to Nereid, frowning and squeezing her fingers one after another. A drop of blood emerged from a fine line like a papercut. "I should've worn gloves. She's sloppy about safety in mechanicals." Sophie shook the blood off into the grass and pressed her thumb over the wound.

Nereid watched fascinated as the little thing finally transformed itself into a key-shaped piece of plastic. After it stopped writhing, she picked it up and peered at it. "So where's the lock?" she asked after a moment.

Sophie looked around, then up. "Uh. There, I think." She stood up and helped Nereid to her feet in front of the floating old-fashioned lock plate. Sophie caught Nereid's hand as she moved to insert the key. "Are you sure you're okay with this? This all boils down to essentially trading your genetic material for a new hand for Wire. I mean, I'll try to prevent it but..."

Nereid smiled and stroked Sophie's hair fondly. "It's okay. Wire has been so unhappy with the prosthetic you built for her." *Besides, it's my fault she lost her hand.* She remembered the way the villain had magically controlled the micron-thin fibers their superhero team's deputy leader (and Sophie's ex) Wire had thrown at him and slashed it back at her. They were just lucky it only hit her hand, and not, say, her head. *If I'd moved faster, taken him down faster, maybe everything would have been fine. And if I hadn't dehydrated the hand accidentally when I killed him*—even thinking about the moment she'd found that she'd killed the man made her wince, still—*maybe they could've sewed it back on.*

"I suppose I haven't been nice about it," Sophie said, a little sheepishly.

"Nicknaming her after that one-armed guy in *Metallic Magician* was a dick move," Nereid said, thinking, *I know you're still pissed off at her for the way you guys broke up, but poking fun at someone's new disability is an asshole thing to do.* "You're better than that and you know it."

Sophie looked chastened. "Sorry," she mumbled, and let go of Nereid's hand. "Jesus, Gogo would write a really vicious song about me if she heard me do that." Nereid thought that perhaps Gogo would go a bit further, given Sophie and Gogo's long friendship and Gogo's disabilities. *Maybe some performance art.* "I don't know why you put up with me."

"Because you *are* better than that," Nereid said, kissing her. "You made it possible for Gogo to learn the skills she needed to build herself all those amazing prosthetics, you helped her crowdfund her music."

"I guess that's why I didn't get why Wire was upset sooner," Sophie said. "Gogo doesn't let anyone forget her legs are 'missing.'" Sophie made quote marks with her fingers and Nereid honestly couldn't tell whether they were sarcastic or not. "I think I've only ever seen her wear the humanoid legs once in all the years I've known her. I guess… I didn't think about how Wire might feel differently."

"Well, fortunately," Nereid said, "we live in a world with more options." She pushed the key into the lock and tried to turn it. The lock responded by humming and vibrating until the air seemed to peel away from the tall brushed-steel door in which it was embedded. The door popped ajar with a soft hiss.

"One has to admire Prudence's theatrics," Sophie said grudgingly, leading the way through the door, sliding a couple of lenses into place over her left eye.

They climbed curving steel stairs that were lined with thin blue neon tubes. At the top, the landing blossomed out into a vast, sprawling laboratory with a ceiling so high Nereid couldn't see it past the bright indirect lighting. Row upon row of black-topped lab benches marched away up a tiered stadium arrangement, displaying intimidating arrays of glassware and complex machinery. The back wall was obscured by taller-than-human-sized glass tubes held by tangles of machinery top and bottom. None of them held anything—or anyone—that Nereid could see.

She tried not to think about the possibility that there might be a tiny Nereid growing in one in a few weeks.

"I'm so glad you could join me!" sang a cheerful voice from somewhere above them.

She was already sliding along the zipline from the topmost tier of the stadium lab benches when Nereid spotted her. A short, round, fortysomething white woman with stylishly short brown hair nailed her landing on the cement floor and grinned at them, throwing her arms wide. "What do you think of Chez Pleasant?"

"It's very impressive," Nereid said earnestly.

"Thank you, thank you," the woman said. "Brainchild, my dear, it's been a dog's age. You're looking good!" The Professor was wearing a spotless white lab coat over a black buttondown shirt, silver silk vest, and black and white houndstooth-patterned wool trousers.

"And you, Prudence, are lovely as always," Sophie said, stepping forward to hug and cheek-kiss the woman, only a little awkwardly. Then they turned to Nereid. "Pacifica Starr, a.k.a. Nereid, I'd like you to meet Professor Prudence Pleasant, life researcher extraordinaire."

Nereid received (and attempted to give) a firm, warm handshake. "I've heard so much about you," she said, thinking of Sophie's lengthy diatribe about the lack of quality mad life scientists these days and the Professor's somewhat villainous but mostly commercial interests.

"I won't ask if it was all good," Professor Pleasant said, with a conspiratorial smile. "I've read a *great* deal about you, Pacifica. Our newest recognized Class 10 paranormal! Distinguishing yourself by saving Wonder City not once but twice so far!" She squeezed Nereid's shoulder fondly. "I'm very glad for the chance to meet you."

Nereid blushed and mumbled, "Thank you." *I never expected a villain to be... friendly? charming? nice?*

The Professor's very warm hand slid from Nereid's shoulder to the middle of her back as she turned to face the room and said, with a grand gesture, "Would you care for a tour?"

Nereid glanced at Sophie. Sophie's face was composed in her habitual sarcastic smirk, and she raised an eyebrow at Nereid's inquiring look. Taking that as Sophie tossing the ball back to her, Nereid said, "I'd like that very much."

"You're welcome too, of course, Sophia," the Professor said, guiding Nereid along the nearest lab bench.

"Of course, Prudence," Sophie said, trailing after them. Nereid was very aware of the Professor's hand and the likelihood of Sophie's gaze upon it.

For the next hour, Nereid was dazzled by room after room of Professor Pleasant's secret lair. The main room, the Professor explained, was mostly for show, but also for long-term bench experiments. The real science, she said, was done in the terrarium rooms. Several were full of spectacularly blooming plants and carefully-monitored boxes of blue and purple butterflies, ethereal damselflies, and other small, lovely, six-legged things.

There was a massive aviary room, with a ceiling that arched at least ten stories above them, full of tweeting and calling birds of many colors, from little brown jobs to bright tropical birds to glowering raptors. "I'm sorry we can't go in," Prudence said, leading them out of the observation antechamber. "I keep them in strict quarantine. So many zoonotic infections affect birds."

Nereid attended closely to everything Prudence (she insisted that Nereid call her Prudence) said for those first several rooms, but her concentration was entirely derailed by the room full of flapcats.

That's what Sophie called them, of course. Prudence had a more complicated name for them. But Nereid was utterly enchanted by the tiny tabby kittens flapping their wing fuzz and making dubious landings on their noses in test flights, while older cats watched them from high perches, their more substantial wings folded majestically as Sphinxes. The sleek calico that dropped heavily onto Prudence's shoulders meowed imperiously, demanding Nereid's hesitant petting. The rambunctious trio of rangy silver adolescent felines divebombing her head distracted her from even the pretense of listening to Prudence's narration.

The room was clearly designed for the cats: cat-trees and ledges high and low, cat exercise wheels that generated a red dot somewhere else in the room for other cats to chase, hillocks of lush grass and small shrubs for them to hide in. Water and food stations were all over the room, as were litterboxes in various shapes and sizes. There were two walls designed to look like cliff-faces with little caves in it for cats to curl up in.

Prudence and Sophie began some mutually patronizing technical discussion of something—the climate control in the individual rooms?—and Nereid ended up sitting on the floor, covered in winged kittens, for a while. As she sat there, happily listening to raucous purrs and acquiring small puncture wounds as they scaled her adventurously, she noticed a shy silver tabby kitten peering at her around a corner. She made the inevitable silly beckoning noises to it and it eventually padded out to sniff her fingertips.

"Oh!" she said, noticing how small the kitten's extra appendages were. "Your wings don't work, do they, baby?"

This caught Prudence's attention. "Some of them don't quite work out, I'm afraid," she said, absently scratching the calico's head.

"You don't sell the failures, though, do you?" Sophie said, frowning down at the kitten.

"I don't call them *failures*, for one thing," Prudence said, lightly cuffing Sophie on the shoulder. "Failures are for you mechanical fetishists. No, I don't sell them. I spay or neuter them and they live with me in the residential wing."

Nereid had finally coaxed the kitten into her arms and was running her fingers through the blotchy markings of its coat. It purred as loudly as the others, and its little stubby wings moved as much as the others' wings did, though they would never carry it around the room.

Eventually, Sophie helped Nereid detach various felines from her shirt, and they followed Prudence into more rooms. There were a few rooms of aquaria full of fish and anemones in electric colors that inevitably drew Nereid in, though Prudence said, "Oh, those are still very experimental," in a dismissive way.

She was attracted to one enormous aquarium full of palm-sized octopuses among a variety of small ceramic castles and what could only be bright plastic toys. At first, they all charged the glass of the aquarium, which startled her, but after a few moments of hostility, they settled into rotating lazily in the water. She was somewhat put off by the way they watched her, following her movements and staring. Her gaze skittered away from their surprisingly human-looking eyes and spotted a small sticky note attached to the bottom edge of their tank that said, *Schedule release.* In another room, she noticed that the organisms were roughly fish-shaped, but had sensory organs on stalks that she remembered reading about in her Extraterrestrial Life course. In all things, she forebore comment. She was, after all, walking through a supervillain's lair. One would inevitably run into some schemes, right?

The rooms Prudence allowed them to linger in were larger environments for eminently saleable cute things, including "dragonettes," "skymice," and flying potbellied pigs. The latter were highly inquisitive and surprisingly affectionate. Every room was lovingly designed to engage the animals in it, with lush vegetation and careful attention to privacy and hide spots.

"You've been very generous with your time, Prudence," Sophie said, gently peeling a hot-pink dragonette's tail from around Nereid's neck. "And your animals apparently love Mary Poppins here, but we shouldn't take up much more of your day."

Prudence smiled and literally bowed acquiescence. "As you wish, my dear," she said, and led them through the labyrinthine hallways to a lavish residential area. The parlor—done in a mock-Victorian style—was adorned with only one (apparently normal) cat, but a couple scampered out of sight behind shelves and curtains in her richly-decorated office space. Before she led them through it, though, Prudence looked at Nereid. "Pacifica, will you be bored by a couple of scientists bandying technicalities? Would you rather head back to the cattery? We could come get you when we're finished."

Nereid was relieved by the offer, despite the condescension built into it, because she could think of nothing she wanted to witness less than the two of them sniping at each other under the cover of technobabble for another hour. *And Sophie can be* just *as condescending sometimes.* "That would be lovely, thank you, Prudence." When the Professor moved to escort her, she said, "Oh, no, don't worry about me, I remember where it is. You two go ahead and talk business."

Prudence looked thoughtful, then shrugged. "All right. We'll see you in a bit then."

Sophie flashed a smile and wink at Nereid behind Prudence's back, and followed the Professor into her office.

Nereid stepped back into the hallway and chose the direction she thought would lead her back to the cattery.

It became obvious almost immediately that she'd chosen the wrong direction, but when she tried to turn back and try again, she was foiled by the fact that every intersection was identical to every other intersection. *Too bad I don't carry any makeup, because making trail marks with lipstick seems like the only way to get around here.*

She wandered around a bit, trying locked doors in a desultory fashion, depressed by the realization that she was completely lost. *Typical Nereid,* she thought. *Stupid, impulsive, etc. At least I haven't killed anyone this time. Yet.*

Then a door handle turned under her hand.

She pushed the door open slowly and carefully, remembering how the skymice room's "airlock" area had been mysteriously open, and a flock of winged rodents had descended on their heads immediately. Fortunately, neither Sophie nor herself were bothered by small squeaky things.

The "airlock" area, as in the other terrarium rooms, was small, windowed, and full of monitoring equipment, though the screens were not turned on. The dark room beyond the windows was illumined only slightly by the antechamber's ceiling lights. All she could see in it was an upright, bulky, roughly human-shaped sarcophagus with a woman's face. The eyes in the face were glowing with a pale blue-green luminescence.

That looks pretty creepy. The first really creepy thing I've seen here. Well, other than the octopuses that watched me. And the extra-large spiders with opposable thumbs on their forelegs. And the… okay, I guess a lot of things here are creepy. Professor Pleasant was, after all, technically a supervillain. She had even had a few run-ins—more than a decade before—with some of the big, high-powered superhero groups, like the Gold Stars and the Guardians. She hadn't come out of those battles too badly—she walked away, instead of ending up in prison—which rated her in the top tier of villains. Despite her claims to only be interested in commercial success, there was a better than even chance she was engaging in villainous shenanigans.

Nereid tried the door from the antechamber into the main room and found it unlocked. *To pry or not to pry, that is the question,* she thought. After a moment's rumination, she grabbed a clipboard from the counter, pulled the door open and stepped into the darkened room. As she gently let the door close behind her, she set the clipboard into the doorjamb at floor level to keep the door from locking behind her. Then she turned to regard the sarcophagus and let her eyes adjust to the shadowy space.

She could just make out looming, complicated machinery and tubing set against all the walls. The tubing converged into larger conduits that ended at the top of the sarcophagus. The floor seemed clear of traps or obstacles; however, she used her water manipulation powers to gather a low fog to see if there were any beams of light that she might break to set off alarms. As she dispersed the fog, having found no visible trippers—*I'm screwed if they're infrared or something, of course*—she realized how easy it had been to raise it, and closed her eyes to better focus on what her powers could tell her.

Professor Pleasant's complex was huge, she realized, and very convoluted—she could almost map it by changes in humidity between rooms and hallways. *Gosh, if I'd only thought of this sooner.* Closer by, this room had a higher humidity than the surrounding rooms, and the sarcophagus was full of water. It also contained a human-sized body. She focused in more closely, could sense the blood being impelled through the body's circulation by a functioning heart, could feel the changes in density and fluid that roughly approximated those she was used to in a human body, though the lungs seemed to be full of water. *Membranes specialized for gas exchange?* she wondered, then was pleased with herself for a bit of scientific contemplation that wasn't from Sophie. *Maybe I do have a learning curve.*

When she opened her eyes, the semi-glowing thing had not moved or visibly changed in any way, despite her vague and ever-present worries about horror movie conventions. Walking very softly, she approached the container.

Standing on tiptoe, she could just look into the glowing eyes, and found herself looking through glass into the face of an apparently sleeping humanoid woman. She was pale-skinned with a fin-like crest rising from the top of her head that waved gently in the water, almost like hair.

Nereid dropped down and thought. *She looks human, except for the fin. Is this someone Prudence has altered? Grown? Imprisoned?*

She chewed on her lower lip for a few minutes, then went up on her toes again to peer in. *Definitely not like any alien species we discussed in my Extraterrestrial Life course.*

Then the woman opened her large, dark eyes and seemed to gaze straight into Nereid's soul with an almost physical impact that rocked Nereid back on her heels. She felt a sudden burst of *OUTRAGE INVASION ATTACK* with a helping of *fear* until she was out of eyeshot.

There was an ominous slamming sound behind her—*That wasn't the door, it sounded too heavy to be that door*—and water began to pour into the room from half a dozen waterfalls that opened directly from the walls. *Oh, shit.* She looked behind her and saw that a transparent wall had dropped across the room between her and the control area. *Of course. And I thought I was being clever by making sure the door didn't shut.*

There was a *lot* of water coming into the room very *fast.* She thought about stopping the flow, but she was curious as to what would happen when the room filled. *Most people would be trying to break out of this oversized aquarium.*

She hadn't yet overcome the moment of panic when water first covered her head—*That probably takes some getting used to*—even though she knew perfectly well that she had a bubble of air around her. But she kept treading water near the ceiling and kept her eyes on the sarcophagus.

After a delay of several long moments, the sculpted woman's face was lined with light, and then the sides of the object were, and then the whole thing opened like an oyster shell, releasing its inhabitant in a rush of phosphorescent fluids and lashing fins. Faster than Nereid could follow with her eyes, the woman swam up and stared into her face. There was another electric moment of contact when their gazes met—*RAGE.* A moment later, the being wrapped her long, sinuous body—no legs, just a long tail—around Nereid and tried to crush her with considerable strength.

Nereid had been braced for an attack, given the initial reaction, but not that particular style. She exhaled hard in surprise and felt the bruising constriction around her chest and arms keep her from inhaling again. She let her body shift away to water, leaving her aggressor holding her clothing, which was not, unfortunately, made of the same material as her superhero costume, which shifted with her. *Hello, Class 10 water elemental type powers, I'm glad for you again.*

Her opponent felt the change, shook herself loose of the drifting jeans and t-shirt, and backed off a short distance. She stared around her with huge eyes, flexing her hands agitatedly in a way that made spines rise on the backs of her arms and claws extrude from her fingertips.

Now Nereid was baffled. *I don't want to hurt her. How do I talk to her?* The woman made a couple of experimental passes with her claws exactly at where Nereid was centered. *Okay, that's impressive, since I know I'm pretty much invisible to humans when I'm submerged in water form.* The woman dived under and came at her from a different direction, and this time, Nereid felt something moving through her. *Okay, she's got water manipulation powers, though not as big as mine. Now what, genius?*

They stared at each other for several long minutes. The mermaid was a beautiful woman, with translucently-pale skin, broad, smooth features, and high cheekbones. Nereid felt as frumpy and freckled as she usually did, despite being made of water.

Finally, Nereid slowly and carefully shaped a bubble of oxygen out of the water between her hands. She stuck her watery head into it and watched the mermaid's reaction. The woman looked dubious but drew a little closer to peer at her.

"Hi?" Nereid said. "I'm sorry I disturbed you." *I'm not thinking about how I can talk while I'm made of water. It makes more sense than how I can* think *while I'm made of water.*

The woman tilted her head, listening.

"I got lost," Nereid said, opting for truth over anything else. *I'm terrible at lying anyway.* "And found this room by accident."

The woman grimaced in a frustrated way, shook her head, and swam back to her sarcophagus. Nereid started to call after her, but stopped herself and watched.

Reaching inside the sarcophagus with her spiny arms, the woman apparently triggered something that started enormous pumps underneath the room. Nereid felt the drag of the drains on her shape, and held herself in place entirely by force of will. She let the oxygen around her head dissolve back into the water, and waited.

The mermaid held onto the sarcophagus and stared at Nereid as the water drained out into huge tanks Nereid could feel surrounding the room. When air touched her skin, the diaphanous fins on her head fell together into straight lengths of dark hair, the spines retreated into her sleek, wet arms, and the tail bifurcated into bare legs. She was a little wobbly standing on her feet, and Nereid had a moment of thinking, "but at every step you take it will feel as if you were treading upon sharp knives."

Nereid let her own shape shift into her human body, and immediately blushed because she'd, of course, forgotten to wear her transforming underwear that morning.

She and the other woman faced each other across the room, equally naked, equally staring. Nereid felt obscurely that it was unfair her new acquaintance was not blushing.

The woman said something in a language that Nereid failed to recognize, except to suspect that maybe it was something Eastern European. Nereid shook her head. The other woman, looking faintly annoyed, said something slowly, in what sounded like a Romance language. Which Nereid did not speak or understand, but could generally recognize. Unfortunately, there was something in her accent that rendered her words unintelligible to Nereid.

Nereid shook her head again, and sallied, "¿Habla usted español?"

The woman shook her head. They stared at each other helplessly, and then both of them started laughing at the same instant. It was the kind of laughter that gets out of control quickly, when one is anxious and embarrassed and relieved all at the same time. In just a few seconds, Nereid had to sit down on the floor because she was laughing too hard to stand up, and her acquaintance was hanging onto the sarcophagus frame with tears running down her cheeks.

Of *course*, Sophie and Prudence chose that moment to show up.

One of the nice things about Sophie, Nereid thought, wiping her eyes and trying to stifle her giggles, *is that she never pointlessly asks if I'm okay. I mean, if I'm laughing, I'm probably fine.*

Sophie, in fact, was standing near her with a smirk on her face, watching Prudence go talk to the other woman. Nereid and her friend caught each other's glances and immediately convulsed with laughter again. Prudence and Sophie shrugging at each other only made them laugh harder.

So it was a few minutes before any sense could be got out of anyone.

Prudence took off her white lab coat and helped the other woman into it, the two of them speaking confidentially to each other, with enough physical contact that Nereid knew immediately that they were lovers. Sophie retrieved Nereid's clothing from where it had scattered over the floor, and Nereid composed herself enough to dry her clothes and pull them on, face burning with embarrassment. Somehow it wasn't so bad when it was just her and her new friend, but to have Prudence see her... well.

"This is Danica," Prudence said, after the scurry for clothing was complete and they were all facing each other like adults. "She contacted me online a few years ago when she suddenly developed an alternate form and a dependency on immersion in water. Her case was fascinating, so I asked her if she'd like to come here for an examination. We've been working on it ever since."

Danica listened for a moment to Prudence with some interest, then looked into Nereid's eyes again. Nereid got that same shock of contact again, the same wordless sense of someone else's emotions. *Must have a limited range? And need to actually see my eyes maybe?* Nereid thought. She concentrated more and stared back into Danica's gaze. It was a bit like falling into a lake, and encountering different currents at different temperatures, with just a few impressions that drew images up from her own mind.

Apologies Anger-Irritation? Acceptance Scientists?—here there was an uncomfortable exchange of the various levels of affection they each felt for their respective mad scientist, and Nereid blushed furiously at both her own intensity and Danica's—*Loneliness Family-feeling Self-hatred Trapped Caged Sadness Attachment...*

After losing a couple minutes of the verbal conversation, Nereid became aware of Sophie nudging her gently, and, with an apologetic thought toward Danica, she looked at her girlfriend. Sophie was frowning, and so was Prudence. "Sorry," Nereid said. "We were... well, not talking but..."

Prudence gave Danica a glance, and her lover shrugged and said something in the language Nereid didn't recognize. Sophie's face cleared immediately, while Prudence frowned more deeply.

Nereid cleared her throat and said, "She told me that she feels trapped here, though she loves you, Prudence. Did you... ask for me to come along to try to use my genes to help her?"

The expression on the mad scientist's face shifted from guilt to anger to sadness to her usual benign half-smile so quickly that Nereid might have missed it if she hadn't been watching for it. Prudence said, in a strained voice, "Yes. I… well, she wants to be able to go home, visit her family, and she can't do that right now. When she's in water, her body changes—as you've seen. And she can only be out of water for brief periods without pain."

Danica took Prudence's hand and squeezed it, and Prudence gave her a tense smile. They said something to each other in that other language, and whatever was said made Prudence's smile relax into her whole face.

Sophie's face didn't so much as twitch, though. Nereid knew that she understood what was said anyway. She'd stopped trying to count how many languages Sophie could speak.

"Have you worked out the terms for what we came for?" Nereid asked Sophie in a low voice. *Please let this all not have been wasted on you two poking each other.*

Sophie nodded. "Prudence has been very generous."

"Prudence," Nereid said, more loudly, keeping her voice steady, "you know that Sophie will have countered accidental collection of my tissue." *Well, she said she'd try.* "But you can have a blood sample, if you like." *I can't believe I'm trusting a supervillain with my genes. The other Class 10s will have a fit. But if I couldn't see my parents again…*

Prudence blinked, opened her mouth, then closed it again. Sophie's hand tightened on the small of Nereid's back. Danica looked a little concerned, and looked from Prudence to Nereid questioningly. Nereid gave her a small smile. *I made a mad scientist speechless. I think that just made my week.*

"Can you promise me that you'll only use it to help Danica?" Nereid said. *No little Nereid clones in tubes, please. Or little octopuses with water manipulation powers and self-image problems.*

Prudence frowned, but this time, it was perplexed. "You've seen what I do," she said. "Why would you trust me?"

"I… don't, necessarily," Nereid said, shrugging. "But Danica does. And I figure, with her powers, she's a much better judge of character than I am." Nereid tried not to think about some of her larger mistakes with judging character.

Prudence gave Danica a long look, and Nereid suspected that silent exchange of emotions was going on. The scientist looked away, but Danica grabbed her chin and brought her face back to her, saying something in a low, urgent voice. There was definitely something pleading in the tone. Nereid reached back to grip Sophie's hand.

Prudence nodded, said something else, and nodded again. Danica kissed her hard, which caused Prudence's cheeks to pink. *And a mad scientist blushing. Another first for me, I think.*

"Yes," Prudence said, turning back to Nereid. "I can promise that."

Danica said something else, and Prudence added, "She says she needs to get back into water now."

Nereid hugged Danica to say goodbye. Sophie shook hands with her and murmured something in a very low voice that made Danica give her a surprised look, then nod and smile. The woman stepped back into her sarcophagus, which was, on closer examination, fairly roomy inside; it extended further back into the wall than it appeared, and seemed to have a computer system built into the walls.

Prudence and Danica's hands lingered together until the sarcophagus started to close up. Then Prudence watched the whole thing come together with a sad expression that disappeared as soon as she turned back to Sophie and Nereid.

Without speaking, they all went into a nearby lab, where Prudence efficiently pulled two vials of Nereid's blood. She deposited those immediately into a freezer vial rack, and then led them out of the room.

Prudence expended some effort to reclaim her chatty self as she walked them toward the front of the complex, and Sophie kindly met her on less feelings-laden ground by asking questions about the power sources and superstructure. Nereid was lost in thought until Prudence paused to duck into a door.

Nereid and Sophie exchanged interrogative glances and then shrugged. Prudence reemerged a few moments later and handed a large plastic box to Nereid.

Puzzled, Nereid peered into the grating of holes at the front. The little silver tabby with the non-working wings blinked huge yellow eyes at her and meeped.

Nereid was startled speechless, tears springing to her eyes. *It must be all that empathic communication,* she thought irritably, scrubbing at her face and finally managing, "Prudence! I can't possibly accept…"

"You'll need to bring her back with you when you come to pick up your friend's new hand," Prudence said, leading them down the hall. "So I can spay her. She's too young for that right now."

Nereid stared at Sophie, who smirked and shrugged. She looked into the carrier again. The kitten, at the grating, made a great effort and managed a tiny, squeaking mew. There was a water bottle and a small litterbox in the back.

Back in the huge laboratory, at the top of the stairwell out, Prudence shook Sophie's hand, and turned to offer her hand to Nereid. Nereid hugged her, to both their surprise, awkwardly and one-handed, her other hand occupied with the cat carrier. *Impulsive, bad, Nereid,* she chastised herself, but Prudence seemed pleased.

"Well, you just let me know if Brainchild doesn't treat you right," Prudence said warmly, and waggled her eyebrows suggestively. "I have an open relationship."

Sophie snorted, shook her head, and started down the stairs. "I have the advantage with this one, Prudence. Being a mechanical fetishist and all."

Nereid blushed all the way outside, then nudged Sophie hard with her elbow as they walked across the field toward Sophie's car. "Jerk," she muttered.

"Of course," Sophie said loftily. "I don't want you to forget, in midst of your big old love-in, who loves you enough to build you some very *interesting* items."

Nereid snorted and handed the kitten to Sophie over the fence. "I don't think her relationship is as *open* as she thinks," she said, remembering Danica's sense of fierce possessiveness.

Sophie held the carrier while Nereid climbed over the fence. "Well, I think Prudence is going to have to learn the old 'if you love something, let it go' line."

Nereid looked at Sophie oddly. *She does nothing* but *let things go. Didn't you notice?* Out loud, she said, "You don't think she'll go visit Danica's family with her?" She safety-belted the kitten's carrier into the back seat of the battered little sedan.

Sophie slid behind the wheel and shook her head. "Prudence has had agoraphobia for years now. That's why she's not a major supervillain, despite having all the resources and ability to try for world domination."

As they drove out of the field, Nereid noticed a bird watching them go. It was a small crow, she thought, until she saw the little hands emerge from under the wings. The bird appeared to be *knitting* something with a slender gray-brown yarn and tiny needles. Then she noticed a few similar birds in higher branches, all watching them, all engaged in knitting.

Nereid thought about *Schedule release* again. *Too bad this area's landlocked,* she thought, deciding not to mention it at all, ever, to Sophie or anyone else. *The octopuses won't be able to hang around like the birds do. What will her octopuses do to pass the time?*

"You didn't try very hard to give it back," Sophie said, gesturing toward the back seat with a jerk of her head. "It's never going to get past the team's security advisor."

Nereid looked out the passenger window. "Oh, come on."

Sophie shook her head. "Not a chance. Everyone knows Prudence."

Nereid glanced at Sophie. *I'm not sure you know her as well as you think you do.* She reached back to put her fingertips against the holes in the carrier, and felt her kitten rub against her. "What's your name, sweetie?" she said into the back.

"How about Spy?" said Sophie with a roll of her eyes. "Trouble? Snitch? Oh, I've got it! 'Spymaster Q. Tattletale, Esquire'!"

Nereid looked back at the kitten, who met her gaze with the same kind of electric impact she'd gotten from Danica. But all she got from this magnetic stare was *Mine.* She scritched the kitten under the chin, causing it to half-close its yellow eyes, breaking the possessive headlights in which she'd been briefly caught. She considered for a moment, remembering how Danica made Prudence break her chatty, cheerful character for just a few moments. Then she said, "You know, Sophie, you're not with another mad scientist right now. You don't have to show off how smart you are, or what an ass you can be."

Sophie looked aside at her, then back at the road. "I've been an ass all day, haven't I?"

"Yeah," Nereid said, then added, "Both you and Prudence, really."

"Well, like you said, we test each other all the time," Sophie said with a shrug.

"Like junior high girls," Nereid said, raising her eyebrows.

Sophie scowled, opened her mouth, shut it, thought for a moment, then said, "I'm sorry." After a pause, she added, "I'm sorry to you too, kitten."

"Mrrrt," the kitten said in a smug kind of way, apparently accepting for both of them.

THE PRADO BY CHANCE
Leia Weathington

Leia Weathington is a writer and artist living in Portland, Oregon. She writes comics and cooks dinner in a little treehouse where she lives with her husband. *The Legend of Bold Riley* is her first book. You can find more information at boldriley.com.

Alex Weiss normally liked to keep her drinking to respectable hours, except for Wednesdays. Wednesdays all bets were off. She leaned against a metal locker in the dingy briefing room of Madrid's INTERPOL office. Her captain, a balding, irritatingly cheerful man, booted up the communications console and waved for quiet. Alex turned her head as if to quietly cough and tipped another glut of bourbon into her paper cup of coffee.

"All right, kids!" It was always 'kids' with this dickhead. "You know the drill. Hang in there while the big boys and girls do their thing and we'll see if they need any assist."

This pudgy, affable fuck. For the past ten years since the worldwide accord designating mutated superhumans the caretakers of mankind, the mundane constabulary had almost never been called in to assist. What was the point, when twelve percent of the global population could fly, lift four times their weight, was telekinetic, become invisible or whatever other weird shit had popped up in the gene pool of late. FBI, CIA, Mossad, KGB, INTERPOL, every powerful and dreaded organization across the globe was gutted in favor of the Übermensch Initiative. Specialist teams of four to six superhumans and their handlers took care of the real police work and the regular humans sat back listening to feeds of their exploits waiting to see what bullshit grunt work might need to be done. Clean up, cataloging ill-gotten goods—a particularly good weekend for Alex when that drug dealer from Sicily got bagged; the coke lifted from the evidence locker helped host an incredible rager—and jailing the erstwhile henchmen not killed in a brutal assault by people who could start fires with their minds and government sanction to do so.

Wednesdays in this time zone were when the Spanish Super Team did their strikes against criminal elements. Several of the younger officers sat forward eagerly when the dispatcher began reporting civilians trapped in a factory fire. Alex had spent three years leaning forward, breathless at the chance of action. Now she took the chance to slug directly from her flask while her colleagues hoped. Sure enough, some asshole called the Falcon of Albania swooped in and saved everyone in peril.

Still, it wasn't Dunhill, Virginia. Thank god she had worked her whole 20's away to get to INTERPOL just to sit around and watch others wield power. This was not what she had expected from a career in law enforcement. Maybe her parents were wrong letting her watch all those cop shows.

The dispatch was winding down to its inevitable conclusion. A smuggling ring broken up, several trafficked women rescued, a few Syrian cultural items recovered. Alex perked up just barely at that. She had joined under the Works of Art division. Works of art were classy, works of art were money. There wasn't any class or money in Dunhill, Virginia.

Works of art could be put in her pocket and sold to very rich people who were smart enough not to commit flashy crimes for the adoring public and insatiable media.

The paltry team assembled closed down for the morning and trudged back to their desks to await the incoming paperwork for their districts from the Initiative's maneuvers. A young woman sidled up to Alex as she drained the rest of her cup. Yvette, recently reassigned from the main branch in Lyons, big doe eyes, soft voice, slight frame. She irritated the tits off of Alex.

"So good all of those lives saved, oui?" Yvette said, gently touching Alex's arm. Alex was entirely certain the French tacked on at the end of her question was a calculated move to seduce a backwater American. If Alex was a younger and less hateful bitch it might work.

"Wonderful." Alex crunched the cup in her hand and tossed it into the nearby bin. "Truly world peace is right around the corner." Yvette looked up at her from under thick dark lashes and opened her mouth. Alex dipped away from her, passing her drunken stumble off as a smooth roll against the locker. "'Scuse me, looks like I've got some old shit to catalogue."

She left Yvette without looking back and went to do the dregs of police work left in this age of phenomenal human advancement. Four more hours of bullshit and Alex could go finish the rest of the bourbon. Hopefully the Saudi exchange student whose window was right across from her studio apartment would have a new conquest for the night. She was less interested in his cock than his taste in brunettes with brawny thighs. Also his predilection for leaving the lights on and the blinds drawn.

A vault was burgled on Serrano street in the Salamanca district. That could have been handed off to the boring ass, everyday police force that nations and cities still maintained, but this call was routed directly to Alex's desk. When she picked up the call, bored and hungover as usual, a reedy woman spoke tentatively: "Inspector... Weiss? Yes?" The English halting and unsure.

Alex answered easily in fluent Castilian Spanish.

"Yes, this is Inspector Weiss. What can I assist you with today, Señora..."

"Barranco." The tentativeness of speaking in another language removed, the voice asserted itself to be older, haughty and moneyed. Alex straightened in her office chair at the thought of 'moneyed'.

"Señora Barranco. What can I do for you."

So a rich woman's private vault was burgled. So what? Petty crime. Barely worth registering in this brave new world of justice. Señora Barranco's description of the steel of her safe melted through, the shape of a human hand clear in the metal, was worthy of register. Then the halting explanation that all the rich bastards on her block kept a sort of neighborhood watch, just as a precaution. From their little get-togethers it turned out that Señora Barranco was the fifth robbery in the month. She copped to having an ancient Egyptian bust stolen from her safe, one that should have gone back to the nation of Egypt after the 2019 accords mandating the return of cultural artifacts to their homelands. The robbery had upset her, but more so the scrap of paper with the house number of another neighbor left in the display case. All the rich were in bed with each other. The favors that came from protecting one another were as delicious now as at any point in history.

"I would be most grateful if you could perhaps look into this for me, ah, discretely." Señora Barranco said, her tone hushed. "It's making all of us very uneasy."

"That sounds a bit like you didn't acquire the sculpture by legitimate means, Señora. It also sounds like you are attempting to pay off an agent of INTERPOL to run a dirty errand for you." Alex fiddled with a pen absently and let the silence stretch for an uncomfortable moment before asking, "And what would have led you to believe that I would flout protocol to get your goods back?"

"A man by the name of Aldof Black." Came the cautious reply.

Ah, Aldof. British expat living in Athens, one of the finest fences for rare antiquities Alex had ever had the pleasure of letting off the hook in exchange for a cut of his profits. So nice to find he still thought of her when good money was within reach.

Alex wrote the relevant information in the notebook she kept in her jacket pocket, assured the señora that her department would look into the theft and hung up the phone.

Alex sat back heavily into her creaking chair. How interesting. Most of the dickheads with super powers wanted to play hero to one degree or another. Super powered petty crime like robberies actually dropped after the dawning of the New Mankind.

Alex did not notify her captain of the call that day, ruminating over the pros and cons of doing so while watching Khalid (she learned the exchange student's name when his mail was misplaced in her box) being ridden by a redhead with fantastic abs from across the light well. Alex swilled two fingers of whiskey in her glass, poured another two on top of that and wondered:

"Why be so sloppy?"

Alex had a few boys in her department. Simon, Diego, and Alberto. Big, dumb things that liked the power that came with being police but lacked the wits to abuse it without getting caught. Alex took the simple brutes under her wing. They were incapable of thinking on their own, yet had proven quite adept at following instructions provided they thought the ideas were theirs. There are some men who love nothing more than a man's woman. A woman that's hard drinking, blue mouthed, and never sexually available but always with the possibility just out of reach. Alex had hidden paperwork detailing Simon's excessive force in 2017, Diego's moonlighting as a bouncer at a mob-run club, Alberto's cuts from Madrid prostitutes in exchange for not being arrested. She listened to them complain about wives and girlfriends, paid for rounds of whiskey they could never afford, gave them flirty looks under her eyelashes from time to time. These men adored her. It was her own little squad within a squad.

They would do anything for her.

The least of which was playing cards and drinking cheap plonk during work hours.

"I may need you guys for some private security soon." Alex said, and picked up a new card. She had always liked the glamor of poker but never had the patience to learn the rules. The boys didn't like Go Fish, but a bit of needling did the trick to convince them.

"Any jacks?" Alberto asked Simon, who made a noise of disgust and handed his card over.

"What for?" Diego asked.

Alex pushed her half full cup towards him and he topped it up. "Been a string of burglaries on Salamanca, rich old dude thinks he's next up for being robbed. Nothing big, just waiting around a few nights, be seen looking intimidating should take care of it if he's being cased."

"Fuck those rich assholes." Snorted Simon. "Two of hearts?"

"Go fish."

"*Damn* it..."

"Come on, Alex, what's the point?" Diego threw his cards across the table. "Private security pays dick. Just call the Initiative and tell em to get a spooky shadow mutant to deal with it. They love that shit."

"Yeah, I'm out. I'd rather get a night's sleep than deal with that bullshit." Simon tossed his cards dismissively at Alberto and leaned back to swig from the bottle.

"You can't just quit when I'm winning!" Alberto sulked. He sorted the jumble of cards and didn't look up. Alex knew things were rocky with the girl he'd been seeing lately.

She nudged his knee with her foot. "Alright, dickheads. Just me and Alberto then. It'll be fun." She gave Alberto a warm smile, the one that softened up hard men like her dad. "Besides a shitload of money split four ways is fine but way better split two."

That got their attention. Simon paused with the bottle halfway to his lips, Diego absently tucked a cigarette the wrong way into his mouth. Alberto was giving her a dopey smile.

"How much shit in that load?"

Alex told them. Diego went wide eyed with surprise and tried to play it off when he lit the filter end of his smoke. He choked quietly in the pause, Simon with the bottle still poised at his mouth.

Then Simon laughed and swigged hard. Slamming the bottle back onto the table hard enough to overturn the ashtray. "Well, fuck! I'm in!"

"Alex and I can just do it. You guys don't have to come." Alberto said sullenly. "We'll handle it."

Simon threw a handful of cards at Alberto's face.

"Fuck you, Alberto. I'm not missing out on that kind of cash."

Alex smiled her best and warmest smile again as Diego tried to discretely toss his ruined smoke under the table. "Well, yeah and we can't just leave our girl in the wind. It might actually be dangerous." He said.

Alex deepened her smile and did the thing where she squinted a bit to make it look as if she felt a deep camaraderie and affection for these people. She had gotten quite good at it.

"Thanks guys," she said, counting the euros in her head. "You always have my back."

◆

She had done this sort of thing before, just a bit of moonlighting as security for the wealthy and paranoid. Unless it was a nightclub (and she refused those jobs after the last one ended with a brawl at the entrance and her brand new leather coat shredded,) the work was easy. Alex and the boys showed up at Señor Delgado's front gate at 10 PM, dressed in black, sidearms prominent at their hips, cheap headsets in their ears.

"Hey, Al, this sweater itches bad. Can I take it off?"

"No," "Alex hissed over her shoulder at Simon. A bent backed old man was making his way down the entryway stairs. "And shut the fuck up. Be professional."

"I think the turtlenecks make us look gay."

"Be professionally *quiet, Diego, you fu*—Señor Delgado!" Alex extended her hand. "Alex Weiss. My team and I will be keeping you safe tonight."

Señor Delgado did not accept her hand shake and instead gestured brusquely towards the front door. Irritated, Alex's waved over her shoulder to her men. They followed her, a billowing hulking cloak of black turtlenecks and cheap haircuts.

It had always annoyed Alex to run security for the wealthy, of particular annoyance ones who had been so for generations. Señor Delgado led them through his palatial estate, noting his valuables, his concerns about a few windows with loose hinges, his adamance that nothing be touched or he wouldn't pay them a cent.

"I'll have one of us at each entrance, Señor. One for the front, back, and side. I understand the vault is what worries you the most, however," Alex cut in over the old man's prattle. "I want to post my best man there on the off chance the thief gets through the rest of us." Diego, Simon, and Alberto puffed up behind her.

"I don't know what you mean, Señorita—"

"Inspector."

"Inspector Weiss. I have no vault." Señor Delgado tapped his cane against the marble floor and squared his shoulders. He squinted at Alex like he had caught her stealing pocket change from his jacket, like she was some low class child. Alex's patience thinned and snapped at his condescension.

"Señor, I know you have a vault. If you didn't we wouldn't be here. Do you want efficient security or your shit stolen?"

Señor Delgado sneered at her coarse language and Alex shut her eyes briefly to muster her professional charm. She breathed deep and smiled, that reassuring smile she perfected to go with her freckles and girlish pink mouth.

"Señor," Alex said. "Let us protect your welfare to the best of our ability. We can't do that if we can't cover the entire premises. Please," She held a placating hand out. "Please, let us keep you and your livelihood safe."

There was a bare pause before Delgado rapped his cane against the floor again and led her to a pocket door. When he pushed a decorative bit of mold-ing the wood slid back, and Alex and her boys descended a stone staircase to the vault. She regarded the solid steel door, turned and nodded to Alberto, biggest of the big bastards.

"Post up here, Alberto. Simon? Take the back door. Deigo, I want you on the front entrance." Diego groaned. "Shut up. I'll take the side garden entrance. Stay in contact over radio, stay alert, stay awake." Alex issued her orders smoothly. She knew the boys didn't care for her bossy tone in front of another man much, but the money these moonlight jobs she found always kept them from openly challenging her. Besides, Delgado was a man who only appreciated other men so it made sense he knew the key points were guarded by them.

"Señor Delgado," Alex clasped his withered hand and smiled through his disdainful glance at her split nails and calluses. "We have the situation in hand. Nothing will happen while we are here." She smiled with her learned warmth even as he took his hand back quickly. "It's late Señor Delgado, please, enjoy your evening. Sleep. I have the situation in hand."

Instructions issued, and Delgado off to his coffin or whatever, Alex took to the smaller garden entrance. It was nice for a few hours. Fragrant jasmine blossoms, a warm steady breeze, bougainvillea gleaming in the half moon, Alex pretending she wasn't some underpaid servant of a global government. This was her house, her garden, her nice things inside. She was just enjoying the grounds before having an expensive night cap.

Then the pop, pop, pop of gunfire at the front entrance, back entrance and top floor where Señor Delgado slept.

Abrupt and awful, Heiress Weiss was Inspector Weiss, and Inspector Weiss had a problem. She drew her sidearm and tried to radio her boys.

❦

Alex crept towards the vault. In the flickering half-light of the emergency lantern she could see the heavy steel door ajar. Alberto's massive bulk crumpled against the wall. Gun held at the ready, low in a tense grip. The gunfire in the upper levels had stopped. She had switched off her radio. She hoped Diego's screams had stopped.

As she neared the vault door on silent feet she could hear a clink and a quiet click, then the soft strains of... Violins? Alex approached sideways into the soft glow of the cracked door to peer inside.

"Please, come in, Miss Weiss." A woman's voice, rich and low came from within. Alex shouldered the door open and raised her gun. It was a credit to her nerves and her training that the muzzle didn't dip when she saw the spread before her.

An old mahogany table laid with antique china, fragrant candles that cast a warm glow through the room. Standing by an ancient record player near the back was the most handsome woman Alex had ever seen in her life. She had skin like dark, polished wood, eyelids dusted with gold, lean, tall, rangy. When she smiled, warm and wicked, her teeth were perfect.

"I'm so glad you came." The woman said. "You've had my attention for some time now. I thought I should have you for dinner."

"I'm uncomfortable with your phrasing."

The woman laughed, delighted. "You *are* wonderful. I'm so looking forward to this!"

Alex was losing patience. She moved forward cautiously, keeping her gun trained on the woman. "Who the fuck are you?" She demanded.

The woman closed her eyes and dipped her head in a minute bow.

"Forgive me, my name is Rachel Aberoa. I promise you aren't in any danger from me."

"All of my men are dead so I'm not inclined to believe that."

Rachel waved a dismissive hand. "Oh, they're just men. You can always get more. Although, I'll tell you Alex, there are much better options."

Alex whipped around as the vault door swung fully open. Three of the automata she had glimpsed in the shadows swinging their deadly arms clipped neatly inside, unbothered by Alex's gun trained on them. They carried platters covered with silver covers. One had a bottle of wine and a white towel draped over its arm. Alex noticed for the first time that they all wore bow ties.

"I used to use regular men for henchmen, but let me tell you it's become so much less complicated once I started making these beauties." Rachel said as the automata set their platters down on the table. They drew the chairs out and stood by dutifully. Rachel leveled a smile at Alex. "Aren't your arms getting tired?"

Alex trained her gun again. "If they get too tired I'll just start shooting."

"Come and sit." Rachel held out a hand to the empty chair across from her. One of the automata pulled it out with a screech. "I promise I won't hurt you. Well, at least not kill you. If you start shooting at me I'm afraid I'll have to defend myself, and please note that it's four against one."

Alex hesitated.

"Keep your gun on the table if it will make you feel better." Rachel said. "But I insist we eat before the food gets cold. I put a great deal of time into assembling the menu."

Alex declined to lower the gun and never looked away from her host as she eased herself down on to the chair. Aberoa only flashed her genial smile and smoothly sat. The silver covers were withdrawn. Alex couldn't help but glance down as the smell wafted up. Her eye twitched. Rachel rested her chin on her wrist and smiled.

"A black truffle risotto topped with crisped jamón ibérico, *genuine* Kobe beef, and grilled asparagus. I'm given to understand you like it."

"Black truffle," Alex muttered.

"I prefer the black so much more than the white. Much less pungent."

Alex startled violently at the pop of a cork being wrenched from the neck of a wine bottle. The automata holding the bottle chirped apologetically. Rachel reached a cautious hand toward Alex. Alex scowled.

"You'll have a terrible time eating with all of your attention on this useless thing," As Rachel's fingertips neared the muzzle of the gun the metal wavered and the grip became hot in Alex's hand. She dropped the gun with a gasp. Rachel caught it easily. "You don't believe me," Said Rachel molding the gun metal in her hands like it was soft clay. "When I said you aren't in danger from me, I meant it."

Alex watched as Rachel shaped the molten metal in her hands. Rachel's fingers were delicate as they sculpted. She cupped her work in her palms, satisfied, and gently blew on the surface. A billow of steam flowed from her cupped hands. Rachel smiled as she placed her work down in front of Alex. The mottled grey and copper had been fashioned into a rippled heart shape.

"After all, you have my heart, Alex Weiss."

The automata poured Rachel a glass of wine then one for Alex, who simply stared at what used to be her sidearm. She didn't look up when Rachel took a satisfied sip.

"Ah, Domaine de la Romanee-Conti. Over 20,000 a bottle." She gently swirled her glass and mused, "If one were to actually pay for it, of course."

Alex looked up, her anger edging into genuine fear. "What the fuck is this?"

Rachel frowned. She set her wine glass down and extended a tentative hand, palm up, beseeching. "It's… dinner. I simply," Rachel sounded tentative and tried again. "I simply wanted to take you out."

"First of all, there's that phrasing again, and second you just killed *three* INTERPOL officers and an old man—"

"Oh, please," Rachel cut in. "That man owns cocoa plantations all over West Africa. He's practically a slaver. Trust me, I looked into it."

"Shut up!" Alex snapped. "Third, you've been robbing houses all over Salamanca to do, what, now? Leave a trail of breadcrumbs for me to follow so you could have me for dinner in a dead man's basement?" Alex sat back momentarily but started forward again as Rachel opened her mouth to speak. "Oh, *oh!* And fourth, have you been *stalking* me, Aberoa?"

A flicker of guilt passed over Rachel's face, a minute tightening of her eyes and mouth. "I wasn't exactly,"

"Then what," Alex gritted out. "Was it *exactly*?"

Rachel shifted. "I saw you a few months ago. In the Prado, by chance. It was after that little terrorism dust up with," Rachel snapped her fingers, trying to recall.

"Uh, I think it was the Star Spangled Motherfuckers and the Mystic Legion that time."

"Yes! That's the one. The Prado had a hole in the ceiling and the Arts and Antiquities Unit was there to assess the damage and make sure nothing had been looted in the chaos. I was there doing some… personal work."

Alex raised an eyebrow at that. "The museum was cordoned off."

"Alright, some highly illegal personal work, let's say." Rachel smiled softly at Alex. "And when I was trying to slip out unnoticed, there you were. In front of Bosch's Garden of Earthly Delights. But not in front really, you were staring at the back of the tryptic. So few take the time to truly appreciate the other side." Rachel shook her head. "The look on your face. Fascinated, sad, hopeful. Like you appreciated the desolation of the landscape and the potential for what could be built there."

"You were beautiful, you seemed interesting," Rachel paused to sip from her wine. "I admit to digging for some information. I was impressed by your service record, in particular how many corruption cases members of your departments were involved in. Never a black spot on your reputation though. Even a commendation back in Charleston for services rendered in tracking down a fellow officer who had been stealing jewels. Shame the ruby necklace never surfaced again." Rachel fixed Alex with a knowing look. "Your beauty was enough to catch my eye. Your cleverness was what kept it."

"I tracked your movements for a time, I thought maybe you would be a problem for me in the future but as I did…" Rachel laughed quietly. "I saw a woman a bit like myself. Smarter than every dumb bastard around her, and smart enough not to show it. I came to admire you a great deal, Alex Weiss."

"I could have machinated a little scenario to meet you, maybe charm you enough to sleep with me, but had I done that it's all I would have gotten, a few nights where we pretended to be people we aren't. You are a woman not easily impressed, that much I can tell." Rachel indicated the vault around them. "I wanted to impress you. And to make you an offer."

"Which is?" Alex asked.

Rachel sat forward, face a picture of excitement. "Eat with me. Talk with me for a while. If you enjoy yourself perhaps you would consider coming with me back to my island." Rachel raised her hands. "Not that I expect anything from you if you did. I'd hardly expect you to be my girlfriend after one dinner, just perhaps the chance to woo you, as myself and not some shallow version of it."

"Even if—" Alex paused. "Wait, you have an island?"

Rachel waved a dismissive hand. "I purchased it in my early twenties. I had always wanted one and I had the skills to obtain it. Learning about proxy accounts and offshore investments was quite a boring experience but it paid off well."

Alex regarded Rachel in silence. She picked up an asparagus spear and chewed thoughtfully. Rachel grinned.

"Alright," Alex said as she tossed the stem back onto the cold plate. "If I have dinner with you, if I talk to you, and I decide not to come with you, what then? You leave me in the shambles of my life and career? How do I explain this shit if we part ways?"

"I have a good cover story for you. Don't worry, a few doctored videos, a paid eyewitness. You can go back to wasting your intelligence at INTERPOL where no one appreciates you." Rachel said. "Choose to come with me and I have a cover story that will leave you looking as pure as the driven snow. A hero copper with a nice pension to be sent back to your little sister back home. Jenny, I believe?"

Alex narrowed her eyes.

"Forgive me," Rachel said. "I'm not used to actually wanting someone to like me. From what I've garnered she seems important to you." That subtle shadow of doubt over Rachel's face again. "I would like to hear about her, if you'd like to tell me. When you are ready." Rachel reached across the table and touched Alex's wrist tentatively, her fingers a warm stroke. "I want to know you. I want to give you the chance to *take* all of the things you want without miles of red tape and bullshit rules. You may not have my abilities," Here Rachel touched the lump of metal on the table and a fingertip shaped impression dimpled the surface like clay. "But a few genetic parlor tricks have never been as important as the intelligence to use them to their full potential. No matter what those puffed up superhumans running roughshod over the face of the globe and their obtuse handlers think."

"I can give you wealth. I can give you a life full of all the things you crave. I can give you a real challenge." Rachel didn't look up, almost shy. "I can at least give you a night with someone who won't judge your darker nature, who will even admire you for it." Rachel did look up then. "I had hoped I would have the same from you."

Alex sat, thinking, in a dead man's basement. The information spread before her: A beautiful woman who owned an island, who had a taste for the finer things and the will to take them. A pile of corpses upstairs she didn't give a damn about even when they breathed. She considered the paths and saw dead ends, mediocrity and boredom at the end of all of them.

All save one.

Alex picked up the glass full of expensive, stolen, wine and toasted Rachel who still looked unsure but hopeful.

"So tell me about your island, Señorita Aberoa."

❧

Of all things, Fort Knox.

The robberies and cybercrime had been rampant in the past few years, glossed over in the media in favor of the showy displays by the Ubermensch Initiative and their battles with super terrorists, aliens, or whatever exotic new threat du jour. Low level accountants were starting to whisper. The flow of economy was disrupted in parts of the world, a growing dead spot of communications off the coast of India. It had been brought up in meetings with world leaders and quickly dismissed. The Ubermensch Initiative would surely catch anything dangerous, just like they had a thousand times before.

No one really cared.

Least of all, the beleaguered and underfunded lead detective to arrive on the scene. He sighed at the emptied reserves and the techs milling about. They were under strict orders to simply catalogue and wait for the arrival of Weeping Eagle and the Appalachian Avenger. The detective snapped his fingers at a watery eyed crime scene photographer and ordered her to take shots of the melted inscription on the primary vault's door. A heart, and inside of it, looking like someone had dragged their finger through paint were the initials: *R&A WERE HERE.*

JAGUAR LIGHT
Susan Smith

Susan Smith is a writer and librarian. Smith's work is steeped in mythology, identity, gender, art and sexuality. Novels *Of Drag Kings and the Wheel of Fate*, *Burning Dreams*, and *Put Away Wet* were published by Bold Strokes Books, the novella "Billy Boy" in the *Outsiders* anthology by Brisk Press.

Night, Portland Art Museum. Jaguar slid through the skylight, the glass melting away from her diamond tipped claws. The exhibit she was after was on the fourth floor, easily accessible for one with the strength and power of the great cat and unconstrained by the gossamer threads of law. Jaguar had toured the exhibit this evening and saw a painting she had to have. An artist she didn't know, CJ Hurley, but the painting had taken her and ravished her senses, the glowing greens of the deep forest catapulted her back to running through the trees on all fours, life crackling from her fur, power coursing along her veins, bursting from her thews, her spirit-self wrapped around with the flesh of the cat alive, alive, alive—the memory trigger was so strong, the decision was simple. She would have this painting.

Jaguar had become a supervillain for all the traditional reasons: arrogance, affluence, and affection. *Nahual* power came from the jade jaguar amulet she wore, from the generations of blood come down from the Aztec empire, the Jaguar Knights of her ancestors. When invoked, the amulet gave Jaguar the senses, the power, the speed and agility of the great cat, but more, it invoked the soul mantle of the jaguar warriors. Like the great cat, she was unconstrained by convention. She was not one to question or place impediments between her desire and its fulfillment; like the cat she hungered and she fed. She wanted and she took. For years the world had been her territory, roaming freely and alone, seizing up any bright beautiful thing that caught her attention, pretty girls, glowing gems, sparkling baubles, leaving it all as easily when the urge to roam seized her.

So many years of inchoate yearning, living from instinct to instinct, blood dark on her teeth, light splintering from her diamond claws, the long dormant call of the true *ocelotl*, the *nahual*—the warrior who could become spiritually and physically the jaguar. The great solar enemies were no more, the empire fallen, the knights gone and the dark smoking mirror the jaguar provided to the sun was lost in the green distant past. What point now, the power, the strength, the call? Let the eternal now of the jaguar spirit take over and let the world be her hunting grounds. It was the price to be paid for the power.

Jaguar reached out, her light-drinking uniform making her a wave of ink in the green shadowed darkness. An icy kiss of her claws and the display case folded, shivering away from the object of her desire. Emotional fulfillment was at hand.

"Jaguar."

The voice was snakeskin on sandstone, dry leaves whispering across the cemetery road. It echoed unnaturally in the exhibit room, circled her hyper sensitive ears. No human voice unaided by magic or virulent science could make a sound that low, a sound that pricked up her spirit self's ears. Jaguar paused mid gesture, a cat with one paw raised. The other hand twitched with desire to clutch at her amulet, the jade jaguar head with the obsidian mirror caught in its open jaws. In the center of the room a swirling began, a viper ouroboros, circling upon itself as it grew, impossibly, into an anaconda, and at last into a figure of myth, a serpent filing the room, jaws great enough to swallow a horse whole. It wasn't illusion; the snake was real. The scent smote on her, a low growl pulled from her in response. Then it coiled out of existence, a hooded figure standing where it had been.

Faced with flesh and blood, Jaguar turned, sheathed her claws and yawned. Out of the corner of her eye she saw the figure glide across the floor, not touching it. Jaguar looked back to her painting.

"You missed the meeting."

A minute twitch of her shoulder served as Jaguar's shrug. "I had other plans. The NWVA sending the secretary out to chide missing members now?"

"The North West Villains Alliance has plenty of members. But you are the one I sought."

Bloodmoon, Mistress of Magic, thrust back the hood of her crimson robe. Something had changed since Jaguar had last seen her at the last NVWA meeting. Bloodmoon was all notepads and Coke-bottle glasses and in a roomful of colorful outlaws came across as a hopeless nerd, LARPing the villain lifestyle. Jaguar was offhandedly kind to her, as a cat will occasionally select an unremarkable human and drop attention on them. It made Bloodmoon absurdly grateful, and she imprinted on Jaguar like a duckling.

They had never pulled a job together. Jaguar's outlawry was motivated by desire and whim, while Bloodmoon kept a closely guarded secret of what she would do with her power, once she found The Source. Jaguar never bothered to ask what The Source was, or how Bloodmoon sought it, and the magic woman merely intimated that they were shared beings of great power and mutual understanding.

Now Bloodmoon radiated power, blazing across every spectrum Jaguar could see or sense. Her spirit self edged away from the swirling serpentine mass in the center of the room, the flowing black snake of roiling, vengeful power. The light of madness shone from the sorceress' eyes. Jaguar felt all her senses stand at attention, screaming warning.

"Your power, like mine, comes from the dark eternal forces. I have been whispering to the things that live beneath the earth, I have sought the wisdom of the snake and the skull and the root. I have done it, Jaguar! I have cracked the problem open like the ribs of a sacrifice! No more need you waste your life opposing Lady Light, Protector of Portland!"

"Fantastic. Mind helping me get this painting out of here before the alarm sounds?"

Bloodmoon waved off the suggestion, her hand, Jaguar now noticed, red to the wrist.

"The guard is dead. I have the key, The Source! I can end the game of villain and hero forever. The spell has been revealed to me, the way to pull all the power from the world, save only that granted by magic. I can kill all the heroes. The world will be ours alone!"

The stars wheeled above Jaguar in a drunken fan of frost and sapphire. She was away, without the painting, bounding across rooftops with the fluid grace of her namesake. The Mistress of Magic had vanished dramatically, testing out her new powers or just showing off. Her words rang in Jaguar's memory. End all the powered beings, kill all the heroes. No one with powers granted by toxic waste, lightning accidents, the bite of radioactive centipedes, creeping changes in DNA, or the culmination of chemical catastrophe would survive. No one born on Mars, or the granddaughter of the ancient gods, the billionaire playgirl vigilante. No one granted powers in a solar panel factory explosion.

No life for Lady Light, the solar powered super Protector of Portland. Jaguar's prime foe, her nemesis, her greatest enemy and longest relationship. The brilliant sun goddess, her hair rayed out in dreads around a face of shining beauty, draped in white and gold and brass flowing garments stitched by hand from locally sourced ethically harvested wool. Lady Light, her reason for coming to Portland, for staying. Lady Light, who used her solar powers to harvest the rays of the sun into light blasts and flight, who led film festivals and vegan cookoffs and lent her image to solar panel co-ops. The spirit of Portland, wrapped up in gorgeous African skin, the embodiment of the Sun. Without her accidentally acquired powers, the solar absorption would incinerate her alive. Every interview in the local alternative press included this offhand fact. Why not? Who could use such a thing to harm the Protector of Portland?

At last Jaguar slumped down panting to rest against a wall, underneath a billboard. The thoughts could not be fled away from. Why the panic? Wasn't this what she wanted, the rule of the night, unimpeded by the solar hero? No more opposition from Lady Light, no more constant struggle, constant grappling, no more smoking mirror to the burning day star. No challenge. No foe. No ultimate game of dark and light, no sensual struggle with the only being ever to equal her, thwart her, hold her attention for more than a few months. No more of the most satisfying relationship of her life.

"Hold, villain!"

Jaguar rolled her eyes. "Oh come on!"

Blazing out of the core of the night, levitating fifteen feet off the surface of the roof was the sun goddess herself, Lady Light. An aura of gold surrounded her, burnished and gilded every inch from glorious crown to incomparable heel. She slowly lowered down, her hand extended in the arresting pose. Jaguar didn't bother getting up.

This non-response seemed to bemuse the hero, who kept a watchful distance, floating just above Jaguar's height, ready to strike out in any direction from the spiky look to her golden aura.

"You will not escape me, Jaguar!"

"You need to be endorsing contact lenses. I'm not moving. I'm tired, I've had a long night."

The golden aura retracted closer to Lady Light's skin, like a shield. She floated closer to the roof. "I know. There was a break in at the art museum, a guard was killed. Rooftop panels opened with diamond tipped claws. You won't escape me."

Jaguar sat up straighter, causing Lady Light's aura to expand aggressively. "That wasn't me! Ok, the painting was me, but I didn't even get that. I didn't kill the guard."

"Is this some kind of trap?" Lady Light asked, glancing at the billboard Jaguar was slumped under. Jaguar looked up and behind her for the first time. Sun Goddess Co-op Solar Panels—help the sun work for you! Cheerily emblazed across a smiling picture of the Protector of Portland.

"No, just a cosmic joke."

"You are letting me take you in?"

"For the first time in my life, I don't feel like fighting. No, I'm not letting you arrest me. I want to talk. Have a cup of coffee with me?"

Lady Light landed on the roof warily. "Coffee?"

"Coffee. No ambush, no break for it. No hero and villain. Just two women talking. I have some huge, Portland in peril stuff I think I need your help with."

"Ok. But make it herbal tea, coffee keeps me up."

They settled on a 24 hour vegan café in Northwest Portland, Moon River. Lady Light turned off her glow, but her flowing yoga inspired costume and Birkenstocks fit in just fine. Jaguar stripped out of her uniform and revealed jeans and a t shirt, both black.

"Why the black uniform, if all you wear is black under it?" Lady Light asked. Jaguar held out the sleeve.

"Light drinking fabric. It absorbs all the light in its vicinity, so it looks black, but it isn't. It's actually yellow, spotted, with green and blue as well. The *ocelotl* are very colorful."

Lady light slid the fabric between her fingers. "Feels like silk."

They took a table in an unoccupied corner, the very tattooed waitress struggling to keep the grin of recognition off her face when she saw Lady Light. Jaguar she barely glanced at. This amused the villain.

"Does it bother you being recognized in public? I mean, no mask, and you look like you would wear that any day of the week."

Lady Light sipped her hibiscus jasmine tea. "I want the people to know me, to feel like I am one of them. That I am here for them."

Jaguar loaded her coffee with milk and sugar, smiling at Lady Light's reaction. "You're not though, are you. Neither of us is. We are super powered beings in a mundane world. Nothing they could do can hold us."

"We have a responsibility to use our gifts for the greater good. Why else have them?"

Jaguar laughed. "Are you for real? I mean, I always expected you to be like this, but you are exactly like this. You are the embodiment of good. Doesn't it get boring, holding back all the time?"

Lady Light put down the cup of tea. "I don't hold back when we fight. No more stalling. What is the Portland in peril story you have to tell me?"

"Ok. You know Bloodmoon, Mistress of Magic?"

The solar hero frowned. "Seattle villain, right? Fought the Rain Man?"

"Yes, and that is an unfortunate name for a hero. She's considerably stepped up her powers and ambition since then."

"What is her evil plan?"

Jaguar paused while the waitress refilled her coffee, and offered Lady Light anything she might desire. It was like a reflection seen in a curved surface, the polite smile Lady Light gave the girl. Not the blazing passionate anger that suffused her face when they fought. This was the mask, this public face. The waitress left.

"She has a spell that will allow her to strip the power from all powered beings." There. Flat, matter of fact. Let the hero digest that.

Lady Light dropped the tea cup. "Can she do that? How? Have you seen it?"

"She can, I think. I haven't seen it, and I'm not sure how she's going to pull it off."

"How do you know?"

"My senses. I'm powered by magic, it makes you sensitive to others. While my powers are very specific, bound by the *nahual*, hers are more amorphous. Magic wielders are a breed apart. There isn't really a limit to what they can do, if they have the spell and are willing to pay the price."

"Why tell me? Is it because you would lose your abilities, too?"

Jaguar shook her head. "No. People powered by magic would retain their abilities. Bloodmoon would never give up her own powers. I get my power from the *ocelotl* amulet, I would be immune. You would be consumed in the solar fire."

"Then why? There wouldn't be anyone to oppose you."

Jaguar sighed, put her hands in her pockets. "I've been thinking about this all night. I live on instinct, so this is out of character for me."

"Teaming up with me?" The solar hero smiled.

"A great enemy is a great gift, it keeps you at the very height of your power and skill." Jaguar reached out and caressed Lady Light's face. "How can anyone be great without great foes?"

Lady Light smiled at the caress, her eyes catching fire. "So you need my help."

Jaguar leaned back, withdrawing her hand from Lady Light's cheek slowly. "No, baby, I need you out of the way while I do what I have to. The paralytic is passed through the skin. It will leave you immobile for now, but you will be able to burn it out of your system in a few hours. Bloodmoon isn't like me, she doesn't live for the fight between us. She wants it over."

Lady Light was left sitting in the café, while Jaguar skinned back into her uniform and writhed with the change into her power self. The transformation the jaguar amulet allowed was multifarious. Like any *nahual*, she could appear as a woman, as a great cat, and as many stages between both. When she summoned her full spirit self the jaguar enveloped her fully, pulling her between the worlds. Every second world sense lit up, scanning for Bloodmoon. Jaguar ran through the night.

The Mistress of Magic had given away the timing of the ritual, but was canny of the location. It took Jaguar an hour to run the spirit paths until she caught the scent of monstrous magics brewing. Of course Bloodmoon would locate her ritual there. More than seventy miles from Bend, in the rugged middle of central Oregon desert nowhere was the skeleton of a long dead volcano. Glass Butte, named for the rivers of volcanic glass seaming the ground. Obsidian. The black mirror, held in the jade amulet's jaws, the symbol of Tezcatlipoca, the god who gave the amulet its powers. God of the north, the night, the smoking mirror, the jaguar. No wonder Bloodmoon wanted her involved. The black glass river would give her immense power, but Jaguar's amulet would help focus it.

The butte stood grey against the coming dawn, surrounded by the rivers of darkness. Jaguar's spirit eyes could see the dark glow rising from the black glass, showing underneath ribbons of rust, mahogany, sparks of silver like stars, glints of gold, the full rainbow culled under a deep red fire. Magic, being channeled, called along the glass river, called to the high country. If she could see that, then Bloodmoon, whose powers had gone Hyperion, could see her approaching like a comet. The question was, would she see the threat?

Jaguar couldn't feel the sharp obsidian under her paws, so swiftly did she flow up the glass river. The height of the hill was breached and Jaguar skittered to a stop. The north end of the ridge was lit up like the aurora borealis, the light blinding beyond the spirit senses and into the material world. Jaguar shifted back and could see it, unaided, her human eyes flinching from it. How did Bloodmoon handle that much power? The Mistress of Magic swayed like a dancer, arms flung wide, spiraling, spinning, twisting like a snake trying to recall limbs from another life. Bloodmoon was drunk on the power, pulling in excessive gouts, churning under the boiling light. Everything that touched her turned red as old blood, clotted, crimson boiled down to black. Even her robes were darkened, dipped in coal oil.

Madness. This was the twisting of the spirit realm, the burning of the material, and for the foulest of intents, the deliberate destruction of power, of life itself. Jaguar knew who she was and had no illusions about it. She was a criminal, a thief, a taker of anything she desired. The only limits on her were the ones she chose to heed, and those were few. But hers was a nature of passion, of desire, not of pure wanton destruction. The great cat is innocent, killing to eat, not for a long nursed vengeance, decentralized and sprayed over all life until the concept of life became abstract and nullified.

Bloodmoon turned her hood to gaze upon Jaguar, and Jaguar flinched. The eyes were gone. Not gouged out, just gone, excised from the original bone and flesh, overwritten, smoothed away as if by a caul. Not even pits of shadow. Yet the lips beneath writhed and Jaguar realized, with a stab of nausea, that Bloodmoon was attempting to smile at her.

"Jaguar."

"Bloodmoon. You've got quite the set up here. Wild how much energy you are putting off. Are you rehearsing for the big day?" Jaguar strolled toward the

Mistress of Magic, trying to keep her voice from shaking. This was hideous, against all of her instincts. She, who had lived for years by them, now had to ignore every sense and urge that her instincts howled at her to flee, to be long gone into the night and away from this abomination. Nothing human could hold this much power without changing, without leaving humanity far behind.

"The sun rises on this day, the day is at hand, the end is at hand, the day of ending. They will die, all will die, let all near them die as well, let the burn come and scour clean all the stain of powers. This will show them I am not to be laughed at, not to be mocked, all will die, all will go out as the sun will go out—"

The looping crimson energy geysered around her, splashing up like a river over its banks, like a stallion throwing off the bridle. Bloodmoon, what was left of her, couldn't hold back what she had summoned. The Mistress of Magic was distracted, lulled by Jaguar's calm approach. That emotional blind spot would end abruptly. Jaguar knew that she would have one chance for this attack. She flexed her hand and unsheathed her claws. Bloodmoon, swaying, eyes gone from her physical self, missed it.

The jaguar has no natural enemies, it stands at the apex of the wild hierarchy in which it lives. It is known to stalk and ambush its prey, pouncing on the unaware and seizing on it with claws. The strength, speed and power of the attack are breathtaking. Unlike other great cats, the jaguar does not go for the throat, rather, it seeks to puncture the skull of the prey.

The diamond tipped claws raked the hood to shreds, tearing away ribbons of flesh as well. They failed to puncture the skull. Jaguar had applied the paralytic to the tips, a futile hope against a being of Bloodmoon's new power. Jaguar felt the claws slip away from the target and sensed the disbelief from Bloodmoon, the hurt, boil into instant rage. Jaguar was on her back, blasted prone with the force of it.

Bloodmoon loomed over her, seething with fury and wounded pride. "How? How can you do this to me? It was supposed to be us against the world!"

Jaguar shook her head to regain her sight, seeing double or triple magic wavering before her. Bloodmoon was already too powerful; she didn't have a prayer against her. She seized the jaguar amulet in her grasp, jade teeth around obsidian mirror. *Tezcatlipoca, Necoc yaotl, Enemy of Both Sides, fill me with your strength.* The river of black glass sang and roared like a cataract breaking free of a dam. When it turns, love turns hard.

Bloodmoon's eyeless gaze fixed on Jaguar now, her attention, her hurt turning the energy around her a vivid green, iridescent as crushed beetles.

"I would have ended them all for you. Ended that sun bitch you spend all your time mooning over. You think I'm blind? She is the reason you came here, the reason you stay! How can the moon compete against the sun?"

"I was never yours!" Jaguar shouted, regretting it immediately.

Bloodmoon swelled like a full leech.

"You will be mine now."

The night, gray and pearl at the horizon, cracked in half. The full force of Bloodmoon's wrath descended on Jaguar, flattening her to the stone. Air, struggle and light went out. Once, as a child in Texcoco, Jaguar had been trampled by a horse. Her uncle had insisted she learn to ride, despite horses being nervous around her. Something in her scent, her mother always said. They could smell the predator. The first horse she was introduced to balked and threw her, trampling her in its terror. So many bones were broken that her mother, *nahual* herself, gave Jaguar the amulet to start her powers and help her heal. That recovery felt like basking in the mild spring sun to the pain that crushed her now. The volcanic glass ground into her bones. Well, it would be a good death, Jaguar thought. Each age of the world is marked by the destruction of the previous age, and by the creation of a new sun. Out of conflict and chaos and night comes the sacrifice, out of the sacrifice, the sun is set in motion. At the last gasp of the fleeing night, on the rivers of black glass, the last age of Jaguar's world came to an end. The stars went out, the night left in tatters like flayed skin, blood dripped onto the obsidian.

The sun rose on the new age, and the world began again. Darkness scuttled, chastened, while in the air above the black glass rivers the sun emerged whole from the chaos of flailing scarlet energy. Gold and brass, amber and white, the royal triumphant aura of the conquering sun, the avenging sun, the solar hero righteously flaming against evil.

Life is movement. Life is change, change through conflict is the realm of the jaguar. The great cat is not so easily slain, not so easily crushed down. The jaguar blazes with life. It is the obsidian, the smoking mirror, that shows the sun sublime solar fire. Thought returned to Jaguar as the wall of magic pressing her down dissipated, shifted to the more immediate threat. Sun goddess? Lady Light, here? How?

The titanic struggle between Bloodmoon and Lady Light illuminated the high desert for miles, shaming the more mundane dawn creeping over the horizon. With the Mistress of Magic's attention shifted away, Jaguar had a chance to press up from the earth, to gather her strength. To view the battle above, hear the singing of the obsidian rise to a pitch. And to get in position.

For all her magnificence, Lady Light could do no more than distract Bloodmoon. Physical force could delay her, but it would take magic to stop her. Jaguar moved. The time between thought and action was gone, her reflexes primed to their utmost spirit form. A flash of muscle and sinew, a low growl, and she was standing behind the distracted Bloodmoon, just off to the right. There wasn't time to signal Lady Light of her intent, and if she was off by a hair's breadth, the unfiltered solar fire would incinerate her instantly. It was a hell of a risk to take. Jaguar laughed in the teeth of hell.

Lady Light swept back her arm to launch a sunbolt at Bloodmoon. The arm swept down, the light sprang forth and crackled white hot, directly at the Mistress of Magic. Jaguar pounced, shoving Bloodmoon away from the sunbolt by a fraction, taking the solar fire on the obsidian mirror in her amulet. The bolt struck the volcanic glass and angled away, into the black rivers all around. There it magnified, turned from white to silver, amber, green and gold, a thousand roiling snakes of power, finally blazing from a thousand origins back onto the confused, dazed Mistress of Magic. There was no way she could hold it; the power lit her up like a torch soaked in kerosene. There was a snap, a fizzle, and nothing left but a scorch mark on the ground.

Lady Light dropped to the surface of the hill. "Is she dead?"

"No, calm your precious conscience. Just banished to so many places, she will take an age to find her way back. You can't kill a being of that kind of power so easily."

"How did you do it?"

Jaguar held up the amulet. "She was pulling all her energy from the obsidian. I used the obsidian mirror to direct all your power into the glass rivers, so she would overload. How did you find me?"

Lady Light turned a look of engaging anger on her. "Oh, after you paralyzed me? I put a sun-tracker on you when you had me feel the sleeve of your uniform."

"You sly dog! That was before I double crossed you." Jaguar said, with admiration.

"I'm good, baby, I'm not stupid." Lady Light's smile was brilliant. "See you back in Portland? Maybe we could try that coffee again, without the doublecross."

"That's the game, isn't it? See you back in Portland."

The solar hero and the great cat raced off into the night.

CHROME CRASH
Mari Kurisato

Mari Kurisato is an Ojibwe Nakawe Native whose native-given name is too long to print here. She's a queer, disabled mother, artist, MMO gamer cyborg. She's also a writer with one self published novel, *Guns of Penance*, a story in *Love Beyond Body, Space, and Time*, and three stories published with M-Brane Press, including one published in the *Things We are Not* anthology. She is hard at work on her next novel. She lives with her wife and son in the Denver Metro region. Her work can be found at *polychromantium.com* and you can stalk her on Twitter @CyborgN8vMari.

It was a drone from her own country that shot her in the back.

The gleaming machine sped as fast as a dart, a tireless hunter chasing unsuspecting prey through the early dawn sky. Its engines were quieter than a whisper as it flashed over grasslands and skimmed the treetops of lush pine forests. At the base of a snow-covered mountain, the craft circled silently over a village of a small reservation, where the people were all asleep.

In the village, a young Anishinaabe woman named Dirae stirred in her bed, and frowned at the sadness of her fading dream. Her lover Sarah slumbered beside her, and the host family the two women shared the tent with were peacefully sleeping on the other side. Dirae sighed at Sarah's loud snoring. She shook her head before sitting up to go relieve herself in the communal outhouse near their tent.

Her toes touched the rug.

At that moment, the drone loosed its hellish gift from a kilometer away.

Missiles streaked into the village. Dozens of people died in an instant, to the shocked screams of children in burning tents. People ignited as they ran; more volleys following the first. The barrage ripped apart flesh, families, and lives with machined precision.

Dirae crawled from the wreckage of her host family's tent, cradling a small boy who was crying for his mother in one hand. She called out for Sarah, but there was no answer. Dirae sprinted toward the dry riverbed, away from the fiery tents and the exploding bodies, the suffering screams. As she ran, the drone noted her movement, twitched, and sent sixty explosive rounds at her fleeing form.

The bullets struck her in the back, and Dirae lost hold of the little boy— though he was probably dead by the time his neck hit the rocks of the riverbed.

The drone swiveled, and dispassionately rained hell down upon the tiny village.

🐾

Tiamatia didn't always hate the world. Once, she'd been into unicorns, science fairs at school, and rereading the local library's collection of Octavia E. Butler's books while hiding from the kids who made fun of her white eyes and her paper-white hair.

But not long after her menarche, she'd started getting the migraines, and then the nosebleeds. And then, when she was seventeen, she had a migraine so bad she nearly vomited, and her family fell dead as they sat around the dinner table that night. Their eyes, nostrils, ears, and mouths streamed blackened blood.

She screamed, called the ambulance, called the police, anyone to help her, only to watch the first responders splatter like scarlet balloons as they stepped into the house. Madness overtook her, and she fled into the woods behind the neighborhood, running barefoot into the snow, terrified of seeing another human being for fear of watching them drop to the ground, as dead as the rest.

She stayed in the forest that night, too terrified to go back home, though she desperately missed shoes. And socks, and human beings. She shivered against the base of a tree, branches pulled over her, the pine needles offering scant warmth. The next morning there were helicopters overhead, dogs barking in the woods, and men yelling.

Tia ran as hard as she could, ignoring her frostbitten feet, neglecting everything but the terror, and the need to get away from people. She ran until she stopped feeling anything below her hips, until she felt fire chewing the inside of her chest. She ran until she was too dizzy to stand, and she crashed to the snow, gasping before getting up.

But no matter how long she ran, how far she forced herself to go, it seemed the dogs were always right behind her. She crawled on her hands and knees, scraping her face, arms, and thighs. And still, the dogs and their masters came.

At last she slumped into the snow, streamers of black ink swarming over her vision, and the hounds bayed, closing in.

Another headache whipped through her awareness, worse than the last one. Blood poured from her nose.

Seven dogs' hearts exploded instantly, and thirty Search and Rescue personnel fell to the ice, lifeless. Tia became, in a matter of seconds, the only living creature within two miles.

She rested, and then crawled away, her head pounding. She made it back to her house, which had been cordoned off with yellow police lines. Tia waited until dark to force her way back into her house.

She stood in the hallway and turned on the light. Hunger gripped her, and her feet burned. But the room spun after a few steps. The next moment she vaguely felt herself falling, hitting a floor that was as soft as cotton.

Tia woke up in a van, an ambulance. There were guards in strange armor, (all glossy and sleek angles of plastic) on either side of her. The guns in their hands were ordinary rifles though, which Tia thought, was just as lethal and scary as the armor.

She tried to move her head, but something held her down. One of the guards jerked, raised an epinephrine needle-looking device that must have come from a Star Trek prop room and brought it to Tia's face. She tried to get away, but she was so tightly strapped in she had no room to even squirm.

There was a loud bang and everything slid to the right. The back of the ambulance and the guards near the door disappeared in a scream of metal and spray of scarlet. Tia felt her ears pop, and then gravity went crazy as the guards next to her vanished. There was a loud bright bang and a blinding flash. When Tiamatia could see again, she was staring at the asphalt, just a meter away from her face. It was streaked with oil and—in places—dark red mucousy liquid.

I must be upside down, she thought. Then more thoughts tumbled out quickly, the way water sprays from a hydrant. *Still strapped into the gurney. Was the bed bolted to the floor? Was there some sort of accident?*

There was a sound of a flag snapping in the wind, and then a muffled cry. Horns honking in the distance.

"Sir, she's still alive," said a man from somewhere behind her.

"...*Help*," Tia said. Rather, she choked it out, finding it harder to breathe.

"Take it easy, sweetheart. Help is here. Can you tell me your name?" A man's voice. Calm, confident, and smooth as a midnight radio DJ's.

"Tiama—" was all Tia said before the world flipped and she was staring at the morning skyline of a strange city.

"Easy there," said a tall, broad-shouldered man with silver hair. "You're all right. Everything's going to be fine." He smiled, and it struck Tia that he reminded her of a vaguely famous TV star who always played the noble underdog politician. She tried to smile back. There was the sound of helicopters hovering very close by.

"O-Okay," she said. Then, "What happened? Where am I?"

The man started to answer, but turned and looked at someone she couldn't see. He put a hand on her shoulder, as if to reassure her. Someone spoke from nearby.

"But I'm from Nine News! Can't I just get a quick statement from him for the—"

"Get that camera out of here!"

Tia looked at the man with the regal sand-colored face, dark blue eyes, and the silver hair, and something odd struck her.

He was wearing a bright blue spandex body suit. Or at least a body-suit top. But he had a white cape, the kind Roman army commanders wore in old Hollywood films.

She giggled. He looked at her, that warm smile on his face.

"Something funny?" he asked, gently.

"Are you a cosplayer?" Tia asked.

He grinned and shook his head. Then he held up the same needle from earlier, so Tia could see it.

He jammed it into her neck before she could scream.

Then she felt nothing.

Became nothing.

✺

Dirae stared at the television as she stood at the bar of the greasy spoon coffee shop, her eyes fixed on the screen. Her reflection in the mirror showed a woman with burnt gold skin, black eyes sharp enough to cut diamonds set below angular, thick, black eyebrows.

Those eyebrows were nestled on a wide, high forehead that was wrapped by generous cheekbones which smoothed her narrow nose down along her leonine face toward her sharp chin, with thin, blood-red lips. Her face was framed by thick, ink-black hair.

She gripped the edge of the bar so hard it had sprouted cracks in the plastic veneer. Her coffee cup was in pieces, and the liquid pooled and slipped into the cracks.

Until she saw the news broadcasts, Dirae treated the distant sensations of urgent dread as nothing more than a symptom of her general unease with her plans to use her powers to raise money. But when the man in the cape looked at the camera, and the camera glimpsed the girl on the ambulance gurney, it hit her as hard as a thunderbolt to the breastbone. The vague feeling of dismay and worry sharpened into a solid certainty. That girl was afraid, alone, and needed help, and the caped man was not going to help her. But worse, something about the girl struck Dirae as deadly, lethal. Dangerous to *her*. The emotional agony that Dirae felt spilling from the girl, the sheer despair cut into Dirae's mind, interrupting other thoughts.

That feeling gelled into action when Dirae saw a drone float slowly across the screen, patrolling the scene of the accident. Dirae flashed back to her teenage years, when the drones killed everyone she knew, and almost killed her. She turned from the bar at the coffee shop, pushing aside people who were already scrambling to get out of her way.

She lightly slapped her hand against the door, and the glass burst from it as the frame bent and tumbled into the street, knocking a bike courier to the pavement. There were screams as people pressed against each other and the back wall of the coffee shop to get away from her.

Dirae stepped outside and let the large trench coat she wore fall away. Her skin began to shimmer, as if a watery reflection of light flashed across her body.

A dog ran up to her and started barking at her loudly. Then it bit her leg. She kicked the animal into a fire hydrant a block away without even really thinking about it.

She *stretched*. She tapped her foot on the pavement. The ground beneath her feet shattered as if a skyscraper had fallen in her footprint. There was a loud cannon shot as the sonic wave broke the sound barrier. A taxi cab and a few stunned pedestrians were flung away, bits of dust before a hurricane.

The coffee shop windows exploded inward, the building itself ruptured and splintered.

She was already in the sky, gleaming chrome flying through the air as she headed toward where the pain and the terror told her the girl might be. She had no idea exactly where the girl was, but she leaned in the direction that caused her headache to get worse. If the girl's telepathy could hurt her from this far away, what harm could she cause Dirae up close?

The air around her wavered as she forced herself to go faster. The skyscrapers she flew by swayed, windows cracking as the air pressure of her passing pulled at them with the strength of an EF5 tornado. With a loud, rolling snap, glass from thousands of windows spilled into the streets as Dirae pushed her body harder, her rage growing the same way the air-frost coated her skin.

As she neared the freeway, the pain, fear and fury built to a fever pitch. She flew low over the cars, searching frantically for the scene she'd seen on the news.

Please let me not be late. Please, not this time.

The girl's pain, her grief, and her dread hit Dirae hard as a wall. Tears froze at the outer corner of her eyes. They should be close by, she thought. They should be right—

WHAM!

Dirae was ripped from the air by a sudden, intense fist of pressure. Her body smashed through a minivan's engine bloc, the pavement below supporting beams of steel, and the pillar of the overpass. She remembered the pain of the drone that had shot her in the back when she was a teenager. She came to a stop after smashing through the roof of a metalworks foundry just west of the overpass, landing hard in a huge vat of red molten steel. Now the pain was almost serious.

Her suit and skin seared away with the heat of the foundry's metal, and what remained underneath was rippling silver, some type of chrome-water substance that fed off her fury and resisted the flames of the foundry pool the same way an elephant resists the bite of an ant. She stood up; the men who were screaming for help fell silent, and Dirae almost laughed.

Her whole body shined mirror bright; even her eyes and hair gleamed silver. For a moment, Dirae imagined the forge birthing a very pissed-off goddess before she leaped into the air as if she'd never been there at all, save for the rain of molten metal she'd leave in her wake.

Dirae punched up through the overpass, smashing aside concrete, steel rebar, glass and the half-ton trailer of a beer truck as if they were all paper cut-outs. Her fist caught the drone dead-on. It snapped in half, then exploded, but this time she'd braced herself against the blast.

Gunfire tattooed a wave of flames across her back, and Dirae spun slowly in the sky, letting the girl's pain and dread that Dirae was forced to feel focus her anger in the moment, as high-explosive bullet shells bloomed into fire before skittering away harmlessly from her skin.

She saw the government thugs, private paramilitary or whatever they were, hiding behind a larger truck that a civilian had left behind as the smarter people realized they needed to run away.

Seven men behind the truck, all of them unloading clips of explosive rounds at her, the shots banging and clanging off her skin. She swooped down low and kicked the truck they hid behind. The truck smashed into an SUV with a loud pop of metal, and the sickening wet-bone crunch of human flesh.

A knife of icy remorse slid down into her belly, but Dirae's fury burned through that. She turned, rose into the skies to see whom she had missed. As if it would make a difference, one of the survivors started shooting at her again.

She waited until the man made eye contact.

Then she plummeted out of the sky toward him, bullets bouncing off her face in a splash of sparks. She stopped in front of him and ripped the rifle from his hands, bending the weapon until the plastic stock of the shoulder guard cracked. He looked at her in his SWAT gear, wide-eyed behind the tactical goggles.

"The girl. *Where* is she?" Her voice was a throaty growl of steel, a bass guitar dancing with a high voltage wire.

He went for his sidearm, fear still driving him like a hammer to nail, and as gently as she could, as carefully as she dared, she puffed up her cheeks and exhaled as if she was blowing a snowflake from her fingertips.

The SWAT cop slammed into the hood of a green Nissan minivan thirty feet away, and sure enough, she heard a bone break. But when he fell to the ground, he screamed.

Alive. Good enough.

There were screams besides his, and sirens. It was all distant TV static to her, though, reduced to white background slush in the grip of the girl's agony, and despair. She strode to the man, picked him up gently as a lamb, and waited until the fog of pain cleared from his eyes. She dared not shake him. When using her powers shaking him would turn him into blood-paste.

"Where," she asked, almost sweetly, "is the girl?"

"Fuck you," he got out between clenched teeth.

One hand whiffed past his face, a millimeter from his ear. Dirae's fist punched through the Nissan so hard it shattered into snowflake-sized pieces by the time it splashed against another car, as if a train had hit it.

"Now maybe you're a company man. Yes?" Her voice was soft as silk hissing down a beam of polished iron. Almost apologetic. "Maybe you've got the party-line drilled deep into your gray matter. And that's fine. I'm not the torturing type, not like your bosses. But here's the thing. If you don't tell me, then I have to look for her, and if I do, that means more of your buddies will probably try to stop me, yeah? And they'll die, and try as I might to prevent it, more innocent people will get caught in the crossfire, and they'll die, too. So the question is, how many American lives are you willing to lose before 'go fuck yourself, I'm a patriot' stops being a comfortable shield, hmm?"

She saw the change in his eyes, the minute dilation of his pupils, the raised brows as his gaze shifted from her to look away. She dropped him to the ground. Twisted around and saw the fist just before it hit her in the jaw.

It *hurt.*

Dirae *welcomed* that it hurt. So few things did, anymore. Not viscerally. Not physically. Physical pain was a relief from the girl's broadcasted emotions of horror and suffering.

She tumbled, smashed through a hatchback, crushed a motorcycle and struck a passenger van, ripping it and the terrified driver into halves.

Twinge.

Then she crashed through the concrete barrier and started to fall. But the caped man with silver hair, the one from TV, was suddenly there, and he caught her by her hair, giving her another southpaw fist to her chest that cracked the sound barrier, sending Dirae's body ricocheting through another overpass pillar. Rebar and concrete chunks followed her, tiny meteors thrown sideways.

The overpass started to slide down at an angle, and cars, trucks and a school bus slipped across the battered macadam like toys, loud pops and cracks echoing as they bounced into each other, the terrified screams of the people drowned out as the concrete began snapping and crumbling.

The icy twinge exploded into a blizzard of panic, and Dirae spun around as she hit the earth, slamming through the asphalt and bedrock, springing back up at several times the speed of sound, a blur of shining silver, completely ignoring the man with a cape as she flung herself toward the collapsing overpass.

She smashed through the windows of the school bus first, picking up three or sometimes four children and zooming out of harm's way to let them fall safely to the grass on a nearby hill. She got all of the children out, and the bus driver, too, but then cars started to tumble over her. She caught one, two, but even though they weighed nothing to her, she couldn't go as fast as she needed to save everyone. That many g-forces on normal humans would turn them into smeared scarlet.

In ten seconds, moving at super speed, Dirae saved two hundred people as the overpass collapsed. Thirty she left to die because they were either trapped or too old to save without hurting them even more. By the time she got everyone out of the wreckage that she could, the caped man was gone.

And so was the girl's presence in her mind.

Dammit.

✄

Tia woke up in a claustrophobic gray chamber that suggested a storage space was converted into a hastily put-together hospital patient's room. A portable heart and pulse-oxygen machine beeped softly from next to the nightstand near her bed. There was a small bathroom with a sink, toilet, and a shower. A bookshelf on one wall was filled with books that belonged in an estate sale bargain bin. The only other thing in the room was a television monitor, behind a thick layer of blue-tinted plexiglass. There were no pictures, no tiny little accent objects that might give it the warmth of a usual hospital. Instead of warm beiges and gentle blues the walls were flat gray-painted concrete. And worst of all, Tiamatia noticed, there was no phone, and no door.

No way out.

❦

The greasy, pearl-skinned man wiped the sweaty hair from his forehead, glared into the television camera, and spoke loudly.

"Surely, Dr. Fronisi, even you can see that the battle between internationally beloved patriot Magnus Dei and this strange flying chrome criminal in downtown Unity City last week is proof enough that Mr. Dei's plan to protect our country is not only a feasible decision, it's the only sane choice we as the citizens of Unity City can dare make!"

He slammed his fist for emphasis. The camera cut to Dr. Fronisi, a man with smooth-boned features, dark eyes and smoky quartz skin underneath tightly cropped, wiry hair. He spoke, adjusting his paper thin glasses as he leaned forward.

"Now hold on there, Dr. Turbat. There's no hard evidence that Magnus Dei is any better than the people he claims to protect us against. After all, who's to keep people like him, and all these other people with these… *powers*, in check? Are we just supposed to trust him because he says so? What makes him so different from this metallic-skinned monster?"

Anahera rolled her eyes and switched the TV off.

"Hey!" said Dirae from the couch. "I was watching that!" She sat up, a pout on her face.

"Yeah, and the dishes from last night are still in the sink, and it's your week," Anahera said.

"Oh, come on, I was busy!" Dirae said as she stood up, carefully stepping around the coffee table and ducking down to avoid hitting the lamp hanging from the ceiling. She bumped it a little anyway, sending the lamplight swinging wildly, and Anah laughed, reaching up to caress Dirae's cheek.

"Oh ha ha, very funny, Anahera." Dirae leaned down and kissed the woman's sand-colored throat, not having the heart to tell her that she had noxiously bad morning breath. Dirae tousled Anahera's black hair, and stared into her dark eyes above the curling facial tattoos, the Tā moko that gave a detailed account of the woman's family, social status, and tribal history, much of it a secret to Dirae.

That's OK, she thought, I have secrets of my own.

"What were you so busy with that you neglected your half of the chores, hmm?" whispered Anahera as she toyed with Dirae's hair, using her other hand to grab Dirae's shirt, pulling herself closer.

There was that splash of icy regret again, sloshing through Dirae's chest.

"You know, overtime hours at work is a thing, Anah," she said smoothly. Technically it wasn't a lie. Not exactly.

"You're an architect, Vi. Not an EMT. People in your career field are known to keep regular hours. Nine to five, not five to nine," Anahera said as she kissed Dirae's collarbone.

Dirae kissed the top of her head and forced the bile back down. She knew considering herself lucky that her silver-bodied "battle-form" rendered her mostly unrecognizable was a bad thing, but how could she risk Anahera's life by telling her the biggest secret she had?

"Yes," replied Dirae as she kissed Anahera's neck again, "but we also do work late on occasion when a client makes late-minute revision requests and pays the firm the rush fee that we ask for. And if Avitas says 'hey Vi, stay late,' I stay late."

Anahera backed up and looked Dirae in the eyes. "Fine. But I don't have to enjoy it, and the sink is drowning in dirty dishes. No more kisses for you until you get them done."

Dirae forced a big smile, ignoring the slimy, cold feeling of shame in the pit of her stomach as she held up her hands in surrender. "Alright, no need to beat me up over it, I'm going." She made her way to the kitchen, the doubtful look on her lover's face when talking about her work shining painfully brilliant, a fire in her mind's eye.

She washed the dishes, distracted by the news report.

🗲

Imperatrax sat on the sterile plastic couch, bone-thin legs tucked underneath her, leaning against the cushions as if she were a rag doll that was just tossed there. Magnus stood in front of her as she stared at a sleeping girl on a wall monitor with filmy, fish-gray eyes.

"Oh Magnus," the corpse-skinned woman said, "don't look so sad. We're doing exactly what we're supposed to. Protecting civilians and keeping dangerous elements," and here the woman gestured to the girl on the screen, "from hurting others. It might be harsh for the girl, but the world doesn't always offer fair choices, just right and wrong ones. Saving people sometimes means keeping some people safe from even themselves. Like her."

The woman smiled a tiny slivered slash of black and red, lips and tongue, and the man repressed a shudder. The pale-skinned woman narrowed her red eyes and wiped slick blue hair from her face, and spoke after a moment.

"What about Entrophasia, for this one?"

"It's better than calling the poor sap 'Brain Exploder,' that's for sure," Magnus said crisply. He frowned, turned away, and did not look at her.

"It breaks my hearts that you doubt me, Magnus. You know what I am trying to do here. What we are all trying to do. The girl cannot control her powers, so it's for her own safety as much as ours that we keep her inside the lowest levels of the Vinculum Aeternum."

The caped man looked back, anger hardening his face.

"Why? So an innocent girl can go mad and be unknowingly condemned to rot there all alone?"

The woman stood up, her body slithering wetly off the couch. For a second he saw the pain hidden in her glittering ruby-colored eyes before she spoke.

"She is hardly innocent, Magnus. Whether or not she knew what she was doing, the law of Unity City is clear; murderers who know right from wrong shall be charged for their crime, regardless of intent or accident. At least here we can keep her safe from those that might try to exploit her. People who would try to harness her powers for their own ends. Just think of what a danger she could be in the hands of some of the monsters that we know are lurking out there."

The caped man clenched his fists, his voice rising, words clipped. "Monsters like that silver woman that I fought? Why don't we take her out and stop the threat she presents to us, to our cause, and to people like the girl?"

"We don't know what that criminal wants, or even where she is. We need to find out more about her, before exposing ourselves. And perhaps this girl is our best hope of helping us find that out, especially if the girl knows the chrome menace."

"All the more reason to go after her now, Imperatrax!" Magnus said, letting himself lose just a little control. He told himself he wasn't afraid of her. He wasn't really afraid of Imperatrax Prime; he was the strongest man in the world, after all… But he knew better than to really show how mad he was, though he suspected she knew.

Imperatrax dropped her jeweled gaze to look at him and just frowned. "Patience," she said, her voice purring softly. Her eyes darkened, the edges of her irises starting to glow milky white. Magnus felt himself swaying before her gaze, and he was suddenly falling backward into a dark pit of the earth. The terror that rose in him was primal and rendered him a child again, back in the days when his father beat him and his mother and…

Any objection Magnus had died in his throat. He nodded and left the room quickly, eager to be away from her.

Imperatrax sighed. Once she had hoped Magnus would see what she was trying to do by his own accord. It upset her that he did not see things her way. But she always knew she'd have to make sacrifices to keep him and others who shared his abilities safe from the larger world. And since the girl—no, since *Entrophasia's* abilities worked as sort of telepathy, primal, weak and untrained though it might be, it was more than enough for Imperatrax's needs.

She sighed, and turned back to the screen, watching Entrophasia sleep fitfully, a wounded caged animal. Imperatrax reached out, singing that same song she used on her husband, so long ago, to bend his thoughts to panic and despair, until he was putty in her hands, so to speak.

Now it was slightly more difficult to use the girl's mind as a conduit to reach the Chrome Menace, but if Imperatrax could reach her if she could saturate her with enough dread, then maybe the silver-skinned woman could be brought to heel. Be made useful.

Perhaps she would even see things the same way Imperatrax herself did, and would join the cause willingly, without having to be turned to it by the force of fear Imperatrax used on her own son.

✤

Dirae's despair grew stronger every day. The pressure of the despair she felt from losing the girl, to the paranoid panic that she'd never find her, ate at Vi. She watched the news obsessively, often leaving the house under the pretense of going to work, and then going to a local coffee shop and spending hours searching the net for any bit of gossip, anything on the girl, or the silver-haired man in a cape. She watched the hours of footage about their fight, the dozens of interviews and opinionated debates the news channels conducted with experts who weren't really that much more knowledgeable than your average Joe..

She spent time wandering the city, shrinking herself down until she was suffocatingly tiny, but it made it easier to travel the metropolis unnoticed—everyone who saw her thought she was a harmless street urchin. Days started to blur together, and the girl's pain and despair that Dirae felt as if it were her own began to crowd out other thoughts.

She stayed away for days at a time, walking the alleys of Unity City and when she did return, she never stayed long. She didn't go inside when Anah was there. She didn't know what to say, or what to do to pretend everything was fine, because it wasn't, and Anah would know.

The nights when Anah was home, Dirae stayed outside, listening, her back leaning against the wall nearest to wherever Anah's heartbeat was loudest. She listened to Anah cry, and she wanted to burst in, and explain everything, who she was, why she was hunting for the girl whose pain wouldn't get out of her head. But it was getting harder just to think straight, through all the agony buried underneath the sickening, lurching sense of panic. Eventually, she stopped coming back every day.

She didn't remember exactly when it was that she came home to see her apartment building burning.

She ran past the firefighters, letting herself stretch until the clothing ripped under her sharply angled muscles, her skin taking on the metallic form. The heat licked at her as she made her way through the complex, careful not to disturb anything structural. But before she even got to her door, she knew it was too late. Her home was destroyed. Still, she searched through the roaring flames, shrugging off concrete and steel beams as they fell on her.

The horror, the despair, all of it came to a fever pitch that sounded like the screams of cars smashing into trains. She grew frantic, throwing a melting refrigerator aside, then smashing apart a wall, beds, drawers. Try as she might, she couldn't find Anah.

She wanted to cry, but in this form, she couldn't. She couldn't do anything. Dirae made her way out of the flaming wreckage, a white-hot lump of female-shaped impossibility. The concrete hissed and burned as she made her way past the stunned firemen and first responders, her body cooling from white to red, to mercurial orange. She stood in the street, as the crowd of onlookers backed away from her.

"It's the Chrome Menace!" someone yelled. Dirae barely heard it. She just stood there, red hot, smoke and heat blurring the air around her. She stood with her head down as she shrank, her skin losing both the heat and metallic sheen. She was naked, but she didn't care.

"Vi?"

Dirae turned at the voice and found Anahera standing on the other side of the street. She let out a pained cry, and started for her lover, heedless of those who watched.

"Oh thank the gods you're alright!" Dirae said. She put her arms out to hug her. But Anah took several steps back, her eyes wide, tears slipping out.

"Y-you're the Chrome Menace?" Anah asked, her voice shaking. She clutched at herself, bending over and sobbing in gasps.

Dirae stopped. "It's not what you think it is, Anahera! Please, I can explain every—"

"How... how could you, Vi? You lied to me! You fucking lied to me!" Anah yelled. She backed away, facing Dirae.

"No! I didn't want to keep this from you, I just didn't want you to get hurt!" Dirae said, the pain and the terror taking hold of her again.

"Stay away from me!" said Anah before she turned and ran away.

"Anah, no, please," Dirae said, weakly.

Dirae wanted to chase her, to stop her, to explain everything, but... no. She had already ruined things between them. She wouldn't try to force Anah to do something she didn't want to. Dirae cursed and looked around, trying to ignore the people taking pictures of her. She stretched, and took her metallic form again, waving a hand at the crowd. Cameras popped with electric fizzles and smoke as people jumped back.

She'd lost Anahera. Only this time, there were no drones to blame, no one else to point a finger at except her. Dirae sank to the ground, and looked up to the sky, the pain burning her in a way the fire could never have.

And there, against the gray clouds, hovering overhead, she saw the caped man, muscled arms folded over his massive chest.

Waiting.

She stretched more, growing to her full height, her skin gleaming, and she rose into the sky, slowly, *slowly*, until she was at his height. They stood still midair, as the crowd below shone lights on them and aimed more phone cameras, streaming for the world to see.

"What," Magnus Dei said with a chuckle. "No cape? No costume? No mask? Did you really expect to hide from us, Dirae Christine Ironfire?"

"Was this you? Was this your doing?" she asked, her voice shaking with rage, like piano wires dangling in a wind storm. She gestured to the burning apartment.

The silver haired man shrugged with a smile. "Luring you out had to start somewhere, and what better place than in front of your lover? Or should I say ex-lov—"

Dirae punched him.

Her fist smashed against his face so hard the people watching below were all slammed against the ground by the sonic boom's shockwave, and glass in all the buildings within a three-block radius shattered from the impact. The street burst open with a squeal and a snapping pop that shook the earth as Magnus Dei's body slammed deep into the ground like a bullet fired into gelatin. There was an explosion as his body whipped through an underground natural gas line.

Magnus shot back up and grabbed Dirae by the throat, his fingers strong enough to bend the metal of her neck. Together they rocketed into the sky, burning upwards through the atmosphere like a blazing missile—because Dei's cape was burning.

She laughed as he pushed her higher, his cape a blossom of flame.

"What, no cape?" she yelled as they flew upward toward darkness. He snarled soundlessly.

They made it into the upper mesosphere, the lack of oxygen taking away the flames from his cape, and his ability to breathe, but Magnus grabbed Dirae's head in his hands and threw her as hard as he could back down into sky below.

She streaked through the atmosphere, a tiny needle of white-hot heat that left a small airplane-like contrail and slammed into the sea near the naval base, causing a spray of water thirty meters high to soak the deck of the Unity City's flagship aircraft carrier. Magnus followed her trail down through the sky and dove into the sea to make sure she was dead.

Dirae rose from the muddy seafloor crater as fast as a lightning bolt, boiling the water in her wake. She grabbed Magnus and squeezed, her muscles expanding and crushing his body as surely as a rolling boulder crushes a pebble. He screamed underwater and inhaled, and in that second instinctive panic overtook him. He flailed and struck and her as hard as he could, the resounding clangs sounding like underwater church bells slapping together. She loosened her grip and he flew towards the sun, towards the sky, tearing through the hull of the aircraft carrier like an arrow through paper. She followed him up through the decks of the warship, water surging after them.

Magnus collapsed on the tarmac of the flight deck, gasping for air, and Dirae landed next to him. Sailors pulled their sidearms and shot at her, but it was like throwing firecrackers against a tank. She ignored them and turned to the gasping superhero who was bleeding from his broken nose and mouth.

"Where... is... the... girl?" she whispered. Magnus looked up at her and shuddered when he saw the expression on her twisted chrome face.

"I'll tell you. Please just. Don't hurt me anymore," he gasped between breaths.

When he finished telling her, she knelt beside him and said in his ear. "You did a good thing. No more pain."

Then Dirae took his smiling face in her hands, and slammed her hands together, the metallic fingers roaring like a thunderclap.

Magnus Dei was dead before he even knew it.

Sailors, airmen, and deck crew stared at her in horror as she dropped the crushed body of their fallen hero to the tarmac. She walked back over towards the holes Magnus had made and let herself fall into the water below.

People in Unity City who saw it that day described what she did as a miracle. Witnesses say the aircraft carrier floated high over the city, water falling from the ship in sprays of mist. The ship swayed like an immense balloon, casting a skyscraper-sized shadow over hundreds of thousands of people who watched where they stood. The massive aircraft carrier was set down in Patriot Park as gently as a mother puts down her child to sleep. No one saw the streak of silver soaring up and away into the sky.

Dirae smashed her way through the concrete barriers and the troops who guarded the doors. She smeared Imperatrax against the wall like a bug, splattered the woman's organs against the TV monitor as Imperatrax pleaded for Dirae to understand what had to be done. The rest was just a matter of smashing her way down to where the girl was. And if there was one thing Dirae was an expert at, it was smashing.

Tiamatia awoke with a terrible headache, and a nosebleed. This one felt so bad it was like the whole room was pounding. She sat up, and the shaking only grew worse. Suddenly, she wondered if it was an earthquake. Then the room began to buck violently, and there was a loud boom.

Tia hid her eyes a moment, not wanting to see any more death. Instead, a giant silver woman stood there, holding out her hand.

"Who are you?" Tia asked. "You're not dead."

"I'm here to set you free," the woman said. "You can call me Violatrix."
Tia smiled and took the woman's hand in hers. Violatrix smiled, hugged
Tia, and then snapped the girl's neck. Tiamatia died instantly, and with her
death, the terror, and the pain faded from Violatrix's mind.

With both of the telekinetics dead, and Anah gone, there was nothing left
to hold her back.

She flew into the sky, a tireless hunter speeding after unsuspecting prey.

ABSOLUTE POWER
TALES OF QUEER VILLAINY!

Check out the whole line
of LGBT graphic novels
and comics collections
from **NORTHWEST PRESS**!
In print and online at
NorthwestPress.com.

Also from Northwest Press...

**The Lavender Menace:
Tales of Queer Villainy!**
edited by Tom Cardamone

The Legend of Bold Riley
by Leia Weathington

Anything That Loves
edited by Charles "Zan" Christensen

Transposes by Dylan Edwards

QU33R edited by Rob Kirby

RISE: Comics Against Bullying
edited by Kristopher White, Joey
Esposito, and Erica Schultz

A Waste of Time by Rick Worley

Mama Tits Saves the World
by Charles "Zan" Christensen, Terry
Blas, and Marissa Louise

**The Completely Unfabulous Social
Life of Ethan Green** by Eric Orner

Fearful Hunter by Jon Macy

Hard to Swallow
by Dave Davenport & Justin Hall